ASH BEFORE OAK

Fitzcarraldo Editions

ASH BEFORE OAK

JEREMY COOPER

24 December

Today I did a beautiful thing: built a rose arch from timber I had first felled and trimmed. My work is not in itself beautiful, but the act of doing it was, the replacement of a fallen frame, an old rose set to prosper.

In the afternoon I cleared the garden path inside the wall to the lane, so overgrown that few signs remained of it having been a way to walk. The revelation of distant lives, the uncovering of previous care for this place by people past, brings me satisfaction. And meaning. Yesterday I dug down below the bottom garden gate to unveil a grey-stone step. Earlier lives are exposed also in renovation of the building. In construction of the new chimney in what has been a barn for a hundred years or more, I found in the wall the contours of an old hearth, confirming the belief that my to-be-home was once part of a row of four farm worker's cottages.

Tomorrow is Christmas Day. I am happy to be living here.

29 December

It snowed again last night. Like yesterday, external silence a prize. At 8.15 a.m., while I was out watching the colour of the sky change with the sunrise above the curve of Cothelstone Hill, the post van drove up the lane, and from my box on the wall I picked up a single welcome envelope. After breakfast I took good feelings up by the cascade to a hidden combe and on into the woods. Many sights: a swathe of green watercress where a stream spreads out to pass through a meadow, kept free from ice by birds. Elsewhere, tracks in the snow of pheasant and fox and rabbit and badger and deer and stoat and vole.

Back home, I identified the footfalls of these different animals in a book given to me thirty years ago by a family friend who used to live down here near Taunton. He was kind to me as a boy – the fact that he knew and loved the Quantock Hills and brought me years ago to this land for a mid-summer walk lends to my choice of settling now at Lower Terhill a sense of balance.

I hope this is real feeling, not sentimentality – a fabrication.

1 January

Hope.
    And fear.
    Together.

30 March

It is March, almost April, and I return to these notes. Work on the adjacent derelict half of my cottage moves ahead, with its solid new roof, window-frames fitted, traditionally done by my neighbour, a master builder.

Discover that burdock is the name of the cabbage-leaved plant I've been trying to eradicate from my wood. It's a kind of thistle, producing burrs – a wild plant with a pedigree as space-filler in both old gardens and picturesque landscape paintings, common in the work of Claude Lorrain. At the annual fair in Queensferry, Edinburgh, the Burry Man covers himself from head to toe in burdock burrs and parades through the streets.

Maybe I'll leave some plants after all.

Jeremy Deller and Alan Kane, artists I admire, illustrate burry men in their book *Folk Archive* and state in the introduction: 'As artists we engage in an optimistic journey of personal discovery (albeit often very close to home).'

16 April

On my first-thing-in-the-morning stroll along the paths through my glades, today I heard, then saw, a lesser spotted woodpecker, upside down near the base of the trunk of the big pine. When it flew away I went over to inspect the spot, and found a hazelnut wedged in a crevice of the trunk. Imagine it will return later to finish off the task of cracking open the shell. I've never seen this bird before, smaller than a thrush, with powerful movements of the head.

A beautifully clear windless sunset, heralding summer, and I walked down to see if the hazelnut was still lodged in the bark. It had disappeared. I couldn't see the broken shell on the ground, so perhaps it was forgotten by the woodpecker and instead found by a squirrel. The bird may on reflection have been a nuthatch, smaller, greyer – lesser spotted woodpeckers are a rarity round here.

Reciting the names of birds and plants is such a British thing to do.

Irritated by my grip on convention.

Only just started this nature-naming business, after thirty years in London, and already tempted to stop.

6 May

Another fine morning. Wonderful the way seasonal change in the fall of light alters the look of familiar
paths. Today, on my pre-breakfast inspection, I found
myself cutting down, uprooting where I could, vagrant
sycamore in the lane – quick-growing trees which
push out brash big leaves across the shoots of spindle,
hawthorn and the dozens of other plants of an ancient
dry-stone bank. This place bears the marks everywhere
of hundreds of years of occupation.

As a boy, in the autumn I loved to play with the helicopter seeds of sycamore, unaware of their invasive
virulence.

And damning streams, another boyhood passion.
There was once a narrow stream here between lane and
hedge.

13 May

It is an ordinary robin, I this evening identified, which sings each evening on the same high branch of the black Italian poplar beside the kennels.

Accept the solitude, I tell myself, if that's how things currently must be. It's enough this moment to enjoy the sight of the candle-like blooms on the weeping bird cherry tree, released this year by my cuttings and clearings to flourish near the bench. The lowest branch of the Monterey pine is precisely horizontal, the trunk vertical, picture-framing the bench which I've had made in hardwood slats, held by a pair of cast-iron ends bought some time ago at the salvage company in Shoreditch, my neighbours then. The trunk of this giant tree is maybe eight foot in diameter at its base, the bark rust-red, fissured, soft.

It doesn't matter what it's called.

Isn't Monterey in America?

I'm perpetually confused these days, when, for dozens of years, I used to be so self-assured.

16 May

There was a handsome young Song Thrush feeding in my garden, diving down from its hiding place in the branches of the Ash to dig for Worms in the lawn, cocking its head to listen. I like the low swoop of its flight between the trees.

I begin to recognize the pairs of individual birds who live here with me at Lower Terhill.

Ash, Song Thrush, written with capital letters at the beginnings of the words – like Richard, or Sarah Jane, the trees and birds are individuals, deserving of my respect, with as much right to be here as I have.

3 June

Watched numerous thrushes and blackbirds feed on the red-ploughed earth out in the park. Beyond the Monterey and bench my eye follows the line of the iron fence, over which it is effortless to step out and stroll. I regularly stand beside one of the big beeches towards the crest of the intermediate hill, from which the under-wood has been cleared, and, as I gaze down at the bench, empty within the picture-frame, see an image of myself looking up at myself looking down on myself, in cease-less solipsism.

Other things happen, other thoughts appear.

11 June

Trespassed again this afternoon onto the hilltops of the Quantocks, where public right of way is banned in precaution against the spread of foot-and-mouth. The absence of man-and-dog for many months means that the flora and fauna grow and breed undisturbed. Saw sixty of the eight hundred head of wild red deer in the Quantock-wide herd resting mid-afternoon in the middle of an open field, accustomed by now to tranquillity, unaware of my approach, their ears visible above the long grasses.

The rabbits, I notice, have eaten to the ground every stem of wild dill.

12 June

Took my book and binoculars out to the bench by the fence to the park. All the time I was there, at first staring out in dull nothingness, then reading, a buzzard was perched on the bare top branch of a douglas fir in the line of trees eighty yards away. It began to summer-rain and I returned to the cottage, to my desk, to these notes. The buzzard will by now also have moved, I imagine.

17 June

Noticed today that the last family pet given an inscribed headstone down beside the overgrown avenue was a spaniel called Scrap, buried in 1967, three years after Cothelstone House, the nearby Georgian mansion, was razed to the ground. Its dilapidated coach house alone remains to mark the grandeur of the past, its stonework and proportions more like Italy than England. The verse inscriptions on the graves attest to the companionship of dogs, ponies and horses, family rhymes, simple, sentimental. The Estate survives, considerably reduced, workable all the same by my landlord. I have lifetime tenure of this large cottage, attached to a small grain store, with an open byre across the yard, the stable-barn along the lane, and a double privy and the greyhound kennels in the garden. A tumble of debris today, the kennels were a luxury home a hundred years ago to the prize pack of hounds which hunted hares down on the flatlands of Taunton Vale.

Five months ago, Mother refused to let me go to Father's funeral, for fear of what I might say about him to family friends.

2 July

Rich, heavy July.

The lawn a rash of white clover and daisy. Running riot at the margins the white bell-shaped flowers of bindweed and bursts of ground elder. Wild raspberry canes are in white flower to the height of my head ... it's endless, endless.

Richness reversed to internal desolation.

Found today on the lower path a chequered blue and black feather, from a visiting jay. Nice if the woodpecker would drop a green feather and the goldfinch a golden tail feather. Since leaving London to make this patch of the West Country my home, on my long walks of discovery I've collected feathers and bones to display in clear glass bowls and tumblers in my cottage, hidden round the bend of a beaten-earth lane.

This whole undertaking, the land clearance and house restoration, the expense of time and money on a property I do not own, is it imaginative or insane?

Why am I doing this?

10 July

Last night deer ate my roses, the leaves as well as the flowers.

Let them. They're off now on the trail of some other delicacy.

I imagine an animal's choice of place to forage is conditioned as much by memories of safety as by the quality and quantity of food. What kind of specific recall, I wonder, do deer have of where they last ate?

They mostly go, I suppose, to where they regularly feel secure.

I turned, not long after writing this, to my place in reading *Natural Goodness*, where the Oxford philosopher Philippa Foot offers an answer to my question, telling of the concerns of Thomas Aquinas for the nature of choice made by sheep in where to eat in a field: 'Aquinas stresses that animals, having perception as plants do not, may do what they do for an apprehended end. Nevertheless he insists that in doing something for an end animals cannot comprehend it *as an end* ... Without speech small children, like animals, are able to have ends but do not see them as ends. And the same point could be made in terms of what is seen to be good. For it can be said that while animals go for the good (thing) *that they see*, human beings go for *what they see as good*: food, for example, being the good thing that animals see and go for and that human beings are able to see as good.'

13 July

Walking along the mown path through the dell this morning, I thought about the damage gardeners do to natural life with their fetish for tidiness – all the cutting and strimming and mowing and poisoning, followed by replacement of existing beauty with crowded inappropriate planting. The narrow path in my wood, which looks like grass, isn't: it's the waist-high wilderness of wonderful everything that grows uncut at its side. Looking also at the shapes and colours of the lane, where I've done little more than dig out the nettles and brambles and cut down marauding infiltration by laurel and sycamore, I understand what anodyne destruction is wreaked by use of machines, the ubiquitous garden brush-cutter and highway tractor-trimmers. This summer I've done almost no work on the land, sat and watched nature take its way, confirmed my preference for the sound as well as the feel of doing whatever I have done by hand. It was only with the greatest reluctance that yesterday I mowed the lawn, wishing to prolong the parade of buttercups, daisies, plantain and clover.

The noise.

Such a horrid noise.

The whine and grind of rotating blades tearing at the grass.

Oliver Rackham writes, in his *The History of the Countryside*, a book of passionate opinion and the observations of a lifetime: 'More intractable than destruction in pursuit of a purpose is the blight of tidiness which every year sweeps away something of beauty or meaning.'

I want to learn to live decently here.

14 July

Taking an impromptu break from work at my desk, I wandered down what used to be the back drive of Cothelstone House, and delighted in an ordinary sight: a blue butterfly in flight. By physically following the flight of this one butterfly, I was drawn back towards a patch of brambles already passed, and made suddenly aware of three others, a painted lady, a small tortoiseshell and a comma sunning themselves in close proximity, wings wide open.

Pleasure also at the flash of colours of the goldfinches in shuttle-flight between lane and apple tree, from where they drop down for a thistle-feast. Four now, the young of my pair already out and about on the wing.

Periodically throughout the summer, watching these sparkling birds, I've thought of a picture which I haven't seen for many years, in the Mauritshuis in The Hague, the city in which I was married. The small oil painting on board is of a bird on a perch, by Carel Fabritius.

In truth I'm unsure what the bird's colour is, fear that, in habitual enhancement of reality, I may in my mind have turned the painting of a greenfinch gold.

This evening, in a review in the *Times Literary Supplement* of an exhibition at the National Gallery, by chance I read that Fabritius did indeed paint a goldfinch. In Christian tradition, it was a goldfinch which pecked irritant thorns from the flesh of Jesus, nailed to die on the cross.

It might be working: this attempt at nature-cure.

19 July

Below the giant Monterey I today found an almost new golf ball. It's the third time I've picked one up there, two white and a yellow, six miles from the nearest golf course. A bird – the cothelstone buzzards, or a loud crow? – presumably bears the prize away, belatedly to discover that a golf ball is useless.

Exhausting error.

I'm curious to know what mistaken instinct suggests to the bird some benefit to be gained by carrying off home a golf ball.

28 July

Hot and sunny early, and a speckled wood, the butterfly which looks its name, toasted itself in a patch of sunlight in the glade, on big leaves of cow parsley. When disturbed, it moved on to smaller leaves of ... don't know what it's called. The butterfly flew up to fight off from its territory a rival male.

The talkative finches returned to the thistles. Amazing how fast and thick these grow in the rubble which infills a mini-pond that a previous tenant dug for the geese he used to keep. I have removed the debris in rebuilding the kennels with Beth Ferendene, a strong, slim young woman, born and brought up locally, who wants to learn traditional builder's crafts to supplement her professional skills as a carpenter and carver. She seems to me to hold within her a sense of belonging to this land, along with my builder Frank Sayer, who, into his forties now, has never lived anywhere else but Lower Terhill.

It's a butterfly day. Three minutes ago a small tortoiseshell flew into the house and past my desk, fluttering at the window to get out, the beat of its wings frantic against the glass. Very gently I enclosed the palm of my hand around the beautiful thing and lifted it to be released into the garden. The brush of its wings against my skin felt like ... felt like?

Earlier I'd seen what I excitedly identified as an adonis blue feeding on horseshoe vetch in the patch of grass which used to be the front lawn of the big house – horseshoe vetch is a low-growing plant with pendulous yellow flower heads, the only thing adonis blue eat. I rang my landlord, Hugh Warmington, to share the news of this rare visitor, and he gave me the name of the officer in charge of Somerset Environment Records and, in time to save public idiocy, double-checking, I concluded that all I had seen was a common blue – which reinforces everything I already know if only I didn't keep forgetting, that the miracle is the sight itself, however 'common'.

Decided that if I'm to continue regularly taking these notes, I should do so in my actual state of no-knowledge, and seek to describe with the eye-of-ignorance what a small tortoiseshell (and a goldfinch, and a leaf of cow parsley, and an adonis blue, the horseshoe vetch, etc.) looks like, what it is that I see, feel, smell. The *Millennium Atlas of Butterflies in Britain and Ireland* says: 'The Small Tortoiseshell is among the most well-known butterflies in Britain and Ireland. The striking and attractive patterning, and its appearance at almost any time of year in urban areas have made it a familiar species.' Oh? Odd, that. When I saw ten days ago, on the wilting blossom of a bramble, turning towards becoming a blackberry (simply so: a black berry which forms as the petals fall from the head of a white hedgerow flower, tight and green to begin with, turning red, growing black and, in a good year, juicy), this creature with wings sloping backwards, like a fighter plane, the scalloped back-edges dabbed in turquoise, the rest, yes, the colour and pattern of a turtle's shell, I didn't remember ever having seen one before. Although I must have, I suppose, for the book's dotted map of sightings charts its presence in every part of the entire British Isles, and it is more than likely that I've several times before been told, or read, its name.

29 July

The family of wrens busy on the ground at the base of the burdock scrambled away at my approach, the young just about taking to the air; except for one laggard which stood trembling at my feet, its mother twittering from behind the leaves of the lowest branch of a nearby tree.

There is a bird which plunges and sashays through the air catching flies, then perches on the ridge of the byre to bang the larger flies against the tiles till dead. After eating, it cleans its beak on a branch.

I fretted at the thwarted energy of a little red-brown butterfly, never stopping, the rapid beat of its wings taking it from leaf to leaf without finding the occasion to alight. 'Stop, please rest, or you'll die. Please, choose a place to be,' I said, beneath my breath.

Later, again seated on my second bench, by the wall, reading *Dying We Live. The Final Messages and Records of the German Resistance*, I look up to see a young rabbit thirty feet away in the middle of the lawn, munching clover. Alfred Delp wrote, not long before he was beheaded by the Third Reich: 'Alas, how limited the human heart is even in the capacities most characteristically its own – in hoping and believing. It needs help in order to find itself and not flutter away like some shy half-fledged birds that have fallen out of their nest.'

30 July

In the dry heat my vegetable patch riots. The endive reaches out longer and longer stalks with fewer and fewer leaves, then bursts into raggedy purple-blue flowers which attract small white butterflies. The sharp-tasting leaves of another salad, rocket, are also shooting up thin dark green stems, ending in four-petal flowers, cream in colour with mauve veins. The orangey-red flowers of runner beans, climbing now to the top of my coppiced hazel poles, look good against their green heart-shaped leaves. See that some have been eaten in places to skeletal webs, so thick were the eggs of the insects laid. The buzz of these insects everywhere. In the soft mornings bees progress in and out of the flowers of bindweed, enemy of the conventional gardener.

These insect lives interweave, touching humans only when we slow and quieten to inactivity. To purposelessness. Very difficult for me to do.

I have so much to learn. Not facts, not all these facts. Stickier things. Treacle. Quicksand. Bog.

31 July

Sitting in the sun, thinking about my sister in New Zealand whilst also looking, listening. It occurs to me how lucky I am that this garden, which has become mine, is mostly green and white. Another white torch-shaped flower has shown itself: the buddleia, following the massed candles earlier in the year of both the bird cherry down by the pine and the white lilac beside the front gate. The new flower of the buddleia has a heavy scent, the petals white, dark yellow heads and pink trumpet stems. I'm lucky because all three – also the valerian which sprouts from crevices in the wall at my back – more commonly come in dark, to-me-less-pleasing colours.

Wonder if a past head groom, whose tied cottage for generations this used to be, *chose* these flowers to be white?

Amongst the half-dozen ever-present darting white butterflies, a flash of yellow. Followed with my eye the brimstone's flight, and when it landed on the runner beans I walked over, to find it perched on the end of a red flower, wings furled, light green on the underside, with two black beauty spots, veined like leaves, shaped on the curve perfectly to the point, and with long strong legs, sharply bent at the knees, yellow like its body. It walked from head to head of the bunched flowers, giving a couple of flaps of its wings, bright yellow on the upper side, to rise to the next bouquet.

My landlord tells me that the tree I've been calling bird cherry isn't. He knows about trees, and yet has never been able to identify what this is.

'Doesn't matter. Must be rare. Lovely thing,' he said.

High up in the tallest ash the sound of a bird I can't see, hidden in the leaves, making the same music as yesterday – a lilting trill, the notes quickening and rising always to the same conclusion. The song of this season. A mother's relief at the release of her brood, in flight to find a territory of their own?

I wish I knew what this beautiful sound means to the birds, to those that sing and to those that listen, let out and taken in without a thought (as we think of it) and yet not, I like to believe, without meaning.

The misting rain of this morning sends up this afternoon, in the heat of full sun, rich scents from the foliage. Two more yellow butterflies have hatched. Like to believe that the over-wintered brimstone, the sight of which I remember being astonished by back in early March, may be the parent of these three seen today, and that, as larvae, they fed on one of the eaten leaves out there in the glade.

To associate myself with the fate of life around me, something I've never before done in all my fifty-five years, feels like a risk. A necessary risk.

Until now I've sought, and mostly achieved, control.

1 August

I do love to hear the call of the buzzard ... keeuuu, keeuuu, keeuuu. It is, by now, *the* buzzard, a distinctively large bird which spends many hours of every day perched on and flying above the trees in the inner ring of my view. The cry plaintive, tension attenuated, refined, matched to the drawn-out spirals of its flight. Don't know in which precise tree he lives (this particular voice is male, I reckon). Don't need to know.

People live near here as well as birds. I just don't speak to them much. Don't have to. Don't want to. Nobody seems to mind.

5 August

Early this evening I went out on impulse for a stroll and met, for the first time, one of the owls in my wood. All I saw was a broad brown back and flanged tail, silent in motion, disappearing within seconds of my appearance, gone to perch in the high branches of the biggest of the sweet chestnut trees, concealed from my view by layers of leaves.

6 August

As I walked to post a letter in the red box on the corner beyond Keepers Cottage, I saw a bird of prey on the top of a telegraph pole (which around here are not high, the straight-trunk size of a small pine). Recognized it as a hunting bird by its long built-for-flight tail, hooked flesh-tearing beak and air of elegant energy. One of the Quantock Rangers happened to pass in his jeep, frightening the bird before I'd had a chance properly to look. Must have been a sparrow hawk, he told me – not a merlin, as I'd romantically imagined, drawn to the name.

I've seen what must be the same bird fly ahead of my car along the lane, skimming from side to side low between the hedges, wholly in control. Like, and unlike, the jet fighters trespassing above the combes of the Quantocks.

7 August

Moles have again been active, retunnelling their crossing points of the path of brick and stones which I embedded in the earth along the track to the far bench. When the moles build their underground roads in unsightly relation to my own ways of passage I tend to stamp their roofs flat, hoping they will opt for an alternative route. The territory is fertile enough to satisfy the needs of all of us who live here. A process of practical negotiation occurs, the dialogue of interaction. No tedious committee meetings, no battering out of a mutually agreeable form of legal words. Live and let live.

Let go, let go.

Please.

10 August

With neat observations I make myself seem rational and urbane.

Far from true.

I'm vulnerable, sinking several times each day into sharp anxiety. Threatened by the tiny everyday.

Can't begin to write what it actually feels like – even writing that I can't do so is soberly expressed, declining the desperation that washes through me.

11 August

As I passed along the path by my cottage door this morning I caught the tail-end dash of a small brown mouse-like creature disappearing into the long grass. If I had seen it before it saw me I could have watched it for a second or two, before it made it to the cover of its hidden run at the base of the wall. On the other hand, I could have been looking in a different direction and seen nothing.

To see without looking.

My aim.

It seems true that if humans move not too fast or boisterously about the place, and stop still as soon as they see almost any animal, large or minuscule, the creature doesn't flee. The other day, down on the fields above the cliffs, it was a hare. The hare doesn't always perceive our stationary shape as dangerous. Maybe, in time, people who seek to live alongside the natural life of a particular piece of land acquire the habit of dressing in appropriate colours, absorb some of the non-human smell of the place.

Living things have their territory. Spiders have their territory. It is the same spider I always see in the corner of the room by the door, and a different spider which occupies the window space.

The three ant nests which I disturbed yesterday in cutting the lawn have not been abandoned. In the clover the ants had allowed eggs to be laid above ground level, where they were exposed by the arrival of my mower. The white eggs have been removed now from sight, taken back down into the earth through remade holes in the top of the nest, the tiny black ants busy again at their disciplined labour. The birds seem not to have noticed this larder door ajar for an hour or two. Maybe there's plenty for them to eat elsewhere at this time of year.

Acceptance.

Nature accepts the way things happen.

12 August

As night falls down by the Monterey pine the bats fly.
I'd forgotten this. They make sounds too. Bat sounds:
high-pitched squealings.

15 August

Work on the house, though slow, is beautifully done. Three people work next door every day, as Frank and his labourer have been joined full-time by Beth Ferendene, who builds rough stone walls with lime mortar, lays reclamation floorboards, does whatever is required of her.

16 August

Though we may seldom see it, life is out there, busy, separate. I caught brief sight today of this other world, when, pulling bindweed from its hold on the long grass below one of the crab apple trees, I disturbed a field mouse, observed for the few seconds it took to cross a mown grass path. Saw it for long enough to recognize a cousin of the slightly darker brown mouse which has strayed into the house a couple of times.

17 August

Another streak of brown in the open, a sleek, super-fast animal crossing the lane. I didn't have time to see its head, but there was a tail. A weasel?

And, in the mid-morning sun, a butterfly with exquisite 'eyes' on the top corners of its wings, dark outside, with bright liquid-shaped centres and splashes, like tears, on the lower wings.

The wings of butterflies fade, grow ragged. Within days, for some, not weeks.

The deadening effect on me of such a sight is out of proportion. As is the elation at seeing healthy butterflies in flight.

19 August

The moles have been energetic in the rain-softened earth. Out in the red plough of the park, in which the lines of sown grass are greening, dozens of fresh molehills have appeared – like the mouths of tube stations, the precise track of their subterranean network unmapped.

Saw scurry from the step to the kennels what I thought might be a child mole. Seen barely for a second, I was struck by the blackness of its body and the pinkness of its feet.

22 August

Whether it is the weeks of early summer rain, or some crop infestation, or a regular look which I'd failed previously to notice, I'm dismayed by the greyness of a field of Cothelstone wheat, ears darkened with mildew. Plucked an ear of the corn and absent-mindedly winnowed it in my hand, and inside the seemingly-diseased husks revealed ripe wheat, rich and deep in colour.

Disguised summer gold, nature's currency.

Two years ago, exploring from the place I rented on Janet White's farm on the other side of the hill, I first took the footpath through the centre of a sloping field of corn towards the spire of Cothelstone Church, with the Jacobean manor house at its side, and cried tears of amazement at the beauty of the sight. I hoped then, in proximity, that shepherd Janet's country-wise contentment would somehow feed down to me.

9 September

There is a robin here which sings to itself. Like a person humming, audible only when close by. An affecting sound, muted, the bird's throat throbbing, its beak closed.

19 September

In the sudden wind the big old oak at the end of the lane
is shedding branch-end twigs, each with several leaves.
They litter the ground: an autumn preface.

Things *are* disintegrating.

21 September

The call of a pair of ravens between the top branches of
two of the sequoia, their bass voices making adolescent
altos of the crows. On a quiet evening, in the slow beat
of their wings as they flap across the park to their nest
I catch the sound of wing feathers vibrate, and think of
the idling engine of a tractor.

What is going on?
    I wish I knew.

23 September

In the mist this morning I hear the rain-shower approach
before I see or feel it, hear drops rattle the leaves of the
trees which descend beside the farm track, then cross
Constance Sayer's garden, reach the big poplar and two
large ash behind my byre, finally to fall at my feet on the
cottage threshold. Until the moment of seeing the rain
splash on the ground I had thought the shifting sound
was something else: aeroplanes unseen in the sky, or a
lorry climbing the road on the far side of Cothelstone
Hill. How I hate getting things wrong.

24 September

A three foot long mole-ridge appeared overnight at the edge of the lawn, almost on the grassed-over path beside the house, where I would have thought the earth was too hard and the passage of feet across the ground too frequent for the comfort of moles. Without hesitation, I rollered the underground tunnel flat. Within two hours the mole had re-excavated. I rolled again.

When I returned after dark from a long end-of-summer day on the beach, the whole ridge had reappeared. This time I left the roller standing all night across the line of the mole's trajectory, and in the morning there was a six-inch high ridge at one end.

Questions tumble. To be answered by watching.

I've always watched, always been on my guard. Mostly failed to see what I needed to.

If this morning I met a mole that could speak, this is what I'd ask: 'You reach this spot via, I presume, a deeper underground network of passages. Why have you chosen this particular place to come close to the surface? Is there special stuff here to eat? Or does rock block your below-ground passage? Why the stubborn plan, whatever the man-made barriers, to excavate this fixed route? Where are you heading?'

Another question occurs: 'Are you a he, a she? Or do you prefer to be addressed as they? Do you live singly or in a clan?'

The mole, efficiently, like a railwayman laying the track's iron curves along the lie of the land, has extended the run another five feet in the direction of the old front porch.

And the bees. I need to speak of the arrival at Lower

Terhill of some honey bees.

The other day Beth and I moved her father's hive of bees from Appleton Farm to the place we'd prepared for them at the bottom of my garden – behind rampant wild-raspberry canes, beneath the black-berried branches of one of the remaining elders, close to a section of the iron fence to the park where bees face the sun to wake them in the mornings to their work. The evening before, at dusk, Beth had taped the bees inside the hive and tied a strap tightly round its layered tiers. In the dark, at six in the morning, we drove Frank's pick-up truck the eight miles to Appleton and together lifted the sleeping hive to place it in the back of the truck, roped it down and set off for Terhill.

It was light by the time we bumped down across the field by the fence to ferocious buzzing of the bees trapped inside the hive. We lifted them over the fence and set the hive onto the brick platform we had prepared. When Beth pulled off the tape from their entrance-slit, hundreds of bees crawled out and up the side of the hive, stood stationary for several minutes as they tested their wings, before making their first flights into the unknown. After our breakfast Beth boiled them up a treat of sugar, donned her bee-suit, lit a pump-gun of smouldering fibre to calm them and then settled the layers of the hive securely into place. After a day in which the bees were busy finding their way around, by sundown there was no external sign of activity, just the inner sound of humming.

Down in a nearby wood a bee-professional from Dunster keeps five of his two hundred hives, and this year one of them produced the most honey of them all.

I'm happy that Beth's bees have safely made this journey.

26 September

A rash of neatness drew me again today, before breakfast, to roller the mole's tunnel flat. It had reached the path by the front door.

I regretted my action.

The mole has refused to be diverted by this idiocy of mine: within half an hour it had noticed the intrusion, and in ten minutes reopened the entire underground track.

I'm glad to have been given another chance to live less rigidly alongside my animal neighbours.

Recognising now the call of a woodpecker, I can look up from my desk when I hear its voice nearby and see it pecking at the lawn – today it was one of the young birds, its head barely red, tail feathers not fully formed.

Am curious to know what form the relationship takes between parent green woodpecker and its child. Earlier in the year I often saw the old pair feeding one beside the other. Now that I think of it, they seem always to have been together, always within sight of each other, keeping mutual watch, and I wonder at what stage they cease to accept the home-staying of their offspring. Or is it the woodpecker couple which moves on, motivated by some impulse to start every year afresh, build a new nest, leaving behind the young birds to find their adult way, housed in the familiar territory of childhood?

Maybe they're not a couple at all, briefly connected merely in parenthood. Ravens, I do know, mate for life.

Anything is possible.

Across the span of the four seasons most birds and animals mature from being produced to be reproducers, some nursing two broods within a single calendar year.

Nature's year measures the same seasonal span for every creature that lives here, whatever the total length of its customary life. How long do woodpeckers, for example, live? There's no reason, which I know of, to suppose that birds retain a concept of time. Nor awareness of intention. Birds retain no sense of what the purpose of anything might be.

I doubt if we, in truth, know better. I've the feeling that purpose is a spectre of man's delusion, that it does not, did not, never will exist, that we've invented purpose in the hope of easing our burden while, in fact, torturing each other with the prospect. We may, quite soon, impale ourselves on purpose, extinguish the human race in our attempt to conquer meaning.

28 September

My boots stand on the quarry-tile floor of the old kitchen here in my cottage. This morning I put my foot into one of the worn leather gardening boots, felt what I thought was a lump of mud, and shook out a small frog onto the mat.

The mole has extended his tunnel by another six feet, heading past the corner of the house.

1 October

While largely ignorant of matters of nature, remembered facts tread water beneath the surface of perception, alongside implanted rules and phobias and fears of childhood. When this morning I saw crimson berries shining like glass, something warned me that they were poisonous. And yet, recalling the neat purple and yellow flowers on the same plant earlier in the year, I doubted this received wisdom. A name sprang to mind: deadly nightshade. Mabey's *Flora Britannica* informed me I've been misled. Deadly nightshade has single purple berries. This is bittersweet, or woody nightshade:

> Popularly known as "deadly nightshade" in many parts of the country, this is not only a misidentification but a misnomer: it is one of the less poisonous members of the family. And, though it is common in shady corners of the garden and has rather tempting scarlet berries, like miniature plum tomatoes, cases of poisoning even amongst children are very rare. The intense bitterness that gives the species the first part of its name (the sweetness is an aftertaste) causes most curious nibblers to spit the berries out immediately ... The leaves, if you crush them, have a disagreeable smell of burnt rubber.

Soon after five in the afternoon, with the wind racing and the sun low in a brilliant sky, I sat beneath the Apple tree, its fallen leaves as well as fruit beginning now to pattern the grass. Picked up my white porcelain mug of tea from the grass and clinging to the side was a ladybird, in the brightness of the sun seeming to be glazed, an inset jewel. Craft-like in form and decoration, crisp, pure, perfectly symmetrical, machine-tooled and coloured.

I've never before noticed white crescents at the sides of the black heads of ladybirds. The precision of this creature's markings astonish me.

The mole has reached an island of wild grasses, where bluebells bloomed in the spring, and after twenty feet of the undulating ridge in the lawn his/her passage now ceases to be visible. What is the ... not the purpose ... the function of this path?

I ask questions of the mole which I'd do better directing at myself.

2 October

During the night, beneath the long grass, the mole turned sharply to the left, downhill in the mown dip along what used to be the path between Mr Blewitt's lawn and his vegetable patch, before later tenants allowed the old man's 'proper garden' to meadow itself. The tunnel is just below the roots of the grass, which the mole pushes up in a hump, with no need for the removal of earth into piles. The grass continues to grow, and the pattern of the animal's trail is curiously beautiful, not offensive at all, the mole's path curling beside my own.

3 October

The mole has veered off to the right, in the direction of
the kennels, and has just dived down into a hollow in
the lawn caused by my earlier assassination of an errant
clump of pampas grass. The mole-tracks extend now for
sixty meandering feet – sixty man feet, thousands of
pink little mole feet.

5 October

Compulsive, this need to name things, so to give them meaning. I name birds and tools and things, while unable to find the words directly to nail a helpful thought about the personal feelings which most matter to me.

Aware, through the books I've ordered, of my interests, the proprietor of Brendon Books in Taunton left out for me the other day a copy of *The Flora of Somerset*, written for the Somerset Archaeological and Natural History Society by a retired naval officer, Captain R.G.B. Roe. His twenty-year project to record the flora of the county was structured around division of the Ordinance Survey Map into square grids of land, for each of which a card was kept noting every growing plant, common and rare.

Reading of this I was reminded of the thought, years ago, developed at the time in pictorial detail in my mind, of taking a large piece of paper up on holiday to Bird How, in the upper valley of the Esk, below the crown of Scafell, Eskdale Pike, Bowfell and Crinkly Crags. On holiday with my singer-friend and her two children, I wanted to draw the outline of the immediate land around the shepherd's kippen, divide the map up and describe square by square every living thing, plant and creature we could between us find. The closer we examined the small stream and stonewalls and patches of bracken and trunks of trees the more excited I imagined us becoming. Sue (aged nine then), who loved drawing, and Bevan (aged eleven), who loved order, I saw being sceptical at first until, in the peace and pleasure of the place, they lost their inhibitions and threw themselves into the project.

Walking giant shapes into the dewy grass on the side of the fell, in imitation of Richard Long, was as far as we got in art-making.

7 October

My house is full of spiders, of varied shapes and sizes. In the corner of a wall by the log burner in the small end room sits a spider I hadn't before noticed, rust-red in colour, with relatively short back legs and pronounced white eyes on its lozenge-shaped body. There is, I am told, not a single spider in Britain which hurts man in any way at all.

Beth will soon be moving from her family home, the farm at Appleton, now sold, to the first of two cottages at the side of the path between the big house and church over at Cothelstone Manor.

9 October

Waking earlier and earlier, wrapped in uncertainty.

In the still-warm sun of a cloudless October morning
the air in the lane and wood reverberates with the sound
of bees collecting the last pollen, which they mostly find
in the spiky light-green 'flowers' currently in bloom on
the older bits of ivy. Big-winged butterflies too are still
around, in sheltered glades pierced by the sun, in summer delusion. The other day I gathered from the wooden
postbox on my wall an envelope of

Landlife Wildflower Seeds
The Butterfly Collection: Cornflower, Field Scabious,
Greater Knapweed, Hardheads, Musk Mallow,
Ox Eye Daisy and Yarrow

My name and address had been written across the printed information on the back of the package. I recognize
the handwriting but cannot, for certain, attach a name
to it.

11 October

It's just a mole, I know.

12 October

Pre-breakfast, I surprised one of the jays feeding by the lower path. Flashing its bands of blue wing feathers, it took flight into the sheltered trees behind the byre, where it maybe knows no human track passes. My intention in clearing, with considerable physical effort, this extra-dense patch of laurel was to create a wildlife haven – this is the first evidence I've noticed of it being used as such.

17 October

If I don't panic, don't allow fear to take hold, nature itself cannot harm me. My responses are the problem, harm-by-self the danger.

21 October

Found beneath an oak on a steep slope of the park my
first chanterelle, late in the season and therefore contort-
ed in shape, but with what I hope from now on to be able
to recognize as the mushroom's characteristic smell of
dried apricot, clear in comparison with one of the false
chanterelles which grow in the pine-needle litter near
my clothes line. There are, as noticed last year, masses
of waxcaps in the old grasslands: yellow and white and
crimson and an electric bottle green.

Parrot waxcap is their full name.

Naming, naming. Saying nothing.

24 October

Looking out into the picture from my bench I witness the pair of buzzards wheel and glide in closer tandem than I've before seen. They are almost touching wings, flying in formation – pilots pushing their body-planes through showground aerobatics, calling to each other.

Jonah was the name of the friend down here in Somerset with whom we used to stay when I was a boy. The bursar then at Queen's College Taunton, in later life he studied to be ordained, and was placed for his first church job as a curate at Cheddon Fitzpaine, off the back road from here to Bridgwater. I've been to see again his bursar's house at the school, where it still stands – although science laboratories have been built on the playing fields beside it. I've tried to find the rectory where he lived at Cheddon, but can't.

I've let him down, it feels.

We roller-skated, my sister and I, around the fives courts on visits to Jonah, steel wheels screaming.

He never married.

I did, years ago, when too young to deal with love. And left her, without any explanation.

26 October

It is the eve of my move into the renovated half of the cottage, a year and two months since work began.

3 November

A wren entered my new study, through the window opened to dispel the night's condensation on the panes. It flew instantly out through the narrow gap, barely ajar.

Lost weight these last months.

5 November

Cutting down a thicket of small dead elm has opened the view from the lane-side windows of my study, and I often now find myself leaning on the high windowsill, looking out at the sweep of sky over the Brendon Hills. Nearby, at the other side of the hedge, I can see the whole of the old orchard, where Will's horses and Hugh's oldest rams graze. At ten, the moon clear in the western sky above the line of oaks beyond the paddock, three of the rams stood in the shade of the single remaining apple tree, and on their backs perched crows pecking at lice in their fleeces. Nearer, below my window, in the shadow of the foliage bordering the lane, I spotted the grey rump of a rabbit. Saw its ears prick where it sat eating leaves, then rise to its hind legs, look around and disappear into the brambled bank behind the hedge.

6 November

Put up in the house today, with Beth's help, two more works by artist-friends. One of them hangs above my Waterhouse table in the spare bedroom.

Waterhouse. Does anybody remember who Waterhouse was?
Who cares?
I do, apparently.

8 November

I've been so happy down here in Somerset these last couple of years and don't understand how, as soon as the final move is made into my home, constructed to my specific requirements, in a perfect country setting, how tension builds and builds.

Where will this tightening end?

I don't know but ... maybe I somehow imagined I was making 'perfection' for myself, and am, inevitably, disappointed.

Mother *made* me seek perfection. Anything less and she was dismissive of me, furious in her disappointment. I had to be good, very good to justify the cost to her of my being her son.

9 November

The third consecutive day part-spent at my new desk in
this slow return to the rhythms of writing. I keep turning my head to the right to look south along the line of
the old cottage roof, with its chimney near the gable end.
It's not the roof, though, to which my eye is drawn but
beyond, to the vast oak a hundred yards away at the corner of the lane, close to the back gate to the demolished
mansion, my eye drawn beyond and above the oak too,
to the sky. The south window of my study is high, four
feet from the floorboards, and tall, another four feet, and
the line of vision from my desk cuts with geometric precision down the new iron gutter of the roof, square to
the big branches of the tree, its trunk rising parallel to
the chimney stack, but higher, a third of the way up the
upper pane of glass. The leaves on the oak look green
still with the sun behind, though I know that many have
fallen and that the green I think I see is closer, from a
different angle, to the golden yellow of autumn. Since
my arrival at Terhill I have constantly admired this tree
and feel privileged to be able to watch it now day-by-day,
to observe the great old thing's seasonal changes near
the close of its life. How old, precisely, is this oak? A
marker on this significant corner at a sharp turn in the
road certainly for three, maybe for four hundred years.
Generations of labourers on the Cothelstone Estate have
watched it grow from their homes here in the four modest cottages which I have made into one person's house.
With four bedrooms, a study and a library, two bath-
rooms and a big kitchen. This building was here before
the tree. Although there may have been another great
tree nearby, since demised. Over the wall into my wood,
recent felling of laurel has revealed, fifty feet from this

giant, an offspring already reaching as high as the neighbouring sweet chestnuts, preparing to play for centuries to come its turn at the role of marker.

10 November

Does purple hairstreak, a beautiful butterfly, seldom seen because it dwells in the high canopy of oak copses, live in my tree? They colonize large old single oaks, the book says. Imagine the time it took someone, some man, some Victorian, on discovering the existence of this secretive butterfly, to observe that – the book again says – the pupae of purple hairstreak fall to the ground and are taken by a particular species of red ant into its nest and fed through the winter.

Evasion. I seek escape by concentrating on nature.

Hiding here in private, inviting nobody to stay.

I dither and sweat at the idea of seeing people. Never telephone anybody. It's better that way.

11 November

Looking into my study on the way to breakfast I see through the window the rams at rest in their places of the night, tight to the hedge. Not noticed them so close before. The paddock is higher, by ten feet or so, than the land this side of the lane, and the rams lie level with my eyes. I see that they are indeed old. One of them stands to piss, and urine flows from the middle of his belly uninterrupted for a long time. The frosts have come, the grass ceases to grow and the sheep and cattle in the fields will soon depend on Hugh to winter feed them.

12 November

The softest of openings to the day, the mist low, rolling East to West from the stream at the base of Cothelstone Hill, thick enough to look like rain, yet lacking the weight to mark the puddles in the lane. Hugh drove by in his green jeep, towing a galvanized sheep trailer, backed into the gate and loaded up the rams. They filed up the ramp without hesitation – whilst the young horses whinnied and raced and leapt all four feet off the ground, unsettled by the departure of their companions.

With both internal doors of my study closed against the draft, the second window behind my desk is reflected in the glass panels, projecting an image across into my stairwell of the paddock, with a horse standing there, framed by the hawthorn in the hedge. I'm mesmerized by the tone and texture of these pictures, the outside inside, the landscape floating in internal space.

The rams may have been taken to the slaughterhouse.

Or perhaps to cover the ewes?

Early mornings remain a challenge, the void inside a struggle to fill. I trick myself into action. Force breakfast down.

Oaks protect their hold in the ground by letting die branches which, if they continued to grow, might outweigh the ageing root system and topple the tree. Poplars, disliked by traditional woodmen, tend to outgrow themselves and fall in full leaf, devastating the trees around them – the lopsided shape of the Monterey pine by the bench is due, Frank's forester brother told me, to a poplar crashing through the left flank of the tree. Two of the topmost branches of my marker oak, on the weather side, are dying back and currently stick out leafless into the sky, like the antlers of a stag. On each of them a raven perches, hefty-bodied birds, shaking their wings, and scraping their curved beaks on the bare timber.

14 November

A blackbird hops from branch to branch of the hawthorn in the hedge at my back, taking in its yellow beak the dark red berries, holding them there for a few seconds and then with a jerk of the neck swallowing them whole. The hawthorn fruit is quite large, must soon fill the bird's crop. A man in Minehead, less than ten miles distant from Terhill, recorded for a Richard Mabey research project the first flowering dates of his hedgerow hawthorn – May-tree, he preferred to call it – between 1984 and 1994, the earliest being 19 April (in 1989) and the latest 26 May (in 1987). Over several pages in his *Flora Britannica* Mabey records other country lore about the hawthorn/May.

16 November

See that mice have discovered my larder. Resting in a basket on a shelf there was a bunch of dry wild oats, once standing in a vase. Every single ear of corn has been removed.

I wonder when the deed was done.

Occasional mouse droppings scatter the shelves, but as nothing else has been touched, these are, I suspect, field mice who have rummaged under the lane door.

21 November

Saw the mouse this morning: dark brown, with pointed nose and rounded cartoon ears erect on the top of its
head. It has eaten the remains of a health food packet
of shelled walnuts, and I hounded it out of the larder,
poking and banging with a stick. I've had enough. After
opening the back door to the lane, I searched for the
mouse and found it cowering in a corner of the boot
room, behind as-yet-unpacked cartons of books, and
chased it towards the outside threshold. The agile animal moved so quickly that I can't be sure it didn't double
back under the boiler-room door.

The mouse miscalculated, got itself into a spot from
which it now cannot easily escape. I know my home so
well, from below the floors to the tiles on the roof, and
am sure that, in time, I'll force the creature to leave.

In London, on cornering a luckless mouse, I impaled
it on a shelf with the kitchen knife, then took another
knife to cut off its head.

The bees and birds and animals and insects of Terhill
may hold some atavistic knowledge that these buildings
are available for use, information which, after my reclamation for human occupation, they must now unlearn.
Until a few weeks ago, flies and wasps swarmed into my
study in search of winter safety, just as the swallows
flew in and out of the stable doors while Frank and his
team sat smoking during their breaks from work. By the
time the swallows return next year the broken windows
of the stables will have been replaced and new double
doors fitted in the open space through which they have
for generations been accustomed to swoop to their nests.
There's a round window in the northern gable which I

will leave unglazed, for the time being. They'll not be homeless.

I need to know inch-by-inch my home, for instant action should anything go wrong. Water. A leak – the devastation of falling water, wet and filth and rot.

Tonight the moon is lower, the mist deeper.

A silent howl, to hold myself sane.

23 November

This morning I saw the dormouse run into the sitting room, where it hid behind the drawers of my small chest of feathers and butterflies. Half an hour later, as I drank a mug of tea at the table, I watched it sitting, head up, paws held to its chest, in a shaft of sunlight on the honey-coloured boards of the hall. When I rose to my feet it ran back into the sitting room, where I heard it in the log basket, which I picked up and took outside the front door, and as I began to remove the wood, out the mouse jumped, to a height and distance incredible for its size.

Where is it now?

Not far away. For it lives here. Along with all the other mice whose acquaintance I've yet to make.

The week ends with the work around the reconstructed part of my house today complete, the cobbled path laid and the red topsoil levelled and dug, to be planted in the spring with native grasses and wild flowers, a mixture marketed by a local Somerset firm as *Butterfly Meadow*. Their label: 'In the nursery we have an old pasture field no longer grazed and which has been more or less left to its own devices wherein both wild flowers and butterflies have flourished. There we discovered the grass species present are of significant value in providing food for larva. With a few nectar wildflowers added to the field we have butterflies from June to September. This is now presented as our butterfly meadow mix containing flowers to feed on and important grasses on which to breed. *Wildflowers*: Knapweed, Devil's-bit Scabious, Common Sorrel, Wild Basil, Autumn Hawkbit, Small Scabious, Betony, Yarrow, Birdsfoot Trefoil, Greater Knapweed, Field Scabious, Brown Knapweed, Common Cats Ear,

Rough Hawkbit, Selfheal. The flowers have been chosen to coincide with the emergence of adult butterflies breeding on the associated grasses. Many other species will be attracted as adults and will vary with area but our observations have included: Comma, Small White, Red Admiral, Peacock, Small Tortoiseshell, Small Copper, Small Skipper, Common Blue, Yellow Brimstone, Painted Lady and Clouded Yellow. *Grasses*: Common Couch (for breeding by Speckled Wood, Wall, Grayling, Meadow Brown, Hedge Brown), Cocksfoot (for Speckled Wood, Wall, Marbled White, Meadow Brown, Ringlet), Small-leaved Timothy (for Marbled White), Smooth Meadow Grass (for Meadow Brown), Meadow Fescue (for Small Heath), and Common Bent (to help create the sward).'

I love lists of names.

In the dark I'm drawn out by the scent of turned earth, remembering to collect from the shed the morning's delivery of bottled milk. Take pleasure in moving my muddied Ford for the first time to its parking place behind the wall, leaving the lane-side of the old cottage free from motorcars.

26 November

Yesterday I was away from my desk all the daylight hours, therefore didn't glance up at the oak, which I now see has in the space of a single day and night shed millions of leaves, the shape of its branches this morning revealed against a blue sky. The light is so bright today that, by contrast, everything in shadow looks black.

On the walk up over the hill this afternoon from my new home to my old, from Terhill to Aisholt, to see Janet and The Old Granary which I used to rent, I picked two crimson waxcaps of exceptional depth in colour, funghi which I've never seen on her side of the hill and believed Janet would find beautiful – which she did, expressed delight with my gift, surprised at their unseasonal appearance. Walked back in the dark beneath the trees of Watery Lane and up the sharp slope of Janet's Middle Hill Meadow, then out across field after field of Hugh's until I arrived at my own gate, the gibbous moon so bright there was never a thought of reaching into my bag for the torch. On crossing the ridge I was shocked by the barrage of artificial orange light spread across Taunton Vale, marking villages which can hardly be seen by day.

Michael, the farm-worker on the Estate, this morning told me that the birds are feeding voraciously. Buzzards are killing grown pheasant, something he's seldom seen before, and the other day he watched a dozen crows demolish the carcass of a ewe, all this despite the mildness of the weather and abundance of food. The sign, Michael's country lore predicts, of a cold winter to follow.

The mouse is back. Unless there were two. Anyway,

within a day of ejection, I noticed renewed feeding on the outer skins of onion, on the stems of pumpkin and on the glue in a roll of swing-bin liners. Upset by the attack on my winter store, I for several minutes banged a stick against the steel sides of the ugly filing cabinet hidden in the larder, seeking to sound-hound the mouse from its lair.

29 November

Changes for the mouse: a new elm door hangs between the larder and kitchen, beautifully carpented by the girl who made my beds and the kitchen table.

Is the mouse resident still? Or has s/he been coming and going beneath the lane door from some external nest to raid the larder?

Frank, confident of his building, claims there's no way in for the mouse, insists my stores are safe.

30 November

I think I might be in trouble.
    Shovel the fear out of sight.
    Mustn't give in.

1 December

Thousands of times though I may walk my paths, the variations are endless. No sight precisely repeats itself. At midday I happened to walk out into the park through the old wooden gate in a neglected corner of my wood and wander in the opposite direction normally taken, northwards down the field-side of the iron fence, where my eye was drawn by an uncommon chirp towards the top branches of the Monterey pine. And there I watched, in bright sunlight, the pair of nuthatch feed. From my customary seat on the bench inside the fence, unable to see up through the dense branches, I can catch only fleeting glimpses of these birds. I didn't know they were still here. Lovely creatures, with solid little bodies, strong necks and long beaks, their chests light pink, heads and backs grey-blue, with white and black slashes around the eyes. They get on with life.

Reading this evening the latest published work by my current favourite amongst living writers, W.G. Sebald, the German academic who teaches in East Anglia. Find that he relates an incident in his character Austerlitz's childhood, trapping moths at night in egg boxes with Uncle Alphonso and brother Gerald. Sebald is as interested in names as I am:

> I do remember, said Austerlitz, that the two of us, Gerald and I, could not get over our amazement at the endless variety of these invertebrates, which are usually hidden from our sight, and that Alphonso let us simply gaze at their wonderful display for a long time, but I don't recollect now exactly what kinds of night-winged creatures landed there beside us, perhaps they were China-Marks,

Dark Porcelains and Marbled Beauties, Scarce Silverlines
or Burnished Brass, Green Foresters and Green Adelas,
White Plumes, Light Arches, Old Ladies and Ghost
Moths, but at any rate we counted dozens of them, so dif-
ferent in structure and appearance that neither Gerald nor
I could grasp it all.

The mouse seems to have departed. The nuts are intact.

2 December

Late last night, in the darkness and silence, while the human residents of the hamlet of Terhill slept, and many of the birds and animals too, I looked out to find the sky covered in weightless rippled clouds, like the marks of receding waves on the sand in a low-tide estuary. The moon had moved to a place where I could not see it, the night air was cool, clear except for this rippling of the entire sky within my view. Something affected the quality of light reflecting from the wet ground, the stillness, the whole scene a uniform silvery-grey, as if wash-painted – like an opera set, reversed reality, day turned arbitrarily into night, the earth turned upside down, sea-sand in the sky.

3 December

Enveloped in mist, the light of the just-risen sun failing to break through, I watched from behind the five-bar gate to the back-lane of the demolished mansion two kennel-men on bicycles escort the Quantock Staghounds up the wet road on morning exercise. The men called in dog-directed voices, the older, capped and raincoated, ahead of the pack, a younger man in a blue anorak at the rear, both straining at the pedals of their bicycles on the hill, backs rocking with the effort.

On a misty morning of peculiar Englishness, in countryside of particular beauty, the purpose of working to keep alive the traditions of the chase must surely be the blood-to-the-heart thrill of riding a horse? Despite my dislike of the hunt, I can imagine the joy of riding on a broad-backed, sure-hoofed hunter out across the winter land to exercise and train a pack of pedigree hounds.

Bicycles, indeed!

The shrouding of my vision as the mists roll through my garden glades leads me to feel invisible. Layers of wet on grounded leaves silence the fall of my boots as I walk. Maybe the illusion today of invisibility concerns sound more than sight, springs from non-hearing of my clumsy human passage. Three blackbirds eating holly berries do not cease to peck as I approach.

I love to move unseen, as if absent.

In the urge to find the occasional answer to repeated questionings, five tree books lie open on my big desk of black ash. The books are: *Trees & Woodlands in the British Landscape* by the master tree-writer, Oliver Rackham; two Collins publications by the equally authoritative and independent-spirited Alan Mitchell, his discursive

Trees of Britain and detailed field guide *Trees of Britain and Northern Europe*; Richard Mabey's *Flora Britannica*; and the Reader's Digest *Field Guide to the Trees and Shrubs of Britain*. From which I learn that only female holly trees bear berries. That the evergreen oak, short branches of which I yesterday gathered for decoration, is called holm in English and ilex in Latin, both of which are occasional names also for holly (Mitchell: 'the hollies have no real claim to the classic name *Ilex* as this was used by the Romans for the Holm Oak'). That there are over three hundred species of holly recorded in Britain, including bacciflava, 'infrequent', with bright yellow berries, a specimen of which grows in the jungle beyond the coach house. That one of the highclere hollies, hybrids between common holly and canary holly, has grey-brown bark and usually forks low.

This last sounds to be like mine, but there resemblance to my tree ends, and I still don't know what its name is. Do and don't mind not knowing.

4 December

Mice are nice, I've decided. Tonight I found that the house mouse had carried each ear of oats up from the bottom to the top shelf of my larder, to store in the least used of places, in the narrow space behind a box of fish cutlery angled against the wall.

Ideal!

I can't think why these ivory handled silver-plated knives and forks continue to travel with me, for I've never used them, will never use them: a wedding present to my parents.

I presume the corn was carried to the secret store in one session at the start and has since night-by-night been eaten. The discipline, the diligence of this little brown mouse!

What paradise the grain stores must have been to the mice of Mountmellick, in the flour mill managed for thirty years by the husband of one of the many elder sisters of my mother, herself the tenth of ten children of an embattled Protestant tenant-farmer at the bog-centre of Southern Ireland. I remember as a boy bicycling down 'miles' of concrete passages beside the giant wooden bins of winnowed ears of wheat, in which we dared to play, sinking each step up to our young knees, fearful of slipping down the open chutes and suffocating beneath a golden avalanche.

7 December

It's only in the countryside, as I walk in steady step through the lived-over landscape of hill-fields and heathland, that beauty feels fixed, immoveable from the middle of this sun-drenched winter's day. In the city it never occurred to me that things seen could be anything other than momentary, a flash of brilliance, ignited and extinguished in a stroke. Here now at my desk, I'm surprised that the biblical sunset lasts as long as it does. Offering time enough to reflect on how many images of war are placed against skies of the same dramatic hue, streaked in orange and purple – *Scapegoat* colours, mirroring a postcard I bought years and years ago, of the Holman Hunt picture in the Tate.

Blood colours.

Last year at lambing, Janet White found on her morning round of inspection a ewe on its back, alive, its blooded udder eaten by a fox, the lamb standing at its mother's side bleating for milk.

8 December

I rose from my desk chair at an unexpected sound in the house and went downstairs to investigate, finding no explanation. Five minutes later the same sound. And I saw flying about the roof of the stairwell a robin. He – unthinkingly, I gender it male – fluttered around, streaking the least accessible wall in the house with rain-lines of shit, then flew into my study and out through the window which I opened for him. There were several more droppings, I discovered, in my bedroom, the bird-stain on my white duvet cover difficult to remove.

This experience has coincided with the emergence into consciousness of feeling that, until now, I've lived alone in a world of my solitary making, self-separated from family and friends. And that now, for the first time in my life, others enter.

What a time it has taken.

Heard today the call of what I know to be a magpie, loud, quarrelsome, a bossy bird. Knowledge of this fact came with the experience of living on the other side of the hill, at Aisholt, where magpies steal eggs from Janet's farm-kitchen table. Here at Cothelstone Hugh traps and kills as many magpies as he can, hating their raiding of the nests of songbirds, and I have thus seldom seen or heard them on the Estate. Even Janet, in frustration, once set up a magpie trap, and captured six, only to find that neither husband nor son would kill them for her. Unable to bring herself to do the deed, she loaded the cage into the back of the Land Rover and drove off six miles to the beach at Kilve to release the birds.

Janet was greeted by laughter on return to the farm-yard, her men claiming that the magpies arrived back home before she did.

Jonah Mitchel-Jones died from the effects of Parkinson's Disease – as my father did, a decade later.

After Jonah's death, thoughtful friends of his gave me several books from his library, which stand at home on these shelves, in their original dust covers, signed and dated in his spindly writing, amongst them: *Sedgemoor and Avalon* by Desmond Hawkins (1954); from The King's England series, Arthur Mee's *Somerset, County of Romantic Splendour* (1941); and *Life of the Wayside and Woodland* by T.R.E. Southwood, revised by T.A. Coward in 1963.

10 December

A Monday night dark and cold, the first of winter. At my desk with a glass of wine and memories of a happy day, spent in the company of two artist-friends from London, down for a song recital I organized last night at Podshavers, the country restaurant I helped set up two years ago.

A comfort to know that it's possible to be normally sociable, put on a good public show outside my mute vacancy.

And a relief that there's no woman around.

Intimacy never seems to work for me.

11 December

This is the third consecutive morning I've rounded
the corner of the garden wall to meet the same bird
breakfasting alone on the few apples which remain on
the ground beneath the old tree. On the two previous
mornings it hastened away, a thrice-dipping flight, as if
mechanically powered, attached to chains hung from a
line of invisible posts across the garden. woodpeckers
have a similar pattern of flight – not the same, though:
faster, the loops longer. Anyway, the sound this bird
made yesterday was different from a woodpecker, with
more notes. This morning I slowed my approach, and
was able to observe the bird, with its pronounced white,
blue, brown and black markings on body and wings.
Not yet full-grown, I felt: because of its slightly awk-
ward movements and the suggestion of plumage in the
process of discovering colour. A young jay, I suspect.
Not that the name matters. Just the fact that it ... yes,
what I like is this: it's a bird which I never see in a flock,
and although a common-enough presence amongst my
trees, is reluctant to show itself. If this is a young bird,
it was presumably born here, and has thus grown up
accustomed to my presence, walking the paths, always
at the same pace and in similar clothes, at regular times
of the day. To this youthful jay maybe I'm a large animal that's around the place, a scraggy mongrel cross
between Will's chestnut horses in the old orchard and
Hugh's glossy black bullocks in the park.

On most nights I hear owls hoot and screech to each
other amongst the trees – exactly how many I cannot be
sure.

From my table at lunch, the sun intense, I spotted a

small owl seated on a branch of the ash behind the byre. On stepping outside it was not there. Back inside I again saw it. In the act of reaching for binoculars I realized that the light fell in a particular way on a knotted turn of the branch. Without needing to check, I knew it was my mind which saw the owl, not my eyes.

While writing this sentence I hear the sound of a tractor, and rise to peer down onto the lane below, seeing in the back of an open trailer Michael with his team of beaters seated on straw bales, on their way to the next pheasant drive. Michael has worked this Estate for twenty years, and is content to labour on for another twenty or more, living with his family in a tied cottage by the Manor, on a salary of a few thousand pounds a year. The man driving the tractor is the old warrener whom I see with his boxed pair of ferrets netting rabbits in my lane. Both these men give the impression of trusting their own sense of value, of cherishing familiarity with this land, of accepting the fact that they'll never gain material wealth. They possess alternative ambition. Michael talks of his desire to secure the return of barn owls to Cothelstone, to which end he and Hugh, his employer, have for several seasons sown wood-side strips with the plants that a particular kind of vole eat and on which these shy birds like to feed.

I like these people. They welcome me, but I find it difficult to make for myself a convincing place in their world.

I try. I try. These notes are part of my attempt.

12 December

Central things unsaid, these words sanitised, a travesty. I ... I can't ... I can't say it.

I do things, plan a novel, make a home, normal sorts of things.

Except nothing *is* normal.

I'm fading.

And I am pleased to be. Despite the pain, it's what I want. To disappear.

15 December

Herzog, the filmmaker, wrote in his *Fitzcarraldo* journal: 'Why do these animal dramas preoccupy me so? Because I do not want to look inside myself. Only this much: a sense of desolation was tearing me up inside, like termites in a fallen tree trunk.'

Imagination carried Herzog through.

I'm stuck with dull words and mind. No way out.

16 December

'This inconspicuous rather than actually skulking little bird': says Collins' *The Birds of Britain and Europe* on
the hedge sparrow, or dunnock as it's also called. Take
pleasure in watching, as I eat lunch, the bird's bluish
head bob and shake, its beak piercing the moss on the
roof of the byre, pink legs wide-astride for balance.
They are secretive, I'm told in *The New Atlas of Breeding
Birds in Britain and Ireland*, nesting in the thickest middle
of brambles and thorn. With a social system the most
complex amongst all our native species, the dunnock is
the main British host to the cuckoo. The precision beauty of this semi-invisible bird of everyday life startles me.

Orange is this year-end's colour, spread across the
sky each afternoon as the sun sets – the quality of air
during these exceptional weeks of weather makes light
into a physical substance, a liquid spilling through the
atmosphere.

Exceptional? In my experience, yes. The whole of
this autumn such brazen extravagance in the colouring
of the leaves before they fall. It must have happened before, and I did not notice.

I'm pleased also with my insistence that every room
in this house be lit by two windows, at either side. From
my bed, without raising my head from the pillow, I see
trees and grass and sky through both windows, to the
west and to the east, and the ever-altering light is indeed,
I feel, remarkable.

17 December

W.G. Sebald is dead, killed in a car crash.

19 December

The night silent as I walked home across the fields in the dark from Podshavers, my restaurant in the old milking yard of an adjacent farm, eyes adjusting to the clouded peacefulness. On up from the gatehouse I heard and felt the crunch of gravel beneath the grass, on the forsaken drive which winds across the park, its route unreadable at ground-high sight, unused for sixty years.

Sebald, I learn from a newspaper cutting sent to me by a friend in this morning's post, collided with a lorry on a country road near his home in Norfolk. His daughter was injured in the accident. He may have had a heart attack.

20 December

Difficult to accept that the others who winter with me here, the fauna and flora of Lower Terhill, do not also have feelings. Maybe they too, in different ways are quietened by this windless weather, set to restorative sleepiness in their leaf-lined homes.

In *Austerlitz* Sebald wrote, I today read:

> Now and then a train of thought did succeed in emerging with wonderful clarity inside my head, but I knew even as it formed that I was in no position to record it, for as soon as I so much as picked up my pencil the endless possibilities of language, to which I could safely abandon myself, became a conglomeration of the most inane phrases ... It was as if an illness that had been latent in me for a long time were now threatening to erupt, as if some soul-destroying and inexorable force had fastened upon me and would gradually paralyse my entire system ... I became aware, through my dull bemusement, of the destructive effect on me of my desolation through all those past years, and a terrible weariness came over me at the idea that I had never really been alive, or was only now being born, almost on the eve of my death.

21 December

Slow down, you're overwrought. Stop, breathe, find your balance.

These things that I instruct myself are easier to say than do.

I know it's bad for me. That worse stuff can happen if I get too intense.

Wish I didn't mind so much about the mouse. Anxiety at not-knowing where it lives, how and when it comes and goes, why it has taken to nibbling an occasional carrot.

Control! Control!

Will it ever stop?

24 December

It's the time of year when the one-time greyhound kennels are most visible at the corner of the garden, a ruin when I arrived, totally restored by Beth and I, her first job at Terhill.

We cleared barrow-loads of rubble, lowered the fallen roofline to its original dimensions, installed a window in the bricked-up opening and made the place, with its three small rooms and two walled yards, watertight for Beth to occupy. The room with a chimney as a workshop, the second to store her Bee paraphernalia, the third a haphazard sanctuary of bits and pieces.

It mattered to me so much to restore this neglected little building.

I'm not sure why.

Remember our excitement at discovering in a messy corner of the byre enough double roman ridge tiles for the kennels, in rounded terracotta. Rarities these days, a hundred years old. They look perfect.

25 December

Soon after nine I cut an armful of holly from my five-trunked tree, the only one for miles around still in berry, and a second armful of variegated holly and ilex from the overgrown arboretum, and walk down across the Cothelstone land to redecorate Podshavers' tables for Christmas lunch at the restaurant. On my way, in the big field beyond the lodge, the wind rises, blowing clouds across half the sky. Although ahead of me the sun shines, rain begins to gust at my back, stinging my ears. I turn to look behind and find that I stand at the centre of a complete rainbow, both its ends grounded in the field I'm in. A solitary figure framed by a rainbow, holding in each hand bunches of evergreen foliage, on Christmas Day.

No better than any other day, the dark hours awake in bed no less fear-filled.

It's the time of year when thoughts of family press for attention.

Can picture, in detail, the cricket fields in winter outside my schoolmaster father's house. See me and my sister playing French cricket in our duffle coats, defending our legs with a bat from attack by tennis ball.

Another memory of these same playing fields. Of clambering on the spectator stands, the woodgrain deep, bleached by the sun. As a boy I stood in mounting excitement with the crowd gathered in front of the pavilion at the end of school matches, to see who might be sent to run around the old building in a spotted boater, notice of the coveted award of Flannels. Boys without their 1st XI colours wore grey trousers, all eleven of the final team gaining their whites by the time of the match against Eton, played out on the MCC pitch at Lords, the school teams occupying for two whole days the England dressing rooms and balconies. Male spectators dressed up in tails and topper, with a Harrow buttonhole of sea-blue cornflower, the stems wrapped in silver foil.

In my head the sun always shines on the cricket grounds of Harrow School.

That's right, I remember now: Jonah ran the Harrow School Clubs off Latimer Road, in West London. My father used to escort schoolboys up to town on Community Service at the club. That's how we knew Jonah, my link with West Somerset.

28 December

An animal has dug a hole in the filled half of my compost heap. With highish investment of animal effort.

Basic things – parenthood, cooking, newspapers, guns – mystify and frighten me. With some – food, intimacy – I'm beginning here to sense the possibility of comfort. As for love, Sebald feels to me a greater personal loss than my father.

Because I never loved him. Whereas Sebald's books I adore.

It's a long chain and I have neither the time nor inclination to examine the links. All I want is to free myself.

See from my file of quotes that I noted, a decade or so ago, on reading Nietzsche's *The Will to Power*: 'The task of spinning on the chain of life, and in such a way that the thread grows more powerful – that is the task.'

30 December

Slept solidly through the night for the first time in many months.

Beside my bed, I like, a lot, the small cabinet with specimen drawers of bones and feathers and shells.

Yesterday, walking with Beth by a stream on the fringes of Exmoor, we watched a pair of birds that neither of us had previously seen. The initial sight was of their flight up stream, inches above the water, dark wings swinging high and low, on each beat almost meeting. Looking down farther along the path through the forest onto the bubbling water below, swelled by melting snow, we spotted the birds perched on a log jammed against a midstream rock. Their heads and tails dipped and bobbed. When we drew parallel, the pair of birds flew in close formation back down towards the place where we first came upon them, and as they passed we were struck by the whiteness of their breasts and by the pointedness of their heads, with longish beaks. 'I think they might be dippers,' I said.

And they were, Heinzel, Fitter and Parslow confirm in their Collins bird book: 'unmistakable for conspicuous white front and habit of constantly bobbing on rocks in midstream'.

Were?

Are.

Still there, if not, then somewhere else, as solid in existence before I saw them as they remain after, out of my sight.

Me too. I'm also still here.

2 January

The mouse is hungry. On New Year's Eve it made its way into Beth's leather bag on the floor by the boot rack, where it nibbled an apple, bit a hole in her pouch of tobacco and gnawed at her wallet and at the paper edges of a cheque book.

What as yet undiscovered damage is it doing to my books on the shelves, and to the works of art stacked in my storeroom?

I've heard of a trap which doesn't kill. Think I'd better get hold of one of these, and remove the mouse to the old coach house, where it can share the food of Will's horses.

Daydream of bare ankles speckled with the yellow pollen of buttercups. They are my own feet and legs, cut-off from sight above the knees, torso-less, running through tall grasses and scattered wildflowers of a summer's meadow. And the paler legs of a young woman, the beautiful legs of Beth, my singular friend, in a separate yet connected dance.

3 January

Spent the day and night at Beth's place, in the cottage she rents beside Cothelstone Manor. Beth worked on the pebble mirrors she's making for sale through a shop in Bath, while I tried to read. It's hard for me to be there. Hard for her too.

5 January

The temperature has risen and January damp descends. Badger tracks turn muddy. No visible growth on land. The fallen leaves lose their crispness, begin to rot, scuffed by animals in search of grubs. The so-said dead of winter feels, in nature's patient way, discrete with life.

It'll come, it will come.

6 January

Walking home from Sunday lunch alone at Podshavers, I veered from the direct path to pass along the banks of an unfrequented stream, so full of bird life that the brambles below hawthorn bushes are washed white with droppings. Dozens, maybe hundreds of birds flew away as I approached. Crossed the footbridge and walked back around the cut oval of Cothelstone's National Hunt racecourse, a residue of the family's historical wealth, liberally extracted from a vast field, planted at its centre with beans.

Called for a tea with Beth on my way home. She remembers going to point-to-points there as a teenager.

We used to go to a point-to-point meeting too, every Easter, one of the family outings I looked forward to, below a bare chalk hillside ten miles from the Berkshire town in which we then lived, my father by then headmaster of the old grammar school.

Although twenty years separate Beth and me, our memories coincide.

9 January

Exactly two years ago, three months before moving into the unheated cottage, each day walking over the hill from Aisholt, when I first began to clear Terhill's woodland wilderness I came across a place of enchantment that I instantly knew I'd never want to touch. A big tree had uprooted itself, its trunk and branches long since cut and carried away, and around the disturbed terrain elder trees had flourished, they in their turn half-falling under the weight of ivy which now festoons the stump and the tangled underwood, creating a nook rich in mosses and ferns and damp-loving wild flowers. In the meantime I have cleared the surrounding territory of nettles and cut back the laurel, unveiling the shadow-limbs of old garden paths, nowhere plainer to see than where the big tree fell, blocking the main thoroughfare of this section of the nineteenth-century arboretum. Redouble my determination not to seek a return to the past, affirms my affection for the curl of my own narrow meanders, crossing and re-crossing the wide straight lines once mapped out by the formal creators of the garden. Strands of ivy have plunged, jungle-like, from a branch of the elder clump vertically to the ground, where they have laid extra roots, and new shoots now grow back up their parental self.

Maybe the ivy will in time become thick enough to sustain itself upright, independent of a host tree.

Bought in Taunton this morning two Live Capture Mouse Traps, an ingenious black plastic square-section tube with an angled bend in the centre, designed to entice a curious mouse by its own weight to cause the trap to tilt and the entrance flap to close. The recommended

116

bait is peanut butter.

Item 4 of *Directions for Use*: 'Check trap regularly to avoid distress to the mouse. The timing of the checks should be no longer than six hours apart.'

Other than the attack on Beth's bag, I've noticed no sign of the mouse in the house since moving the vegetables to an inaccessible larder shelf. I intend, all the same, to set the traps before going to bed and, in mouse-respect, to check when taking my early morning piss.

10 January

5 a.m. and the mouse traps are empty, peanut butter untouched.

Wake at 7 in terror at half-asleep images of water pouring down the walls, caused, I saw as I rushed in my dream upstairs, by the implosion of a radiator, opened up to its steaming, copper-gut innards.

After a break of several years, my nightmare has returned: I see my home disintegrate, reduced to rot and rubble by floods of falling water.

After an afternoon preparing the paddock behind the stables for transformation into an orchard, I'm disheartened by the extent of damage to the land by abandonment of agricultural rubbish. Pickaxing below the surface I unearth broken bricks and rolls of bailer twine and sheets of plastic and bits of iron and great lumps of concrete.

It will mend, the land will mend, with my care.

11 January

Caught a mouse last night.

At least I think I did.

Just before going to bed I found one of the traps closed, seeming to feel heavier as I carried it to a window. It was dark, though, and I couldn't see if a mouse jumped to the ground. Why didn't I put on my coat and boots, take a torch, release the trap down by the garden bench and watch what appeared?

I'm left in uncertainty.

Little, if any, of the peanut butter has been eaten.

I don't understand myself.

12 January

No doubt this time! On late-waking found a captured dormouse, which Beth and I carried down the lane and let out at the centre of the cobbled coach house yard. The mouse did not wish to leave its black box for the unprotected light, kept turning and turning inside. In the end we had to shake it out a touch roughly, and it sheltered for a moment behind the heel of my gumboot, before careering in desperate leaps for the undergrowth at the base of the nearest wall.

How did this appealing little creature – beautiful dark-brown flashes, I saw, on the nape of its neck, narrowing to a point along its back – experience the trauma of imprisonment?

I cannot know.

13 January

Twenty-four black rooks are resting in a double row along the top branches of the old oak, silhouetted against a heavy blue-white sky.

14 January

Catch myself standing for many minutes, head cocked, staring at the end ridge tile of the kennels, and recall the man I periodically used to meet in London on my way to swim each morning at 7.30 a.m. at the public baths in Ironmonger Row, a youngish man wearing an old-fashioned pair of corduroy trousers, navy blue woollen sweater and tweed jacket, standing stock-still on a corner of the street, eyes fixed to the meeting of sky and building, in a gaze of intense enquiry. I never saw the man move, although he was always alone, and must, I presume, have arrived and departed unaided. He was cared for, his black hair washed and cut. A man in his mid-thirties, helplessly at sea on the City Road.

15 January

Another (greyer) dormouse (big liquid black eyes) now lives down at the coach house.

Trapped.
    Like the troubled man in the City Road.
    Like me, entangled in morbid thinkings.

Nobody but I walks up over the hill from Terhill to Aisholt, and the cross-country route I choose to take through fields and woods feels private, mine. On a moonless night I experience a lightening of the spirit as memory of the shape of the land leads me to unseeable gates at the far sides of switch-back sloping fields.

This knowledge is in part physical, sensed by the limbs and muscles of the body, and in part intuitive, a feeling for the shape of the land and for the appropriate passage of man and animal across it. Knowing that on Aisholt's fields I follow not only in my own footsteps but also in those of Janet and her sheep, and of innumerable other country people over hundreds of years before her tenure of the farm, I let myself believe in and be guided by my sense of the travelled way. Tucked into a border-bank of Beech, the stile out onto Aisholt Common from Middle Hill Meadow is invisible to me until close enough to touch – there it is, though, in the pitch dark of the shadow of the trees, precisely where trust in my feet takes me.

When unseen branches comb my hair I do not, not for a split-second, flinch, so confident do I feel in the acceptability of my presence.

Unusual, for me.

18 January

They were out last night with their searchlight mounted on the back of an open Land Rover, shooting foxes.

This morning, at dawn, I hear in the cleared glade behind my byre the death-screech of a pheasant and see, through my bedroom window, a fox and his mate slink off home with their kill.

Good!

21 January

Out before eight this morning and hear more birds singing. It's mild for the season, and I'm up a little earlier than usual. Perhaps I awoke to the day less anxious, less preoccupied, and am therefore able to listen differently.

Let me try to break the circuit of uncertainty with direct description of what I saw. Of what was. Of what is, these January mornings at Lower Terhill:

It's quiet. Not soundless. Quiet. That goes for the colours too. Monotone? Maybe. There are blunt edges to the picture of the lane and paths and hedges and trees this morning. Everywhere is wet. The sky is grey, substanceless, against which the outlines of trunks and leafless branches gain no perspective, are unable to impress on the eye their volume. Although the light is soft, the sun not yet risen, it is day already, beyond dawn. The birds have, I suspect, been singing for some time. I find I can visually follow the sounds of song to their source, sensing, as I watch the small movements of head and the broader shiftings of position, that several of the birds are carrying on what we would call, human to human, a conversation. The character of the light is such that I cannot identify the colour of any bird, am uncertain of actual shape, do not know the name of what it is which this morning sings with both control and abandon. Not a big bird. A finch of sorts? No matter. Enough for me to see the little head thrown back and the beak open amazingly wide to trill after trill.

Better?

29 January

Saw today a flock of birds rise from the hedgerow and wheel at speed, in close formation, down and up and in and out and away.

I go on and on about birds. What am I actually saying?

31 January

Wind batters rain against the study windows. Darkness has fallen, obliterating the giant oak at the end of the lane. With windows fore and aft, I imagine I'm on the bridge at the wheel of a ship which powers itself through the storm that's been brewing since conception.

Melodramatic?

Feels true, though.

1 February

In the night the wind blew down the sole remaining apple tree in the old orchard, beneath which I watched last year from my study rams shelter from the sun.

With the fading of the rain and wind and the rising of the air temperature over the last few days the bees have woken, their hum so resonant, so vibrant that the hive seemed to tremble, as if about to take off and orbit the garden. Hundreds of bees crawled up the front of the hive, stretching after the weeks of sleep, brighter in colour and bigger after their well-fed rest. It's in the winter, I presume, that they guzzle the honey, self-made from the pollen which last year they exhausted themselves gathering.

Or are these bees a new generation?

Another sign of life: big lime-green catkins have appeared on my favourite hazel tree. A twig from the tree lies on my desk, shedding yellow powder on the black ash. The hazel bark too is spring-coloured, a growing-green, different from the as yet lifeless-green of other trees, with tiny leaf buds pushing through. The end bunch of four catkins, each three inches long, is thick with pollen-dust – a shake and twirl of the twig and lines are drawn across my desk.

And the rest? The bulk of life, the stuff I see and think and decline to write about?

10 February

It was one of those days of grey skies and windless rain, soaked in melancholy, when the blood-beat slows, spring hopes forgotten. In the walk to Podshavers for Sunday lunch, in the lower field a hare hunkered down beside a tuft of grass growing in the unploughed stubble and did not rise to run until I came within a few feet of it. Eyes lowered, frowning at some faraway thought, I heard the hare before I saw it, pounding across the ground towards the safety of a distant hedge. On my return, in the same state of mind, in the same field, I lifted my head at a soft chirp in front of me, to catch sight of the pale tail feathers of a bird as it flew low above the stubble to hide in the long grass on a ridge-division of the field.

In the middle of an unpromising February day, were both hare and bird in some animal-way turned in upon themselves, less attentive than customary to their surroundings and to the danger of human approach? I can imagine a metabolic process of response to the circumstances of the day which made the hare and the bird not wish to summon the energy to move until absolutely necessary. I might, after all, at the last moment have changed direction, leaving each peacefully to lie low and safe on its warmed patch of earth.

'Wish', though, is a consciousness-word, primed by feeling and thought. Birds and hares *are* whatever they do.

I try, I try. Try to observe. Try to be interested.

It's getting blacker inside. Soon I won't be able to see myself at all.

14 February

A mild, mostly sunny day, in part spent digging up nettles from the verge of the lane and from the woodland glades.

What will spring and summer this year reveal?

The lane, I discover at my nettle labours, used to be cobbled from wall to ditch, in its heyday part of the home farm on an estate of model proficiency. For sixty years now, since before the war, not a penny has been spent on Lower Terhill, the tenanted farm buildings allowed to deteriorate until no longer of use. I like today's haphazardness.

Time, it takes time, we all need time.

Patience.

In a few years I imagine my home at first sight looking as if it might be abandoned, on keener gaze understood to be occupied with gentleness. There's nothing I want to do but wait, wait and see. Wait and we'll see, we will see.

22 February

It's begun: the press of Terhill's trees into life. The tall-est tree behind the byre, seen from the kitchen table, has gained in weight of silhouette against the sky, caused, I discover on picking up a branch fallen to the ground, by the springing open of green buds, from which red fingers poke out, to be extended in time to soft-pink cat-kins. And down in the wood I notice a round puff of fluff has emerged from the buds of a tree split at its bowl into half-a-dozen trunks. I happen to know what both of these trees are called, one a native hybrid, the other an eighteenth-century import. Nothing gained, though, from naming them. Indeed something lost, I feel.

You cannot lose what you never had, a friend once said to me. I'm afraid I may never have had something vital that I've always needed.

Don't know what it is that I lack.

Fearful that, whatever it is, I may not survive with-out it.

23 February

Mice in the traps on three consecutive nights, eight caught in total to date.

A branch of one of the hawthorn bushes in the lane is in flower, in February.

Hailstorms today, the wind so strong and cold that the windows of my study mist over, then clear as the sun breaks through, and mist again with the return of the hail, the cycle several times repeated. By now the wind has dropped, the sun sets beautifully, and the buzzard preens its tail feathers, perched on a high branch of the big oak.

I love the call of a buzzard.

This time it doesn't speak as it flies away, wings slowly beating, back towards its home in the trees by the stream in the park. I've never before seen this bird so close to the house, the largest and therefore the oldest, the grandfather, I reckon, of the Cothelstone buzzards.

24 February

Last night a mouse must have knocked the trap before entering, for this morning it was closed but empty. Two days ago I blocked the gap beneath the back door. The mice seem to have other entrances and exits. Or I may have closed their only route to their homes outside, leaving those already inside with no choice but live here with me.

I'm confused, hesitant about what to do. Best perhaps to ditch the trap, unblock the door and let them freely come and go.

What am I frightened of?

It can't be the mice. They're the carrier of my fears, not the cause.

Like a child in a fairy tale, the darkness chills my blood and I dare not look.

Silly, I know. Because whatever it is, once accepted, might be manageable.

I doubt it, though. At the heart of things I'm almost certain that it's ... that I'm in trouble.

25 February

It is blackthorn, not hawthorn, which flowers earliest, Beth tells me. She suggests I record the hedgerow locations on my walks, to return to in the autumn and pick sloes for gin.

3 March

At midday the wind drops, releasing the sun quickly to warm the air. The bees are busy, returning to the hive with yellow sacks of pollen high-loaded in balance on either side, just in front of their wings.

Can't be much these days on which to feed. Maybe the gorse, which is in flower – much the same colour as the bees' gatherings.

The daffodils and primroses are also mostly out, a less dense yellow.

4 March

Managed to shortcut the cycle of batterings in bed this
morning and rose in time to listen to the seven o'clock
news, while I ate a quartered orange standing in my
dressing gown by the kitchen sink.

On wandering through my wood, pre-breakfast, I
again had to fight off the enveloping blankness.

No, not fight, not the old flailings for escape, more
like pushing aside, fold by fold, a grey weight of
helplessness.

The grey blackens at each removal of protective
layer.

Terrifying.

Saw a field mouse scuttle across one of the paths and,
on stooping to examine the ground, found the hole from
which it had emerged in the loose earth of the 'wilderness' and, six feet away, across the grass-growth of the
old gravel-bedded path, the other hole down which it
bolted.

Beth knows that I'm somehow not well.

I wish never again to retreat into the belief that I can
face this pain alone.

5 March

Beth's mirrors have sold out in Bath. She's busy making frames, from old iron.

6 March

Stood this afternoon at the double doors to my study, through which the grain once entered to be milled, and watched Frank hang a new door to the stable. A stocky man in his mid-forties, he has lived all his life here at Terhill, and as a boy had wanted to become a shepherd, inspired by the wisdom of an old man on the Estate who looked after the flock and with whom he worked in spare moments from school. He has learnt other skills, become a master builder, who applies himself to each task of his trade with a quality of attention seldom these days seen.

8 March

The trees, I can see, will again grow leaves this year. They mightn't have. I really didn't think they would.

It's raining hard and I drink my coffee inside, at the kitchen table, thumbing *Flora Britannica*. Read that the Scots used to recite:

Ash before oak, the lady wears a cloak.
Oak before ash, the lady wears a sash.

In Surrey they appear to have believed the opposite, predicting drought when the ash came into leaf before the oak:

If the oak comes out before the ash,
'Twill be a year of mix and splash.
If the ash comes out before the oak,
'Twill be a year of fire and smoke.

9 March

Within minutes of rising from my bed, unrested, with shrouds of uneasy dreams wrapped around my head, I watch in gratitude from the kitchen window two rabbits – a couple, they seemed – lollop in and out of the hedge, unaware of my presence ten feet away behind the glass. Early mornings in the lane are theirs, foraging on the verge, a couple of jumps from their burrow amongst the brambles.

A little later, dressed by then, wandering out to collect my post, I inspect the spot where one of the rabbits had for several minutes sat, and see that it had made for itself beneath the dogwood roots a leaf-upholstered bed.

12 March

In the blindness of anxiety I fail to see the signs around me of new life. The other day I wrote this paragraph in a letter to a London friend:

> An image has entered my mind: of a body so red and raw from head to toe with open wounds that the only possible form of survival is to lock itself away in the dark where nothing, not a beam of sunlight, not a breath of spring breeze, not the gentlest of intimate human touch can be allowed entry for fear of the agony of contact. This pain is real, it isn't imagined.

Pairs of birds, I see, have registered their territories, selected places to nest. In the human calendar it's almost Easter. Will eggs then slip from the song thrush, sharp and shy and alive in its nest in the hedge beneath my study window?

At Easter, as a child, I loved to bite off the ears of chocolate bunnies.

13 March

It looks as though there'll be dozens of foxgloves this summer in my cleared glades, their pale green leaves stretching up where the light now reaches down to warm the seeds that have maybe lain dormant for years. Good to see signs of nature's benefit from my presence, in a small way to compensate for other truly terrible intrusions: how I loathe the sound in the lane of my two combi-boilers lighting up, pumping fumes into the air through low, horizontal flues – their awful noise, here in this beautiful place. I gasp at my ignorance, at my stupidity. All for the sake of 'convenience'!

Why oh why didn't I insist on pursuing one of the alternatives?

I hope I can forgive myself.

Hard, very hard, I've always found, to tolerate my own mistakes, to feel acceptable as anything less than perfect.

I'm frightened.

Patience, patience. I'm still a child ... less than a child ... I'm a seed, an egg ...

Nonsense!

Diversionary defence in words.

14 March

I am unwilling to plant, disinclined to sow, all I wish to do on the land here at Terhill is clear the ground of invasive weeds and underwood and set the earth free to bring forth whatever wild flowers may there lie hidden, buried alive.

18 March

Awoke at five to the sound of foxes barking. Surprised to sense some possibility of rest, of release.

19 March

At midnight, in the fields, I smell the safest moments of my boyhood, at Erkindale, my grandmother's working farm outside Rathdowney, in County Leix, at the centre of Republican Ireland. Here at Terhill I smell the same wet wool of sheep, my landlord's large flock of pregnant ewes pattering ahead of me for half a mile in the dark across Cothelstone Park, and every step of the way I breathe the wake of their scent, taking me back to Ireland.

Aged seven, I was the one at Erkindale who found, in the snow on Christmas Eve, the ewe missing for two days, silent but alive at the centre of a hawthorn thicket. It was I alone who stood with the animal, in mourning over the body of its stillborn lamb.

21 March

These recent days I've seen and heard the Terhill life around me but have not digested it, so far away have I fled in my head.

A mild morning, and as I sat before breakfast on the bench beneath the pine, the flight of a wood pigeon registered in a way I've never before consciously noticed. My mind is so trouble-tired I cannot summon the energy to describe the bird's dead-weight swoops in flight – I did see it, though, and am grateful.

Coming back to the house, heard such a loud buzzing on the path by the side of the kennels. The noise came from above my head, and I looked up to see that hundreds of Beth's bees were gathering pollen from the tiny white and yellow flowers of the big willow.

I'm glad Beth keeps her bees here, not over at her cottage by the Manor.

24 March

In the sun this afternoon I saw a butterfly, the first of the year. And hundreds of flies.

At the end, now, of the day, I hope I might have drawn a safety line in the sand.

25 March

At mid-morning one of the two feral cats seen from time to time out and about at Terhill, the big marmalade, trotted through my gate with a baby rabbit in its mouth. The rabbit squealed and kicked, to no avail. The cat disappeared behind the byre, to silence the cry of its prey.

27 March

A mouse-proof bar has been fixed to the bottom of the larder door, and still food is being eaten.

And today I found my house mouse's home: in the middle of a cardboard box full of mugs and tumblers, wrapped in London by the removal men in superfluous masses of paper, quite a bit of it shredded in the building of a nest. My industrious companion had stored the pine kernels at the bottom of a glass, with shredded paper on top, most of the wrapping paper still intact.

What energy for self-preservation, emptying one by one the kernels from the half-used packet on the top shelf and bearing them down to the box on the floor, and then deep inside to the secret glass store!

I wonder if the mouse's intention was to hide his supplies from other mice passing by on their hunt for food?

Don't know what distances mice travel to forage. Thought of them as communal, but maybe they're solitary. Maybe my mouse had not yet discovered that there was no way in and out of the larder. Or maybe it had, and was pleased to be left alone to sleep at ease beside its glass jar of pine kernels.

28 March

My house has more than one mouse. Last night the small bowl of nuts which sits on the oak table in the kitchen was emptied. Having destroyed the one, it seems there's a second nest, another mouse larder. Noticed that paper has been torn from the packaging of pictures stored in the boiler room. I moved pictures and boxes around but couldn't see the mouse-home.

They live so privately, protected.

How many mice are there, trapped now inside my house, barred from the larder, fearful of starvation?

29 March

On the third consecutive day of clear blue sunshine I walked from room to room after breakfast opening every window. Later, returning for coffee from work outside, I found a bumblebee stranded on a stair, unable to fly, wings ineffectually whirring, front legs clawing the air. The big bee had an orange body and its legs, with backward-sloping hairs, moved like the mechanical arms of an articulated crane. I slid a piece of paper underneath its feet and lifted it into the garden, where it crawled away to hide. To recuperate.

I imagine bees may have self-healing powers.

If not, with damaged wings the bee dies.

Life is precarious.

Struggled for three days now to make a mini-meadow of wild grasses and flowers from the stony clay soil outside my front door. Raked and sown and rolled and watered with the best of my care.

30 March

I came to Terhill with the intention of making for myself a home, not a work of art.

That's what I've done, though, I'm beginning to feel: made from the found-materials of this place a piece of sculpture.

The image before my eyes when I moved into this house is almost realized. My builders have completed their tasks and cleared the site, only the final touches remain for me to do and then, despite my sense of imperfection, of disappointment, it may be time to tell myself that it's done. Time to sign and date the work and move on to the next piece.

I thought I was creating perfection.

7 April

By hand, from a gallon can, I water the red crust of earth that is meant to be my butterfly meadow, twice a day, pacing back and forth, close to hopelessness.

I continue because ... because I continue. With the thought, as I shake the last drops from another empty metal watering can, that it might just be this drop, or this drop, or this drop which nourishes into germination a sown-seed, that it might be this step and crunch of heel, or this step, or this step which nudges the barren ground into life.

The curled bright green leaves of a camomile plant, Beth points out, already push through at the meeting of two cobbled paths close to the front porch. In the grip today of terror, I nevertheless manage to dream of drying the flowers of this plant from which to make an evening mug of tea. Should not a single one of the seeds I sowed survive, this patch of land is in itself capable of regeneration, nature tells me.

I listen ... I'm listening ... can't be sure I hear, the din inside distorts everything.

The butterfly I saw late last year protecting a particular patch of sun-speckled woodland seems to have survived the winter. How is it possible?

On the ridge of my roof two young birds are perched, chirping, wagging their long tails, the white and grey of their feathers intermingled, the traditional pattern of their species awaiting definition. These mottled fledglings, fresh from the nest, brimming already with confidence in flight, at sight of me dip off home, frolic as they go in the wind. The air is clear. I see this, see nature celebrate.

None of this matters. Not really. Not to me.
   All this nature-talk is a ploy, attempt at escape.

10 April

In the old half of the cottage this afternoon I shifted the plain furniture back into place, made up the beds, beeswaxed the stairs. From the window of the little end room my eyes followed the orange wing-tips of a butterfly as it fluttered in bumpy – here-and-there, uncertain – flight around the perimeter of the lawn. The sight reminded me that the other day Morris Blewitt dropped by to take a cutting from the cooking apple tree – against which, he told me, he used as a boy to play cricket. An electrician, youngest son of the head groom at Cothelstone, he had rewired the family's cottage for his diploma test. It is working still, I tell him.

Feathers. Sticks. Stones. Bones. Gatherings from the walks I no longer make up into the hills. Tomorrow I'll set them out where they used to stand on the shelves and sills of the Blewitts' old cottage, ready for artist-guests.

11 April

Each day I water the cracked earth. By the time I've finished, the bit where I began is dry again. I stare down at stray signs of life in the drying crust, at tiny pairs of lobed leaves, sturdy-looking despite their infant frailty. I wander off to inspect the untended tracts of bulldozed earth at the far side of the wall, and see that the same plants have a toehold there too. Don't know from where they come, can't imagine how anything grows.

12 April

Today, kneeling on the cobbles of the path and placing my eye parallel with the ground, I see that there also are, there really *are* wild grasses growing where I've raked and rolled and sowed and watered. I check, several times, unable to believe that I may indeed be guiding into life a butterfly meadow on this abandoned patch of damaged land between the cottages and the byre, where oil leaked from a tank and farm debris was dumped and bonfires of derelict timber burnt to ashes.

In the angled evening light, the iron-red earth is seen to be lightly washed with uneven strokes of green.

14 April

A sturdy dark-feathered bird with thick neck coloured slate grey and stylish black hooded mask worn over
the eyes and front of its head strutted across the roof of
the byre to peck at and pick up in its beak twigs fallen
from the ash. The bird was testing material for its nest,
looking for the driest strongest piece – as big as it could
manage to carry. It fiddled until the selected twig felt
balanced in its beak, and then eased into flight, disappearing over the roof of the cottage. Several times the
jackdaw journeyed back and forth from byre to ... I was
inside, and didn't see where this season's nest is being
built.

Birds know trees.

Ash twigs must have qualities that appeal to the jackdaw. And the species of tree in which to make its home
will also have been specifically selected, some birds better than others at choosing safe spots.

Trees for feeding, trees for observing, trees for shel-
tering, trees for grooming, trees for courting. Amongst
themselves, do birds distinguish by name-call the trees
of their homeland? Only five native trees in England:
elm, oak, ash, yew and prill (these days known as hazel).

What do birds *know* about trees?

A foolish question. Even jackdaws, amongst the clev-
erest of birds, 'know' nothing.

Dozens of different birds live here with me at Terhill,
and I see them day by day, admire the beauty of their
song, the brilliance of their various patterns of flight,
am breath-taken by their physical agility, yet will never
understand how they function, why they exist.

This thought doesn't please me.

15 April

In the midday heat a little blue butterfly flew close to the ground back and forth across the centimetre high tops of the wild grasses of my infant meadow.

The sun shone down all afternoon on my line-full of white cotton sheets, which I found, on gathering them in, to be spotted with beads of fly-shit.

18 April

In the lane the quickening of my breath at a whiff of wild garlic, released, I saw on reaching the spot where it grows, by the recent passage of some animal, crushing the slick leaves whilst rummaging in the earth for food.

And then, almost instantly, the descent from pleasure in nature to pain within self.

My brain is numb, exhausted, at a loss for words. I recognize the grandeur of the sunlit shapes of giant white clouds careering across the sky and wish, without hope, that one afternoon I might find that I can again rejoice in them.

19 April

Up in the fields on the hill behind the house I saw this afternoon the first of the season's swallows. It had been difficult to set out on the walk, overcome as I am by ... whatever it is, this pain.

The state isn't new, it's been with me for years. Always used to be able to pull myself free, outrun the threat, now I can't. Just can't see any means at all of ... Can't make sense.

I hear the blood beat through my skull, nothing else.

Or maybe there's too much else. Cascades of fragmented feeling.

Out there on the hill, in a sheltered hollow I lay down in the grass and wept, curled my body into a foetal ball and shrieked.

20 April

No need in recent days to water the butterfly meadow, for at intervals it has rained.

All through the wood my eye is drawn to the threatening growth of nettles and burdock and thistles and ground elder and bindweed and hundreds of sycamore saplings.

21 April

Saw a fat rat visit the compost heap through the tunnel
I months ago noted had been dug beneath the board-
ed sides. The mouth of the hole is black, the compost is
black, the rat is brown.

22 April

On the gravel path at the side of the house this morning as I collected the mail, I was halted by the sight, close to the toecap of my shoe, of a dead bird, with white flashes on its folded wings and bright pink chest. Drops of blood fell from the Finch's beak when I picked it up, its body warm.

On the green patches of the red earth of my 'meadow' several blades of grass have attained an inch in height.

23 April

Last night the mice made their way back into the larder. Found mouse droppings also on my desk.

On a morning when the young cabinet-maker of my beds, my green-oak kitchen table and my elm door here at Terhill gives birth in a Bristol hospital to her first child, I allow myself groans of despair at a few mice. How pathetic! Central city life gave me the illusion of control – the pain of facing here in the countryside the failure to sustain this habit of order feels closer and closer to insufferable.

Need to find 'the courage to be' – the responsibility mine alone, nobody else can do this for me.

It's serious.

Very.

A tiny triumph: in tightening panic as I waited for the return of Beth to help, I myself cleaned out the larder of non-food storage boxes and, while doing so, located and blocked a hole in the ceiling where electrical wires rise from the fuse box into the in-between floor space and out through the wall. The last place in my house to be made mouse-proof?

Watched from the window-seat on the landing half-a-dozen dazzling goldfinches chase each other through the still-leafless branches of one of the two big ash trees at the back of the byre.

Not long ago such sights raised smiles of joy at living here.

Now nothing.

24 April

Words they flee too.

25 April

Small birds fly regularly in and out of the byre. I as-
sume they're nesting. But maybe they feast in there on
spiders. I've looked in vain for the nest. I'm not always
sure what the birds are, although I do not doubt the
fact of often seeing a robin pottering about the byre.
Sometimes, though, I think I see sparrows. At other
times chaffinches fly between the chamfered posts, their
beaks full of insects with which to feed their young.

Can be certain these days of nothing.

26 April

Morning. It's a pair of robins which lives in the byre. Both birds have red breasts.

Despair.

Early afternoon. The leaves of the big oak are a mustardy green.

Late afternoon. Despair.

Despair.

27 April

Must accept that there's no 'getting better', that in feeling fear I am being me, that this is where I am destined to learn to live, with the moles and mice and birds.

Unlike them, I know not how to feather my nest, make myself comfortable.

Long for rest.

By any means.

29 April

I continue with the construction, from hazel branches coppiced last year from the hedge in the lane, of a runner bean trellis. Like the look of what I've made, interwoven, no string. Later I hand-saw logs, gather kindling and stack uncut branches to dry in the byre. I'm busy outside all afternoon. While having supper I watch a blackbird gather worms from the rain-soaked earth of the butterfly meadow, close by, just below the window. The worms twist around the bird's yellow beak while it hops about, head cocked, listening for movement in the earth.

2 May

Yesterday I heard then saw two larks hold their seeming-stationary place high in the sky above my head.

3 May

At seven o'clock this morning, with the sun's beams warming my face where it rested on the pillow, I wished to be permitted to lie there and die. Three maybe four days it would take me, I reckoned, if I declined to drink or eat. I was serious. I am serious. It's what I want to do, be left in peace to die.

Please, look for some other form of letting go, an alternative way of escape: Beth sought to persuade.

Later, I rose from my bed on an impulse to mow the paths that wind through the glades of my leased land, my borrowed territory. Then found myself clipping Mr Blewitt's funny box hedge. Felt that I was ... Something about benign shaping, about acceptable self-representation.

Don't really know what I've done, what I will do, what I can do.

4 May

Four rabbits munch on the grass in the old orchard, the setting sun angled so low that its rays shine through their ears, which glow pink. The fallen apple tree bears blossom, I'm astonished to see.

5 May

My mother's anger burns inside me, burns my insides.
    Does it?
    Probably.

6 May

Unable to feed myself lovingly. It has become difficult to cook and eat anything much at all.

7 May

Three days of sun have bleached yellow many blades of the young green grass at my door. It looks too far gone to revive in today's rain.

8 May

Typical of me to have pre-imaged an aesthetic death, a refined, quietly-smiling letting go! I must somehow know that if I am to carry on, then my hurt, caged, enraged, can no longer be contained. I claw with my hands at the ribs of my chest to tear myself open, set myself free. I growl, howl, hiss, spit. I cower and pant, like a creature from the forest, blind, unminded.

I'm sick of the shit of deceit.

I've stopped behaving.

9 May

I am ill. Feel a poison inside me, in my stomach, upwards flooding to my heart, a poison which I must suck
out of myself before ...

11 May

All along the lane the hawthorn is in its full May flower.
A fledgling robin, born in the byre, is learning to fly.

14 May

Two afternoons ago a swarm of bees alighted on a low branch of the purple Lilac tree in the nearby garden of Terhill Cottages. Beth put on her protective bee-suit and ... no, I'm again wordless.

17 May

The bees! The swarm of bees! The bees, they survived!
Are busy at life in the second hive!

   Strange the way they marched up the planks of wood
into the hive, and then slowly emerged to cluster on
the front of the hive, hanging there through two nights
and a day of rain and wind. They were dead, I dreaded.
Had lost their queen and, alone, could no longer exist.
With the appearance of the sun they revived, and were
enticed by Beth's trail of sugar to take over the home
prepared for them.

18 May

There are dozens of mothering ewes in the parkland beyond the iron fence. This morning a fox sat for several minutes beneath the herringbone stone wall of the demolished house, watching the sheep and their lambs wander past within a few feet. He noted, with pricked ears, my presence on the bench a hundred yards away and, in his own time, sloped off into the wood.

19 May

The bee story is many-layered but my head is tight, will not release the words to communicate.

Three cats live here now, in the old part of the cottage, old Thomas and the brothers Bert and Dennis, competing for territory long in control of the feral twosome, a marmalade and a tortoiseshell. The move from over at the Manor of Beth and her cats to live in the original half of my cottage is another story for the telling of which I lack the energy, the will, the desire.

I've lost the spirit.

7 June

Today.

23 July

In my absence – first at Musgrove County Hospital to be stitched up, and then confined to the mental unit in Rydon House – things did grow in the red earth outside my door. Grew green and tall, unfettered. It was I who nearly did not survive.

3 August

The clover and dandelions and things grow mostly from seeds retained by nature in the soil, little, as far as I can see, from my sowings.

Next year?

The butterfly meadow may reveal itself next year.

Patience, with my damaged self.

4 August

The cats have made themselves at home. The other morning I saw from my bedroom window, in the day-opening sunshine, Dennis at play in the yard in front of the byre. He tossed into the air the cadaver of some creature captured in the hedgerow, jumping with it, all four feet off the ground, willing it back to life, wishing to prolong his one-way game of cat and ... young weasel, I discovered once dressed and out, its front paws with toes as expressive as the fingers of a bookish boy, white-furred from chin to tail down its long tummy, brown with charcoal streaks along its back.

The screams I occasionally hear in the night are the death-cries of murdered baby rabbits. On the garden path and in the lane I frequently find the unpalatable body parts – liver, gizzard, shit sack – of voles and field mice, and the drab-feathered corpses of birds. Few song-birds nest now in the garden.

Are the byre's robins dead?

The feral cats, who kill only to eat and thereby live in relative harmony beside the birds of this place, have retreated from proximity to the out-for-a-lark domestic threesome, supplied twice-daily with their pet-shop delicacies, killing for the thrill of it.

22 August

Don't write much. There isn't much to say, my head bubble-wrapped in medication.

Although it was, as I knew at the time, a bad thing to do, I'm still sorry I didn't succeed. I knifed my wrists in the wrong direction, didn't wait long enough for the bottle of aspirins to send me to permanent sleep.

I lament my failure.

2 September

I'm lost at sea, anchorless, rudderless. Winds blow, warm supportive winds, but I've mislaid the sails. I was convinced that I wished to cast anchor in this beautiful harbour of Lower Terhill, unaware of how far away I internally am from the shore.

I begin to understand that I must first seek a place of safety inside myself, must find some anchored buoy within my own person up to which to tie, and from there reach out to connect to the land. Must build jetties, bridges across which to journey back and forth, wrapped in oilskins and sou'wester against the storms, head erect, eyes bright in the mild moonlight.

Ugghh! The temptation to wrap it up in fancy words! When the reality is plain ugly, my action unforgiveable.

7 September

Poorly attended-to through this spring and summer's alternate bouts of hot sun and sharp rain, my cleared woodland threatens to return to wilderness. Since my return I've attacked the giant nettles and burdock, sought to contain the bindweed, cut back surging laurel. Yesterday, while pulling out streamers of rampant brambles, I wondered at my habitual failure to harvest the wild fruits of the countryside, the hazelnuts, sloes, whortleberries, garlic, rose hips and myriad others. This afternoon, a basket on my arm, I walked over to Schopnoller Farm, where the hedgerows are laden with blackberries, and spent two hours wandering here and there, content in my seasonal pursuit. On returning home I gathered some windfalls from the grass below the old tree and made blackberry and apple crumble.

Aged fifty-six, this is the first time in my life I've cooked a 'sweet' of any kind; never baked a cake, made scones, rice pudding, lemon tart. A simple act, of purpose and pleasure.

Made aware that physical ease *is* possible, replacing the tension and distress my body has endured for the last couple of years.

9 September

Change, incremental change. Seasonal shifts. Play. Joy.
Words placed on the page as they come. A walk in the
rain of today, after a weekend of sun, the last warmth of
summer.

Cats enjoying their play in the yard.

Wish I could watch and listen to the life around me
and be filled, fuelled.

Must partake, participate in the here-and-now – in the
here at Erkindale, where another also lives, Beth, the
owner of the cats; and in the now, not the rescheduled
past or the pre-written future.

11 September

It's September the 11th.

The hawthorn trees in the lanes are thick with crimson haws, the sky with fighter planes, on exercise to mark one year since the Twin Towers assault.

13 September

This morning a neighbour died, Ollie, the eldest brother of builder Frank. Ollie lived with their mother
Constance in the oldest wing of the farmhouse at the
head of the lane. Aged forty-seven, a large-limbed
grey-haired man, slow of speech and step, Ollie had seldom left his mother's side.

I will never again see the two of them pass below my
study windows on a Wednesday afternoon, wheeling
their barrow full of bags of rubbish to place for collection at the crossing of our private lane with the narrow
road.

In the Estate house in which Constance has lived for
almost fifty years, there are several sixteenth-century
plaster relief-panels of figures and flowers. The first of
her nine children to be born is the first to die. A child
for the whole of his life, an overgrown boy, Ollie needed
to die before his mother, his guide to recovery from the
seizures by which, without warning, he was regularly
floored.

Not yet, though. He needn't have died today.

14 September

We call ourselves human beings. Not easy, I find, to live by our name. Human-doer better describes the way I've existed.

Beth lets her cats 'be'.

I can't.

Can't permit them the freedom to wander unchaperoned in my half of the house, am unable to accept their clawing at the kelim on the sitting-room floor. Looking back to childhood, I'm afraid I allowed myself to be made to 'behave', failed to assert the need to unfold feelings, the desire to expose my own person. It's a bit late now. I'm frightened. More fear-filled even than I must, at the very beginning, have seen my mother to be if I misbehaved.

I once wanted to love my mother, a long time ago, and suffered for it.

Important to remember, for safety's sake, never again to love.

15 September

I woke at dawn to the intermittent cry of some animal in the yard, loud, articulate, not a sound I recognized. A stoat, fighting the cats? I didn't get up to investigate. Lay in bed and thought: how rigorously I defended myself in Charlotte Road from the world, how cut-off in actuality I was in London from the day-by-dayness of other lives, alone there in my fortress, two-way contact with those young artists an illusion.

My sanctuary. My prison.

For fifteen years a place at least of safety.

A bay of the byre is piled high with cut branches of ash, cedar, pine, laurel, elm, elder and sycamore, stored in the dry, waiting to be sawn into logs. I enjoy the sorting and carrying of the wood in from the stacks that I've raised over the last two-and-a-half years in selected spots of the cleared wilderness, and find comforting the autumn sight of it now from the kitchen window in the open-sided byre. This afternoon Beth has also been placing things in store, stacking on my larder shelves her jars of blackcurrant, damson and plum jam, made from fruit gathered from trees in our garden.

Distracted by my troubles from care this summer of her bees, Beth neglected their health and when last week she collected the honey found the main hive infested with wax-moth and the swarm in the second hive dormant. Two jars are all we have of home honey.

17 September

Walked over this afternoon with Beth to pick sloes from a stretch of blackthorn in the hedge two fields this side of Schopnoller, on the branches of which, while blackberrying the other day, I'd noted the sloes clustered as blue-black as grapes on the vine. Drawing down with the handle of a walking stick the thorny branches to within reach we picked under pressure, distressed by both noise and smell of two giant tractors approaching closer and closer, the blades of their hydraulic cutters reducing the wild wealth of these great old hedges to mangled nothingness, square-cropped to a quarter of their height and half their width.

Three weeks ago, when a comparatively mild attack by tractor blade was launched on the hedgerow of my lane, the shape and composition of which I tend, I felt personally brutalized, doubted my strength to survive, feared I might be forced to abandon hope of creating here a life of self-respect.

18 September

Seated at midday on the bench outside the kitchen door I know that it is this precise spot that I must return to when my mind dreams escape, from here that I must learn step-by-step to walk. As frail as a baby, the flayed muscles of my neck strain to hold upright my head on my shoulders.

Phrases too neat, too reasonable. Nowhere near what it's really like.

19 September

Today found myself drawn to pick up from the cliff path
at Lee and bring home to place in the baize-lined drawers of my specimen chest two small black-tipped white
feathers.

20 September

Another culinary first: cooked this evening a shepherd's pie, flavoured with rosemary and sage, the herbs I most like to use, in pleasure at snipping sprigs from the two old bushes rescued from strangulation by bindweed. I made too much and ate too fast, while listening on Radio 3 to a concert recorded a month ago at the Edinburgh Festival, of Alfred Brendel playing two of Beethoven's twenty-three *Diabelli Variations*.

Found myself at supper noting in my diary, from a leaflet which has lain unread for a week on the kitchen table, the dates of several meetings of the Somerset Wildlife Trust, of walks and talks, on dormice and damsel flies.

My attention was drawn back to the radio by the voice of Stevie Smith reciting her poem *Not Waving But Drowning*, which the presenter insisted on describing as 'universally familiar, a cliché'. I do hate this cultural snobbism, sneer-nosed disregard for recollection of the impact – shock, in my case, at the poet's resignation to pain – on first hearing this well-known poem.

Because 'everyone' knows that Brendel plays brilliantly the Diabelli is 'nobody' meant to listen?

Confusion.

I'm confused.

Beneath one feeling another lurks, and hidden beneath that a second, different, contradictory feeling, and a third, and a fourth, and ... Hold on. Breathe. Take a deep breath. Must hold on and also let go. Stevie Smith sounded like a ... The music sounded to be ... What am I trying to say?

The pills which I'm being made to take put a fuzz in my head. Although they do sustain a kind-of appetite.

21 September

Walked up through Cothelstone Wood to Paradise.

Enchanted to see, at close quarters, a badger. Watched it scuffle and snuff amongst the dry undergrowth in the shadow beneath packed plantation trees. They're big, badgers. Not surprised their tracks in my copse are well worn, from heavy night-time traffic in search of food.

Looking down from the high slopes of the waxcap field I saw that a white double-poled marquee has been pitched in the middle of the parkland grass, five minutes walk across the fields from Cothelstone Church, where this afternoon will be married the sister of the man who rents the cottage adjacent to Constance Sayer's. Sebastian is his name, a solicitor and a fisherman, keeper of a boat on the Estate's lake. Their wedding guests on this Indian-summer Saturday will barely believe the evidence before their eyes, transported to the centre of a landscape of old English beauty, not a road, not even a path in sight, a pasture-roll away from the Jacobean jewel of a manor house and its attendant church.

Off over the hill from Aisholt, when I first walked across these fields to Cothelstone I cried, wept tears of longing to share the idyll of this land with a loved other. Did not, at the time, know I'd live beside this view. Could never have envisaged what I'd do to myself in the woods this June.

22 September

Been feeding the cats this weekend. Thomas – large, handsome, slate-grey with white bib and paws – has a urinary infection, and is fed special food to prevent crystals forming in his bladder, from there flowing on to block the urethra, leading to rupture and death. The 'boys', Dennis and Bert, tabby twins, are small and lithe. They kiss-lick each other's faces and bums. Dennis's short front legs are white.

I've grown particularly fond of Thomas, whose watchfulness I respect.

Like the old half of the cottage, prefer Beth's home there to my own here.

23 September

Ollie was buried today, beside his father, in the plot in Cothelstone churchyard his mother had reserved for herself. The second-youngest brother, Herbert, head gardener at the National Trust's Thompson Park, read to the full congregation an address of memories and messages dense in the unsentimental strength of this family's closeness. At Herbert's side stood another of Constance's sons, the tallest, a supportive hand placed in the small of his brother's back.

Beth and I walked home arm-in-arm across the fields, conscious of our tread in the footsteps of Ollie and his mother on their regular trips to tend the Sayer graves, bearing clippers and hoe and watering can. We took tea and sandwiches in Constance's neat garden, the daily focus of activity in her life with Ollie. Sebastian told me that last Saturday the bridal pair spent their wedding night in a large army tent, separate from the marquee, pitched in seclusion at the edge of the lake.

Inside the church at Cothelstone are two sculptural tombs: in unpainted stone, the recumbent thirteenth-century images of a crusader knight and his bride, her feet resting on a stylized squirrel; and in alabaster, the Jacobean effigy of a later Stawell couple.

Tim Warr is also buried there, a Somerset rose growing up the porch in his memory. I knew Tim, a housemaster at Harrow School until retiring with his wife to a cottage in nearby Cushuish. While alive he stocked and fished the lake at Cothelstone. A rugby international, Tim re-visited time after time during the week of his death the try he had scored for England at Cardiff Arms Park, toppling out of bed onto the floor as he dived in his mind across the line.

Boarding school myths, ever-enduring, difficult to obliterate.

25 September

Reading Tolstoy's *The Death of Ivan Ilyich.*

28 September

The berries on the holly are already reddening. Not all the swallows have yet left their summer nests in the stables.

29 September

On the outside of the window pane, their black bodies silhouetted against the sky, two spiders together weave a web. The sight surprises me. I find I'd assumed spiders live alone. But they don't; they cohabit, it appears.

Not necessarily.

The web is not the spider's actual *home*, it is the equivalent of a fisherman's net, the means of entrapment of food, the making of which they undertake in company. On other occasions, when disturbed, I've seen spiders scuttle into holes and crevices where it's fair to presume they live, breed, bring up their numerous progeny. Separately, maybe, as single parents, thus to affirm my image of spidery solitude.

30 September

Beside the outline of the old drive to the demolished mansion down which I walk on my way to eat at Podshavers, where it passes the lake, a row of horse chestnut trees drop in the wind conkers at my feet. I've adored since childhood the sheen and swirling layers of colour on a conker fresh from its shell, pith adhering white and soft around the conker's crown.

3 October

I am startled on my morning walk up Cothelstone's hidden combe by sight of the bare white side of a tall beech. Then notice that its sister tree, which for decades had sheltered its bark from rain, had fallen in a storm and has been cut up, stacked ready to be carted away. Within a winter or two lichen will have formed, moss grown, turning the bark of the surviving tree green.

Alone for supper I turn on the radio mid-concert, to hear the bird-song rhythms of a Messiaen piano piece. This is followed by his *Quartet for the End of Time*, written and first performed in a prisoner-of-war camp in Silesia in 1944. Messiaen himself played the piano, in partnership with the only other captives who were practised musicians, a clarinettist, a violinist and a cellist. The notes tell the story more graphically than words, the clarinet sighing loss and loneliness in its solo movement. They played at Christmas, praised and privileged by the camp commandant.

I saw Messiaen many times in the years before his old-age death, when he regularly attended London concerts of his music – with his second wife, Yvonne Loriod, the pianist, an ex-student of his at the Conservatoire. She performed all Messiaen's later piano premiers.

Much of the music I loved, still love.

I miss his beret in the auditorium.

Miss being there myself, confined down here in Somerset.

4 October

Encountered a herd of close to fifty red deer on the upper fields. On sight of me they were shepherded by a grand-antlered stag into a central pasture safe from people, two large fields below the path to Lydeard Hill and a distance above the top slopes of Bagborough Gallops. A calf baulked at jumping a barbed-wire fence over which the older deer had hopped, and ran in panic back and forth, back and forth, separated from the herd. No mother came to help.

More Messaien on the radio tonight, the *Turangalila Symphony*, with Pierre-Laurent Aimard, a pianist whose concerts in London I used always to attend. Recall the joy of a previous time in my life, when I walked of an evening not across fields for supper at Podshavers but through the City and over Blackfriars Bridge to listen to music at the Queen Elizabeth Hall.

One unforgettable Sunday morning I heard Aimard play all twenty of Messiaen's solo studies *Vingts Regards sur L'Enfant Jesus*, written shortly after the composer returned from the War. The experience, its intensity and beauty, took performer and audience down paths in the world seldom visited.

I've lost this breadth to my life.

Aimard played without a score, I remember. Seem to see, in memory.

Unlikely, I now acknowledge. Though I do really think he did.

5 October

Felled diseased elm and invasive sycamore all afternoon. Ever since moving in to Terhill, I've wished to
upend the sycamore near the head of the lane, but judged
it too tall, at least fifty foot, its trunk sixteen inches in
diameter, wider than my biggest bow saw. Today the
task felt within my grasp. It fell, as intended, across the
road. I had to stand on top of the wall and pull the tree
towards me, jumping aside as it toppled, falling with a
crash that would have crushed a passing car.

It didn't feel dangerous.

6 October

Constance – I hear from Frank – talks aloud at night to Ollie, as if he was there.

7 October

Alive spiders eat the dead.

8 October

On the night of his funeral Ollie came to sit for twenty minutes on the side of Constance's bed, to comfort her. She couldn't see him and he didn't speak, but she felt the familiar weight of his sixteen stone frame rock her bed. She spoke to him, so Constance told us when she dropped in today for a mug of tea beside the Rayburn in Beth's kitchen, on her way home from the chiropodist. Ollie couldn't drive because of his epilepsy, and Constance has never learnt, so a friend who lives in a nearby Estate cottage had dropped her off at the end of the lane. While Ollie lived Constance didn't bother much about herself, had not given a thought to getting rid of her bunions. She has a thick, rich-white head of hair. Janet does too, on the other side of the hill.

9 October

This morning I didn't want to leave my bed, wished to sleep forever.

10 October

Part of me *is* a child, silent in a corner, refusing to be comforted, declining to be touched. Out of reach.

12 October

I'm in no external danger. This place is safe. Mustn't panic.

14 October

Two years ago I clambered onto the roof of the byre to cut back a branch of the big ash which, before my time here, had battered in the wind a sizeable hole in the ridge. The ash has pushed out a thicket of new growth close to the point of my saw-cut. Over the rest of the tree the leaves spread loose and expressive, here they lie close and tight and ugly.

Beth's bees have flown both their hives. Unless they're dead.

16 October

Sometimes my whole self goes numb. Which is dangerous because, cut-off from feeling, I don't notice when I'm hurting myself with mistaken thoughts. An internal match to the blisters which regularly appear on the fingers and thumb of my right hand, through careless touchings of scalding tea and coffee pots, the burns unfelt because the nerve I severed at my wrist has yet to regrow.

There's no way out. I can't wall myself up again in solitude, I've got to go on.

Right now I just can't quite see how, or where.

I will, though, I will.

17 October

This afternoon I felled the eucalyptus tree by the old washhouse, an alien to this land, with its peeling skin and toxic foliage. I set methodically about my task, lopping branches one by one, clearing as I went. The tallest section of the tree in falling missed by inches the washhouse chimney pot.

I do not regret the tree's absence. About this I can be clear.

Ambivalence is unavoidable, and yet I've never accepted it.

It has been nigh impossible, late in life I begin to understand, for me to hold in consciousness conflicting emotions. I imagine that I long to share shelter from the storm, but as soon as the waves carry me close to the shore I turn, instinctively, and swim back out to solitude at sea.

Not surprising that four months ago I almost drowned. The danger doesn't go away. I remain on the brink.

Writing to myself is meant to help.

It doesn't.

Does the opposite.

19 October

The giant Monterey pine's canopy of branches, which rises in tiers above the bench by the iron fence, protected me from a sudden fall of rain, dropping vertically from a cushion-shaped cloud, charcoal-grey with silver scallops. The sheep pattered in file down from all corners of the park to shelter beneath the birch trees by the banks of the stream – with the exception of a single ewe, which declined the collective will and stood its ground. The shower was over soon after the most distant of the flock had reached shelter. The independent one continued eating, while the others slowly spread out again across the hill in quest of the sweetest grass.

Before returning to my work on the raspberry canes I tore with my bare hands the ivy from the creviced trunk of the Monterey, already in the two seasons since my previous attack reaching higher than the tips of my fingers as I stretched above my head to grab its tentacles.

20 October

I've broken my promise to Beth.

Assumption of responsibility to care for me during my recovery was her choice, taken on without pressure from me. In doing so she made only one request: that I promise to warn her if ever I again felt like harming myself.

I agreed.

And didn't tell her. Couldn't. Otherwise she'd have stopped me. Put me back in Rydon House.

I failed, though. Lay naked this afternoon in a hot bath with a Stanley knife to my wrist and tried and tried to cut and plunge and twist. Red handle of the knife against white skin of the inside of my left wrist, the point of the blade pressed down. Pressing hard, in the right direction this time.

I couldn't do it.

The water cooled and I got out, dried myself, put on my clothes again and negotiated the remainder of the day.

22 October

Unforgivably, in weak seeking of attention, this morning I told Beth what had happened two days ago.

She cannot trust me now and every moment I'm out of sight will be frightened of what I might do.

24 October

Flies congregate in my study, the windows spotted with their excretions. I regularly rise from my desk to open the windows and let out the flies.

The flies, which are nearing the end of their lives, often fall on their backs on the window-sill, wings ineffectually whirring, and I pick them up by their legs and release them into the air.

Some days I achieve nothing more.

I've been apart from my wife for over twenty years, more than twice as long as we were together. We married young, in joy and belief.

Stupidity and confusion caused me to leave her, for no apparent reason.

I was frightened, not of not loving her, as I maintained at the time, but of love itself. In anticipation of pain from the obligations of love I turned aside from intimacy. Such a mistake. She's so engaged. Sparkles.

27 October

After a night and a day of high winds the two crab-apple
trees are bare of leaves. Tiny apples manage still to cling
to the crooked branches, the fruit bright yellow against
the grey-green coating of lichen. Can see the beauty. Do
not feel it.

29 October

Used to say that, on principle, I do not miss: people; places; work. A delusion. A deceit, maybe. A defence, certainly.

Having never been able to grieve, I am full fit to burst of sorrow.

5 November

The shooting season has returned. The woods and combes out there in the view are shattered today by gunfire.

28 November

The days and weeks when I write nothing, this is when the hard stuff happens.

The little I do write is worthless.

Too distraught to speak.

Tears. Tears.

And worse.

2 December

There was a moment, a moment ago, when I felt I might have something to say, to myself, here on the page. About wheelbarrowing horse manure from a weed-covered heap piled by Will in the yard of the broken-down coach house to empty onto Beth's vegetable patch, which she has recently extended by digging over to ... The words aren't there; if they are, I can't find them; the will isn't there; I'm not interested in a single word I might say to myself.

Paralysis. Of the spirit.

A sort of death.

31 December

My New Year's resolutions are: not to smoke, not even Beth's roll-ups; and to write here something each day, something I've observed, something I've seen. Anything. Writing just anything may keep me alive.

Janet lived as a shepherd for three years in New Zealand, spending part of the time on a deserted island two miles off the western coast in the north of North Island, to which Maori fishermen helped transport her stock of sheep and cattle in open boats. She loved it there, sea-swimming every day from her shack by the bay. Until a young shearer she had met earlier in her travels arrived with a shotgun, threatening to kill them both if she refused to marry him. A bullet lodged in Janet's shoulder as she rowed away in a hidden boat, barely escaping with her life. He was sent to prison.

The incident plays a small part in Janet's autobiography *The Sheep Stell*. Writing helps.

1 January

An owl hooted in the dark this morning, later than I remember hearing before, at six-thirty, when I awoke.

Up and breakfasted, I opened the front door at the first sight of the sun since Tuesday, low in the sky, shining through the trees. Everywhere wet. Drops of water lined themselves up along the bottom edges of the leafless branches, rainwater glistening on the ground, on everything garden-planted, on everything built, on every man-or-nature-made bit and piece of this place of mine. Windless. The world sparkled. A single drop of water on a pine behind the byre, the light refracted in a particular way through earlier drops along its path, shone bright turquoise from where I stood. The simple beauty of light and water. When I shifted my stance the colour vanished and this drop became indistinguishable from the infinite others.

2 January

In the wood at the side of the waxcap meadow lives a bird with a thrilling winter song.

Don't know what bird it is.

Silly to feel bad about my ignorance. I do, though.

Pleased, on my return, to find myself picking out from the nature books on the shelves by the kitchen table E.W. Hendy's *Somerset Birds and some other folk*, a wartime publication, of 1943, and noticing in the chapter on the Quantocks that 'combe' is spelt 'coombe'. In the Shorter Oxford English Dictionary, 'coomb' and also 'combe' are both marked obsolete, 'not found in OE or ME literature, but occurring in charter place-names belonging to the south of England, many of which survive'. Hendy describes the combe (I'll continue to use my spelling) at Huntsridge branching out into four oak-clothed 'goyals', or wooded valleys, a terrific word of which I've never heard.

Standing by his Rayburn on Christmas morning, Frank lost consciousness, fell to the ground and banged his head, awaking twenty minutes later to find himself stretched out on the floor beneath the table. He called one of his sisters, who drove him to Casualty at Musgrave, where an infection of the inner ear was revealed. Frank looked frail, vulnerable, when he called by on Boxing Day. His father died at the age of forty-four, of a heart attack, and Frank has always feared that he'll go at the same age and in the same way. He is forty-three.

3 January

At the kitchen sink, doing the dishes, I watched a rose-breasted bullfinch and its mate fly down to perch on the stems of old dock and peck at the seeds. This patch of land bordering the lane I've let run wild, to the delight of the birds – to my delight too, in them.

I'm fortunate in my neighbours, closest in one direction Frank, the master builder, and in the other, at Keepers Cottage, one of the Quantock Rangers, whose wife is a gifted practitioner of Shiatsu. This morning I paid my fourth visit to her, and felt the tension in my muscles begin to ease a little.

Rest.

I'm so so tired.

4 January

Fifteen minutes ago it looked as if it was going to snow. The sky has lightened. My stomach flutters.

I've always wanted *not* to be English. With all this drivel about the weather.

5 January

Sharp frost, clear blue sky, no wind. Everything outside, the birds in the branches of the birch, white pancakes of ice suspended in the ruts of the forest tracks, everything I saw reminded me ...

No, now I'm making it up, fabricating.

Not *everything*. There was one moment, only. Maybe two. The first: when I stopped in the high wood, aware that if I stood still I'd be able actually to see the birds singing in the trees, the light at a perfect angle. And I did. Saw and heard things, saw nature, heard things of beauty, the nature of things. The second: the sporadic drill of a woodpecker heard not seen on a raddled oak in the middle of a ploughed field, two-thirds of its branches dead, white, like bones, the bent bones of an aged man. Three moments, not two. The third: in a wood on the way up from Grub Bottom another oak, also old, shaped like ... Won't say, can't describe what I saw. Unlike any tree I've ever seen. An image to hold privately in mind.

A muddle. Not too bad, though. The day has passed, with three things worth remembering. Hold to reality, if I can manage it.

6 January

Walked to Kingston St Mary, five miles away, for the first session of the New Year with Jim Wilson, the psychotherapist I see three times a week. On my way back I noticed the shape of the ancient oak trees in the park here at Cothelstone. One leans at an angle, blown askew maybe a hundred years ago, by then two hundred or so years old, the major branches already fully formed, only its highest limbs changing direction to correct for the accident. The trunk on the weather side has expanded, a root partly exposed, like a muscle, extra-developed in strength and size to take the strain of the tilt. At another spot two trees stand close together, their fat trunks by now only a few feet apart, the entire upper parts shaped as two halves of a single tree. They must, I presume, be exactly the same age. I've seen these trees hundreds of times, have admired them, but never before looked at them as I did today. If one fell the other would soon die too, of loneliness. Like Gilbert and George.

7 January

A cold day, yet I sweat, in anxiety at this afternoon's meeting with Dr Ahmed, the psychiatrist in charge of Rydon House, the man who prescribed my electroconvulsive therapy when I was confined in his care. After an emergency appointment at the Clinic a fortnight ago, I declined to raise to the maximum a second dose of anti-depressants – he had wanted to double my 75mg dose of venlafaxine, even though I'm already on the highest recommended dose of mirtazapine.

The effort of holding myself steady, of refusing to take the spiral descent to despair, imposes a strain on mind and body. Sleep, when it comes, is disrupted, unrestful. My muscles waste.

Admit to Dr Ahmed that I still regret my failure to die last July, less than a week after I'd convinced him to let me go home after my first stay at Rydon House. I lied, then, impressively. At least I try, now, to tell him what I feel to be true.

I think he wears a hearing aid, concentrating hard on what I say in answer to his caring questions.

8 January

Beside me on Beth's sofa last night Thomas rolled over onto his back, head and one paw dangling, and I tickled his tummy. He purred. Bert and Dennis chased each other around the room. The cats love a coal fire in the evening, and the quiet company of Beth and me after the to-and-fro of her visitors over Christmas.

10 January

Missed a diary day. Will continue again daily, not squander the whole New Year's resolution. A lapse, merely.

Wish this afternoon's feelings of numbness had missed me, could be dismissed.

11 January

Blackbirds in the frost strip the hedgerows of haws, I manage to notice as I stare at the lane from the windows of my study on another winter's day of neglected beauty.

No mouse in the house this year.

12 January

Bright green fronds of moss are scattered across the white frosted lane below the old oak, torn from its branches by birds hungry for beetles and lice.

I want to reach out to my London friends, to write and share what has happened.

I need people to know.

Not yet, though. I can't tell them yet.

Six months ago I was taken by ambulance to hospital, sirens wailing. Broken, a wreck, distraught at finding myself alive. Some friends must have heard, from other friends. A few of the closest are in touch with me. I'd like to be able to take my place again on the merry-go-round.

14 January

I can function, my body works when my mind asks it to. Attacked with the aid of a double-ladder borrowed from Frank the ash overhanging the byre, grown heavy again in the two years since I last trimmed the branch that threatens the roof.

I've not lost my head for heights, nor my balance and agility, yet I'm so so fragile.

It's difficult to eat, impossible, it feels, to cook, take all my meals next door with Beth.

What happens to me? Can it really be reaction against my decision to halve, rather than double, the daily dose of venlafaxine? Why do I panic, draw the darkness down around me? Neither rest nor nourishment do I give myself. How will I survive?

16 January

See nothing. I let nothing in. NO ENTRY. There's nothing. No note of song, no flight of wing. No word to write.

21 January

Given up the daily entries. No point.

27 January

Walked this morning the five miles to and five miles back from Kingston for my Monday 10 a.m. appointment with Jim. In the fresh earth of the track where it bends beyond the end of the lake, I followed the pawprints of a family of badgers, small, medium-sized and large. All my strength sucked dry on the road, exhausting the hope that something will happen to help.

1 February

On the way to Jim's this morning I convinced myself that this would be the last day I'd see him, determined in the afternoon to end my life. Planned to place a bale of straw and can of petrol in the back of my car, drive out to a remote valley on Exmoor, drench the seats and the straw with fuel, unscrew the cap on the tank, lie back in the driving seat and light a match.

The car – which I hate, a blue Vauxhall – would blow up, and finish me off, if I wasn't already done in by the flames.

I was not in any doubt, felt relief at the decision. This time I'd make no mistake. And so I said my tired, sad kind-of goodbye to the man who had held me through so much. He knew, I reckon, what was on my mind.

I remember telling him, several times at different sessions, of my belief that, when all else falls away and life comes to feel unliveable, we are each left with one last legitimate choice: to be dead. Nobody had the right to stop me.

He had agreed. Simply suggested that the time might not yet have come, that there were paths of possibility still open to follow before arriving at this irreversible resolution. In the end, though, if it became truly impossible to live, then I had the right, of course, to die, he said.

It was a comforting thing to be told. Helped me believe in him.

And I didn't kill myself this afternoon. Wasn't ready. Not quite. Didn't trust myself enough, suspected I mightn't be making sense. Put the bale of straw and can of petrol on the back seat but didn't start the car, drove nowhere.

17 February

A voice, my voice, whispering in the dark.

18 February

Please please let it be that by writing this, to myself,
I'll stop panicking. For the moment. For this moment.
Please.

28 March

Many days away from this self-telling. Return in despair. Can I write myself upright? I need to raise the eyes of my mind from the ground at my feet, the earth bare, dry as dust.

I could try and describe how I feel.

Terror. Hot terror. Cold terror. I'm terrified of feelings.

Six days ago I wrote, by hand, in ink-from-pen in an occasional notebook:

> I cannot write myself free of despair. A fly buzzes
> between the half-closed blind and the glass in the
> window at my back, against which the sun beats.
> I've raised the blind, squashed the fly, and the sun
> warms the back of my neck, glints on the right lens
> of my spectacles, in which, if I look to the side, I see
> my cheek reflected. The hairs shine. While up I let
> out another fly at the window to my left. I prefer not
> to kill the flies which are drawn to the windows of
> my study, the sunniest afternoon-room in the house.
> Only one half of each of the three windows opens,
> and when the flies obsess on the closed side it's hard
> to persuade them to move over; I scoop at them with
> cupped hand, but they usually refuse to be shown
> their route of escape; and then I squash them, guilti-
> ly, on the white bar of the window frame.

Repetition. I've said all this before. Round and round my thoughts revolve, in tightening circles.

29 March

Be specific.

A month ago I started work, three days a week, plant-ing hedges for Rich Ince's country conservation firm. It was Carl Freedman, a regular visitor from London, who made me respond to Rich's helpful offer. 'You'll do fine. Everything you have ever done you've done well. This too,' he encouraged. 'The most difficult thing'll be convincing yourself each day to go!'

Turned out to be true.

The mornings are ridiculous, my bed a tumble of self-hate. Doubt about my adequacy at this simple man-ual work, out in the country air, steepens each day. You'd have thought it would get easier. Not at all. It's a tougher and tougher struggle.

2 April

I don't want to cook and I don't want to be cooked for, I don't want to speak or be spoken to and I don't want to be silent or be silenced, I don't want to be seen by anybody and I don't want to be left alone, I don't want to live and I don't want to die.

Are there limits to paralysis of will? Or is this passivity, this adoption of victimhood, this cutting back, cutting off, this retreat to claim a state of nothingness, this resort to depression, is all of this in fact a ferocious act of will?

Who am I punishing? To whom am I declining to communicate?

I do speak, though: I ask for help, and refuse to accept it. Sensing my own powerlessness, I seek to force those around me also to feel impotent. Hate this. Hate what I'm doing. Yet keep doing it, over and over again. Rolling over and over again in my shit.

Beth continues to resist defeat. Strained to exhaustion by the pressure of my unstraightforwardness, by the endless push-and-pull, by the unanswerable flow of my tears-without-words, she nevertheless grows steadier in the pursuit of ... In pursuit of her own identity, stronger in peeling back the protective layers which separate her from acquaintance with her own nature. She's working at it.

I feel undeserving. Worse, I despise my despair, feel despicable in my self-inflicted distress, am ashamed.

Guilt.

Shame.

'The courage to be is the courage to accept oneself as

accepted in spite of being unacceptable.' Paul Tillich's words are often with me these days, in the hope of somehow finding the courage of which he writes. In another quote, noted a decade ago, I see he used the word 'annihilate'. His book, in paperback, its pages yellowing, is again out on my table waiting to be reread – as yet managed only a dozen or so paragraphs on anxiety, at the heart of his argument. For years, by now, I've seen myself in danger of being driven here there and everywhere by the threat of annihilation. And with the relief of recognition of Tillich's words had imagined the threat to have receded, believed I was out of danger.

Not true. Thinking isn't feeling. And I *feel*, these days, close to self-extinction.

Won't flee.

Must see it through.

It? What is 'it'?

24 April

Yesterday I shocked myself.

This morning, in aftershock, I cover my eyes with my hands, do not wish to see, be seen.

Yesterday, in fevered haste, I dug up with a pickaxe all the wild sorrel from the 'butterfly meadow', believing it to be young dock beginning to go to seed. While busy searching out every young shoot, I puzzled why this was the only dock in sight that extended upwards green stems ending in bunched pinky-red seed-pods. The roots too were different from the other dock I'd attacked. I kept returning to the task, spotting more shoots nestling in the grass.

Sorrel, the wild flower book tells me, is of the dock family. I tasted the leaves from one of the dozens of small plants thrown from the barrow onto the pile of garden debris, and found the sorrel cultivated by Beth in her salad patch had the same slightly lemon tang.

Wild sorrel is perfect, exactly the kind of plant I want to see grow from the seeds desperately watered and tended at this time last year. Some grew close to the path, others were scattered amongst the dominant clover. Thought I'd done well, on a day of distress, to tackle the task with thoroughness.

Sorrel is too prolific to have been entirely eradicated, I afterwards noticed, with relief. Enough, I hope, remains to speckle the to-be-meadow.

Next year maybe it will revive.

I write of this to seek to calm myself. Such a terrible mistake. Difficult for me to accept it of myself. To make such a mistake feels unforgivable.

25 April

Maybe I'll survive my failures. Maybe they're not terminal.

29 April

Picked a handful of leaves from the remaining wild sorrel to add to a green salad for lunch for Beth and me.

30 April

Seeds of burdock, I discover, were amongst the 'Wilderness mix (for the harsh environment)' in my selective order of two years ago from the Countryside Catalogue of YSJ Seeds, the wildflower specialists near Chard. So: some of the burdock, the spread of which I despairingly seek to control, cursing its presence in my wood, I myself sowed. Since then I've visited YSJ's nursery with Rich and two of my co-workers, to collect plugs of marsh marigold, primula and other plants for the project at Glist, one of the jobs I'm helping with at South West Silviculture.

Been working for Rich for two-to-three full days a week now for three months, hedge-planting, way-clearing, spiral-guarding, tree-planting. Fitter physically.

Emotionally I'm ...?

It's been like this all afternoon: I write a word and then can't think of another, keep repeating the syllables in my mind, hoping that whatever it is I want to say will emerge from my head ... my head ... my head ...

No, it doesn't come. Must stop or I'll panic.

Mustn't panic. Panic is the worst.

How can I help myself get through such days as these?

Almost every day, these days.

There was a point, a purpose. I wanted to describe the nursery, its air of abandonment, of apparent chaos, and then to tell of their expertise at gathering and propagating the seeds of wild flowers, and to record the ambitious work at YSJ. They know so much, care so much, are dedicated, thoughtful people.

I envy them.

Envy Rich.

Envy Phil and Timothy, his two full-time workers,

who never let a task defeat them. They all, it appears to me, especially Rich, belong to ...

Words flee, thought veiled. Tempted to blame the drugs for the clouds billowing through my brain.

6 May

Beth is away for a week, on holiday with a friend at a resort on the Red Sea. I'm feeding her cats, talking to them, caressing them. And I do care, especially for Thomas, the big grey cat, a neutered male: Tom, the ex-tom.

Earlier in the week I mowed the paths through my wilderness wood, and today in the late afternoon, the sun's rays low and golden, strolled down the cut paths and sat for a while on the bench facing the park, where a herd of black bullocks presently lives. Tom followed me, padding in my footsteps. He's deliberate in his movements, studied. I was surprised when he chose to sit, tail curled, ears pricked, on the rustic table made for me by Beth.

'Hi, Tom. Hello, Thomas,' I said. 'How are you?' and lent forward to stroke him.

He purred, without turning round, and continued his observation of the cattle.

I wonder whether cows wonder?: one of twenty-two postcard-sized colour photos of cows made last year by Keith Arnatt in response to their reappearance in the countryside after the lifting of foot-and-mouth restrictions. Good to like work by artists I like.

10 May

Beth is back, brown and beautiful.

The filling I had done in a tooth ten days ago has dropped out, and the time-switch on the central heating has broken, minor grievances that weigh heavily.

12 May

Monday morning.

I'm not sure I can write.

I'd been thinking that it's the one thing I can do with my life.

I'll write myself alive again, I thought.

Can't.

Must.

How?

Why?

Because I need to block the slide into thoughts of suicide.

I *can* function.

On Saturday night we met Rich and his wife Suki, with my SWS colleagues and their girlfriends, at the Crowcombe Arms for a staff supper, at which I talked normally, appeared relaxed, joked, looked to be enjoying myself.

And last night, despite my state of gloom, I cooked Beth and me a cottage pie, with ratatouille.

It was the same in Leeds last weekend, accompanying Carl on the journey north to see his father, a street musician whom he hasn't spoken to for seventeen years.

I functioned.

And now this vacancy. What happens?

Must go to today's appointment with Jim in Kingston.

Dead mole on the path by the byre. Intact, no sign of a wound. Grey body already stiff, though soft to the touch, with short flat tail and almost-human front paws stuck onto its torso like the hands attached to the shoulders of a thalidomide child, damaged at birth.

Last autumn, walking down the Strand, I dropped in to the Courtauld Gallery shop to replenish my stock of museum postcards, and bought a card taken from Joseph Gerstmayer's watercolour study of a mole. Bought, as usual, five copies of each chosen card, one of which I've kept. Have been doing this since 1984, collected by now in a dozen large date-bracketed envelopes recording shifts in visual mood.

13 May

Took five attempts to get to Rich's house in Over Stowey for work this morning, a fifteen-minute drive away. Turned the car around five times, on each occasion almost arriving back at home. Turned again, repeatedly, almost reaching him. Glad I made it in the end.

Rich seemed pleased too.

14 May

Warm and wet, plenty of sorrel has revealed itself in the long grass of the butterfly meadow outside my front door. There are some butterflies too!

15 May

Drove this morning to an appointment in Wellington with the dentist, who informed me that the filling is intact.

Dug up thistles all afternoon.

16 May

Rain on the roof, big drops, a sound that reaches me. It's stopped now. My brain is corrugated cardboard.

Delete. A word on a key.

Notice its shape, the form of this particular configuration of letters.

Not seen 'delete' in this way before.

That's all. Nothing more.

17 May

Start. Shut Down.
  Thought I might rescue the day by writing, but can't.

18 May

Bought the wrong-sized postcards on a visit yesterday to Knightshayes Court. Dithered before deciding. After all these years of collecting the standard size postcard, I can still get it wrong. On discovery of the mistake I tore them up, unwilling to endure sight of them stacked ready to send in the wire tray on my desk, a record of foolishness.

In my Thames & Hudson furniture book of 1987 are two photographs of designs by William Burges for Knightshayes, and one of the interior of the library as executed by J.D. Crace, following rejection by the clients of Burges's incomparably more adventurous proposals. This was my first visit to Knightshayes, a National Trust property forty minutes drive from here. Billy Burges used to be one of my Victorian heroes, would be still if I still cared. Saw there the giant satinwood cabinet sold by me in 1981 to the NT, designed by H.W. Batley, similar to a prize-winning piece of his in the Paris 1878 Exposition Universelle.

19 May

Palestinian suicide bombers were at their terminal work again this weekend in Jerusalem.

I've stayed in Jerusalem several times, once for three whole months, in the ground floor of a large old house ten minutes walk from the Damascus Gate. It was a happy period of my life.

20 May

Carl Freedman's next exhibition in Charlotte Road is six paintings of cats by Fergal Stapleton:

> The paintings are lush and affectionate. Each one is a still, a motionless silent screenshot. In sequence they make a blow-up animation of sorts. The cat has been painted with veneration but you wouldn't want to call them religious paintings. Yet the title of the show – I SHALL ARRIVE SOON – is clearly prophetic.

Beth is laying the floor of the arbour in a mosaic of cut pieces of roof tile and terracotta bricks and the green ends of glass bottles and odd bits of salvaged stone. Her work is a delight, obsessive. The arbour itself she has constructed entirely of curved branches of Laurel, cut down by me over these two and a half years at Erkindale.

I loved the time I spent as a boy with my grandmother at the original Erkindale, occasionally for Christmas but usually for the longer summer holidays, out all day with Uncle Dave, bringing the cows in for milking before dawn, shutting the geese, hens and turkeys in to their huts at dusk. Neither he nor Auntie Dinah ever married, never left the farm. Not easy lives. Dinah was slow, stubborn, quarrelled with her much younger brother.

I can't remember at the time taking in the fact of my mother being the tenth and youngest child. Granny was too thin, and bent, too ancient for me to register her as Mother's mother, dressed in high-necked ankle-length black, grey hair drawn into a bun, eyes sharp, broad country-Irish brogue, loud cackling laugh.

When I drove down in March to Lymington to stay with my mother in her flat for two days and a night, she showed me two group photographs taken of the family spread out across the steps of the veranda, one from before she was born. We also turned the pages of her wartime album: a tent hospital in Basra; the Sphinx, visited on leave from front-line duty with Field Marshal Montgomery in the North African desert; the Al-Aksa Mosque and Wailing Wall, on a wartime trip to Jerusalem.

21 May

Despair is too elegant a word. There is nothing salvageable from the pit of refuse I dig for myself. To call it the 'despair of depression' flatters, inaccurately describes my pitiful state. Pity. Self-pity. Horrible.

Refusal of joy.

Rather than get out there and join in, rather than make the effort to ... to conserve butterflies, say, I turn my thoughts to death. I allow myself to think ... No, I *choose* to think of self-murder rather than face the ordinariness of my failures here at Lower Terhill. I cannot let go, cannot relinquish ...

What? What can't I relinquish?

The illusion of omnipotence?

That's intellect-speak. It must be something else.

It's something basic. But I don't know what.

For the greater part of today I couldn't see myself cooking, feared that I really won't much longer survive this warfare with food. Can't count the number of times I've had to leave supermarkets in a panic attack, without being able to decide on a single purchase.

Got out a sirloin steak from the freezer, purchased last Friday at the fine family butcher in Bishops Lydeard. Put it away again, as Beth doesn't eat steak, and I wanted, if I was going to make a meal, to cook also for her.

Decided to try salmon.

Surprised myself by producing a cucumber and tarragon sauce, incorporating the juices of the foil-sealed grilled fish, served with leek, celery and aubergine ratatouille, boiled new potatoes and steamed broccoli, followed by strawberries and cream!

I can do it. Don't want to, but I can.

To cook a decent supper for someone is an act of lovingness.

I'm unwilling to love, don't trust myself sufficiently. Which maybe helps explain why I'm reluctant to engage with food.

23 May

Hit a car yesterday evening in the narrow lane beyond
Bishpool, on the way to swimming in the school pool
at Quantock Lodge. More accurately, the other car hit
me. We hit each other, let's say. She was driving too
fast, while I, for once, was not. Gerald, at the garage in
Bishops Lydeard, reckons the insurers will write my
car off, paying me at the most a thousand pounds. In
January the metallic grey 1800cc Golf cost almost three
thousand.

24 May

Close my eyes, cover my face with my cold hands. Dissolve. Disappear. Am still here. And not here. Absent. Where have I gone?

Beth and her cats have lived here for a year and a week.

25 May

Carl is down for the Bank Holiday weekend. After supper – cottage pie cooked by me, and pear and chocolate tart baked by Beth – we three, on Beth's insistence, went out into the twilight to set free a crow she'd seen earlier in the day in a wire cage in a clearing amongst the trees where the big house once stood. The trap was primed with carrion to capture fellow crows, drawn to investigate. By upending the cage and blocking open a hinged flap, Beth managed to release the crow, which flew low across the ground to the sanctuary of a hazel thicket. Crows attack pheasant chicks, thousands of which will soon be transferred by the breeder into several giant pens scattered across the Estate. Beth dislikes even more than I do Cothelstone's ritual shoots, the 'game' of slaughter, and said she wouldn't have been able to sleep knowing of the crow trapped in the wood. She believes that there's room for all of us, that nature adjusts, finds a balance, if we let it. She avoids hoovering up spiders and lifts woodlice from the kitchen floor onto a piece of paper to shift them to the byre.

I too tend to avoid killing woodlice – because I like the way they roll themselves into a ball under attack, tucking their multiple legs inside sort-of-armour-plated bodies.

This morning I'm afraid I'll be punished for the transgression of saving last night the lives of crows, fear that Hugh Warmington, my landlord, will know we're the culprits, will be angry. Anger frightens me.

26 May

When Beth's father dropped by for tea today, he pointed to the wild sorrel and asked: 'Is that what we used to call sour grass?' As a boy, during the war, on Scout Club outings, he picked and ate sorrel leaves to slake his thirst. Rupert is his name, a retired surgeon. He lives in Crowcombe, fifteen minutes drive away, with his second wife. Beth's mother died three years ago, aged fifty-six. As a young nurse she had fallen for one of the NHS junior doctors, for Rupert. My mother was also a nurse when she met my father, a man of similar temperament to Beth's Dad. Similar in looks too. They'd have enjoyed a round of golf together. Neither of them believed our mothers were as unhappy as they both claimed to be. These men, like others, were mistaken.

My right hand is getting better at doing up the buttons of my shirts, suggesting that the severed nerve of thumb and first three fingers may regrow.

27 May

Making their presence felt in my butterfly meadow
are maybe a dozen plants each with several dark green
necks snaking towards the light, ending in tight oval
buds which, in the sun, are one by one opening. I'm fond
of them: the sunburst yellow of their dandelion-like
heads close up again at night. They are already taller
than the highest grasses. I'm not sure of their identity.
Amongst the YSJ wild seeds which I sowed are common
cats ear and rough hawkbit, either of which they could
be, according to the Collins dictionary of wild flowers.
Beth has lent to me a larger format book of her mother's which I like a lot: *The Concise British Flora in Colour*,
published by the Ebury Press in 1965, with a foreword
by Prince Philip, which forty years on doesn't irritate
me now as it would have done then: 'The dedicated and
painstaking skill which has gone into each plate in order
to ensure complete accuracy in colour and detail will,
I am sure, make this book invaluable to both amateur
and professional botanists.' The names here given for
the genus *Hieracium* differ: rough hawk's-beard, mouse-
ear hawkweed, swine's succory, etc. I'm pleased with the
sound of this plant's possible names.

Telephoned Hugh to confess our act of crow-sabotage.
Without hesitation he accepted my apology.

Easily forget that I've been a landlord myself. On moving into my Victorian furniture factory in Charlotte
Road in 1985 there was nobody living on my side of the
street. My ground floor tenants operated till late at night
a traditional City printing press, and an East End seam-
stress on my first floor made lingerie, Best Curve Ltd

their company name, nightdress-makers to the Queen Mother.

The ground floor is in the only part of the building I still own, Carl my tenant, with his contemporary art gallery.

28 May

Radishes from the garden, washed and left to dry on the white sink leave behind drops of pale lilac water of an astonishing hue.

For over a year, other than working visits to my restaurant Podshavers, I've taken almost every meal with Beth, usually cooked by her. Until recently, tears poured down my cheeks while seated at the table in her kitchen, through the connecting door from mine. Silently, on and on, night after night. Without cause or explanation. She used to hold my clasped hands in hers. There was nothing either of us need say.

29 May

The first night of summer, warm and still. On my walking-way to Podshavers I plucked from the edge of a field a handful of wheat, in multi-shades of green-on-the-turn-to-yellow. Slim, tender. In the country air, not yet sedated by heat, a scent of eagerness, of possibility. Lying in bed on my return, the quiet of after-midnight was shattered by the roar of my Combi boiler, bringing back up to temperature its internal tank of water. As loud, to me, as an aeroplane. I hate, how I hate this sound. Two new flues from my cottage invade the lane, destroy its peace. Destroy my peace.

Unforgivable to install such a thing. One in each section of the house.

An insult. Nature deserves better of me.

In the post a letter from the Bishpool woman's insurers, blaming me for the accident.

From the field behind me the snort of a horse. Will's pedigree mare progresses at the side of her nearly-grown child, step by step across the field, their necks arched out and down to pull at the grass. Will and his family are being evicted, after renting for seventeen years their cottage, two paddocks and the stables in the coach house yard. Will refused his landlord's fair offer of an alternative home for his horses, took his landlord to court, and lost.

30 May

Set out straight after an early breakfast up the hill with basket and knife to gather mushrooms. Last weekend Carl and I picked what we discovered to be a St George's mushroom, marked in one of the reference books with a black chef's hat as 'choice', the highest grade of edible.

Again warm. Ahead of me, on the grassy farm track through the park, sat a pair of wild duck. They flew away as I approached, leaving behind a feather, almost transparent, white incised with shaky brown lines. Good to be finding feathers again. Counted sixty-seven deer, in the usual place. No mushrooms, though. It's been too hot, I reckon. In my unrelaxedness I didn't properly look, soon turned round to hurry home.

Slowed only when I noticed, in the small field below the disused quarry, the yellow flower I like seeing down in my butterfly meadow, and stopped to pick a bunch. They stand now in a vase on my kitchen table. In the Ebury Press book, readers interested in learning more about *Hieracium* are advised to study an article published in the *Journal of the Linnean Society in London* by a Mr H.W. Pugsley, in which he identifies two hundred and sixty different species.

What devotion. Was he married, was he a father, was he wealthy enough not to have to work for a living?

Helping Beth lay her crazy paving to the arbour, I hit the index finger of my left hand very hard with a hammer. The nail is black the flesh blue. It hurts to type.

31 May

Nine days now without a car. It hasn't yet been inspected by the insurance assessor. Another couple of weeks, probably, before I get it back – if it's not written off.

This is not the cause of my tension, of the pain in my body every morning.

Need to remind myself that my front door opens onto a meadow-full of golden buttercups and white and purple clover, as well as russet stems of sorrel and yellow heads of hawk-weed/bit/beard, with several other wild plants yet to bloom. And that in my woods maybe a hundred foxgloves are already in flower, mostly mottled mauve, some creamy-white, and scores of giant umbellifers.

Nourishment.

1 June

For twenty years I've been a full-time writer and in the last sixteen months I've written nothing of the slightest worth. A few letters, and this irregular journal, this vain, vacant talking to myself.

Running out of postcards. Want to drop one in to Francis, Hugh's brother-in-law, who lives in a nearby cottage, thanking him for yesterday's gift of two rainbow trout, morning-caught by rod and fly from a boat on the lake, cooked by me for supper, stuffed with fennel, doused in white wine, and wrapped in foil.

I'm improving.

Don't wish to telephone, much prefer to write a card. I can choose my words, make a distinct impression.

Control.

3 June

Bicycled this afternoon to Taunton for my appointment with Dr Ahmed, at which I spoke of signs of a new steadiness over the last ten days. He asked if there was still nothing I looked forward to, nothing I've these days achieved which has brought me joy, contentment, satisfaction. He chose these three words carefully. I shook my head. And then corrected the denial: 'Yes, some satisfaction. A start, maybe.' Dr Ahmed advised keeping to the daily dose of 150mg amitryptiline and 45mg mirtazapine, at least until our next meeting, in August.

4 June

The other day, walking back from a Jim session in Kingston, I passed a woman hauling herself with the help of two sticks along the lane towards her parked car. Her face was a uniform chalky white, the skin taut, her short hair grey. The smile she gave me wiped from her features the mark of pain. 'You'll be home before I get to my car!' she said, playfully, her eyes alight. Today, on my way to therapy, approaching fast from behind on my bicycle, I saw the large letters ASDA printed in black on the back of her green T-shirt. She works, I guess, on the checkout at the superstore in town.

5 June

This studied ordering of words on the page is designed to conceal rather than reveal the truth, to flatten out feeling. Like crops of cabbage hidden beneath sheets of plastic stretched across nearby fields, unseen, my fears flourish.

The thrice weekly visits to Jim also centre on concealment, despite the show of openness.

Don't know.

Do know that I'm frightened, sweat-beads forming on my upper lip as I write. Things are not as they seem. What I say is of nil significance in itself, just a device to keep me going.

Nothing ends, ends nothing.

The ASDA lady lives in a row of semi-detached Council-looking houses built on the top side of a slope, with a bank to the road and angled steps up to their garden paths. Today I noticed that Taunton Deane Borough Council have dug out the bank to provide a single parking space for the invalid's car, close to the iron banisters on steps leading to her cottage. The road is narrow and steep at this point, and other residents drive off to the left into a parking lot some distance from their front gates.

I like bicycling. In my home lane I saw a small animal shuffling about at the base of the hedge. It didn't hear my silent approach on Beth's almost-new bike. A tawny brown animal, its back arched in motion, about twelve inches from rounded face to the dark-brown tip of its tail. Aware, at last, of danger, it reared on its back legs, revealing white bib and tummy, then darted, quick as silver, for safety. A stoat? Don't have a book in which to check.

Watched two hares feed and play in a field in the crisp early evening light on my walk to Podshavers for supper. Thought of Philip Webb's drawing of a hare given to Morris to weave into a Merton Abbey tapestry. At dusk hares are abandonedly athletic in their movements, jumping and strolling and sitting and rolling, then haring off in one direction then another.

Left over from my premises, I own a Morris & Co. painted tile of a hare, designed by Webb, presumably.

Names. Everything has to be named, in order to exist.

7 June

On this day last year, 7 June 2002, I slashed both sides of both wrists repeatedly with a sharpened carving knife. Nine separate scars straight and white, bearing the dotted marks of over forty stitches. I will do no such thing again.

Love the tail-feather flash of yellow in the dipping flight of a bird up the lane ahead of me. Love the gold glow at the transparent centre of an insect's long tapering body, its tinted wings whirring at the closed kitchen window. Reach across the sink to let it out. So much to note. However long I live here I'll never cease seeing things before unnoticed.

Ripples of optimism in the stagnant pond.

8 June

The blind tricyclist, I call him. Because of the expression on his face, eyes hidden behind black glasses, and his hesitant relationship with the roadside, hearing the approach of cars without clearly seeing them. I coughed this morning as I approached, to warn him of my presence. He did smile to me as I bicycled past. Never does when I see him and his wife exercising their dog on Pound Lane. He can barely walk, his legs spindle-thin, bowed, unsteady, supported by sticks. Lone tricycling he wears the brightest of fluorescent racing gear.

Sebastian, the lawyer, my weekend neighbour, sings to his baby as he wheels her down the lane on their afternoon walk. On his return I sometimes see him labouring to push the three-wheel stroller up the tractor tracks through the fields from down near the lake.

Maybe I'll ask him to teach me to fish?

No, best not. Don't want to have to speak.

I've been thinking of taking singing lessons: a better idea. To learn to accompany my favourite bass passages of the St Matthew Passion, and to sing out strong and loud the *Dies Irae* from Verdi's *Requiem*.

9 June

Driving down a country road in the Cotswolds I spotted a handwritten sign to Rodmarton Manor. The name was familiar: the house in which Leonard and Virginia Woolf once lived?

It was open to the public, and I drove in.

Embedded in a path in the herb garden a shard of white china, with what I see as a small heart-shaped leaf resting on it. I pick it up, and find the shape of a heart has been worn in the glaze, the earthenware body of the broken dish nature-veined by the passage of time – inanimate, yet kind-of-alive – the beauty of fragments. Ordered beauty inside the house: furniture and ceramics and textiles made by masters of the arts and crafts movement, Gimson, the Barnsley brothers, Waals, Powell, and others.

A misplaced memory: soon realize I know of Rodmarton from my dealing days, nothing to do with the Woolfs, built for the Biddulphs by Ernest Barnsley.

An unexpected joy to wander around rooms occupied by a family whose love of the objects created this semi-secret place – objects which I too once loved. The house continues to be lived in and maintained by them, unaltered, the wood of floors and beams and furniture faded, a little dry.

The Woolf retreat was not here, it was in Sussex, near the home of Virginia's sister Vanessa, wildly decorated for her by Omega Workshops. My mistaken naming of these houses annoys me.

Drove on to Thompson Park, the National Trust property at which Herbert Sayer, youngest son of neighbour

Constance, is the Head Gardener. He lives in part of the converted coach house, with a lovely internal garden of his own, in which I heard his children playing.

All the postcards at Thompson were in the new NT style, too big for me.

The two Rodmarton cards which I bought were perfect. Back home, I picked out from the big black and gold bookcase in my bedroom Virginia Woolf's diaries: she took a lease on Monks House at Rodmell in September 1919 – Charleston, of course, is the name of Vanessa Bell's nearby home, the Bloomsbury set's rural signature-piece.

Good to know what they're called.

I gave the heart-fragment to Beth, a gatherer of the remnants of earlier lives, to reuse in her work.

11 June

A swarm of someone else's bees has moved in to Beth's hive. On the threshold lie dozens of dead drones, cleared out by the new residents. After supper, strolling down my freshly mown paths, I put my ear to the side of the hive and hear a peculiar whirring.

Earlier, at breakfast, saw in the morning sun that spiders have woven webs across the outside of every pane of glass in the window by my kitchen table. The webs are so delicate they can be seen only when the sun shines at an angle.

I miss my artist-friends in London, wish I was again involved with their street-events, partying, their creating of stalls of amazement at the Fête Worse Than Death.

12 June

I need more bookshelves, don't have the space to set in place books newly bought. Keep putting this off, unable to decide where the shelves could best be built. Will have to rearrange post-war fiction, all of which no longer fits in the bedroom bookcase. I need to feel that every book I possess is rightly placed.

On the lane today a bluey-green egg, broken, the colour so delicate. A blackbird's? Do crows as well as magpies raid the nests of smaller birds?

13 June

Seen several more of the glowing-centred insects – they have yellow and black striped legs and their bodies end in a dark bullet-shaped tip.

Find myself returning in mind to the Rodmarton visit, picturing the pleached apple trees in the walled garden, as firm as girders. High on the walls of the dining room are hung lustre plates painted in blue on cream with views of the building. Lovely things. Elsewhere, wedding photos, a collage of cut-out helmeted heads of members of the local hunt, and framed snapshots of favourite dogs: a host of family mementos. The house is their life, I can feel it. The wife, in a ragged straw hat, was seated at a table in the sun outside the front door, selling tickets and postcards – the same woman appears in the photos as a young bride forty years ago.

In the unaltered coach house country teas, homemade cakes, elderflower cordials, scones and clotted cream are served at metal garden tables, on a miscellaneous mix of china services.

I don't envy their life at Rodmarton, not at all, happy though I am that the place exists.

Jealousy I rarely feel.

Hard at times though I find it being myself, there's nobody else I'd rather be.

15 June

While washed sheets dry in the sun I decide to turn my mattress, for the first time since the bed was carpented for me two years ago, of figured ash with ebony pegs, in the 'muscular gothic' style which Pugin's genius spawned.

The cats, I see, now that the days are warm like to lie in the long grass. They flatten patches of my butterfly meadow. It doesn't matter, the grasses will right themselves after the next rain, and the cats look luxuriantly at ease, pleased with their lot.

Alex is staying the weekend. We walked across the fields to Cothelstone, and I saw in the churchyard that a new tombstone marks the grave which Ollie Sayer shares with his father, of grey granite, chip-carved with the image of an overhanging oak, and inscribed:

> Happy memories of our Dad
> The death of him was very sad
> In our hearts he will remain
> Till the day we meet again.

The flowers in three vases by the headstone are fresh. Primroses, no longer in bloom, grow at the buried feet of the two men. Alex and I walked on up through Cothelstone Wood and down an ancient drover's track to Cushuish, from there across the bountiful fields of Bewick Farm to lunch on Sunday roast at Podshavers.

After lunch, we returned through the great meadow by the lake and passed close to a lamb sleeping in the sunshine.

Not asleep, we discovered, but dead, its stomach bloated, lips drawn back from its mouth, in and out of which flew huge black flies.

16 June

At this time last year I don't remember my wilderness being overwhelmed by trails of robin-run-the-hedge. It's everywhere, climbing up and pulling groundwards the tallest cow parsleys, sticking to my jeans as I pass. Galium aparine is its official name, also known as: cleavers, goosegrass, kisses, sticky willy and claggie meggie's. Seems to feed off the air itself, rootless, rampant – I haul in, as a fisherman draws from the sea his nets, armfuls of the stuff; impossible to control, suffocatingly dense, a menace. In a week or two the goosegrass will be a mass of small white flowers, seed spreading. Must learn not to fret at these seasonal bursts of nature.

It's odd, unknown to me until after I'd moved to West Somerset, that the Warrs had lived in retirement at Cushuish. Tim Warr joined the staff at Harrow School in the same year as my father, 1948, for both of them their first proper jobs on being disbanded from the army. His support for me as a child though seldom direct was never in doubt. On recent holidays in the Lake District I've regularly hiked past a previous house of the Warrs, once visited as a boy, at the top of a remote vale in Borrowdale, without electricity, accessible only by rope bridge across a stream. The clothes he wore, the smell of him, the texture of his face, his welcoming voice ... I hear and see him still, can touch my own astonishment at his holiday home. It must have felt wonderful to be one of the boys at school invited up by Tim and Phyllis, his wife, on adventure holidays.

The Warrs' two sons and I were sent to Harrow, at minimal fees to the children of teachers at the school. Few of us subsidized boys came to terms with Harrow's

ethos of privilege, some of us disturbed for years afterwards by the connection.

17 June

In the lane, as I wheelbarrowed up from the abandoned coach house more loads of manure, I saw a fledgling crow, its mother flapping about nearby. As I approached the mother flew away over the hedge, whilst the fledgling hopped into the verge to hide at the heart of a fern. The same happened a second time. By my third approach the mother had disappeared from sight and the fledgling merely stepped aside to let me pass, scrawny blue-black feathers in disarray.

By dusk it may have learnt the trick of flight and saved itself from the foxes.

18 June

These days have witnessed the revival of my plan to make an orchard of the paddock below the farm stables. Beth and I are studying lists of West Country apples – although there's plenty of time to decide what to order for the December planting. Intend to include the biggest type of old English pear tree in a corner of the butterfly meadow, in front of the byre, in my line of sight here through the open half-glazed door of my study and down out of the window on the landing at the turn of the stairs. A tree-in-its-own-right, which happens also to be a bearer of blossom and of fruit, will stand as visual herald to the orchard.

Returning to my desk I register on the upper shelf of my steep-roofed corner cabinet, for the first time in ... I don't know how long, at least a year, I guess ... the presence of a terracotta jug decorated with turquoise, ochre and black enamel stylized flowerheads, an object I've always loved owning.

19 June

Today I bicycled past a small rough-earth field in which camomile and poppies thrive. Last year there were enough yellow and white heads of camomile growing here at Terhill for Beth to brew home-grown herbal tea: a languorous summer-holiday smell when I passed her kitchen. This year there's almost none. Much of the ground must be too rich now for camomile, decades of leaf mould and garden compost a natural breeding ground instead for nettles, cleavers, bindweed.

Butterflies like nettles, bees bindweed.

Oh, yes: the bees have a queen.

My fridge has been repaired, painlessly, not a difficult job, done by a man-with-a-van from Wellington. The Trafalgar Cinema, a single screen family-run 1930s survivor, is in Wellington. So is the best greengrocer in the district, an excellent fishmonger and a decent delicatessen.

20 June

In the lane I met an old man on a bashed-about quad bike, leading his flock of newly shorn sheep, at their rear alone a small black and white mongrel, beautifully respondent to the shepherd's requests.

Partnership.

21 June

Midsummer's day, lucid, hot. Near the close of a morning's steady work clearing cleavers, as I passed near the large sycamore to which one end of the hammock is attached, it occurred to me how much better things would look if I cut off the four lowest branches that swoop almost to the ground under the weight of the tree's big sticky leaves. Didn't hesitate, straightway fetched the bowsaw and a ladder.

Can't imagine how I've failed in three years at Terhill to effect this simple improvement, the sight lines in my wilderness-of-a-wood transformed.

Awareness.

Confidence.

23 June

Today Beth and I planted two fig saplings against the south-facing wall at the top side of the parking space, one nursery-bought, the other a sucker separated from the enormous old tree in Cothelstone's walled garden. Needed a pickaxe to dig holes deep enough to secure the plants in the rocky ground, a terrain they relish.

24 June

Hops begin to trail the twisted laurel arms of Beth's arbour, varnished seat-slats shaped on the curve, log-feet inset below the crazy-paved floor, like no other I've ever seen, strange and beautiful.

26 June

I've given up my conservation work with SWS – I'm cack-handed and clumsy, able at last to accept that it's not for me.

It saved me, though. Saw me through. Hauled me to my feet.

I've switched instead to sorting out Rich's accounts, and am happier for it. Driving back from Over Stowey on completion of the current batch of paperwork, beyond Bishpool Farm, close to the corner of last month's collision, a squat game bird ran ahead of my car, neck and head swaying from side to side with the earthbound effort, until it took flight, tail-feathers spread, bright brown, guiding the elegant airborne course of its escape. Would love to pick up a fallen feather from that tail.

A partridge?

Bit by bit I'm becoming not too awful a cook. This evening: black cabbage from the garden, and other local things, nothing special, except for the fact that, not long ago, I was convinced I could never ever enjoy making a meal for myself. On my own, without Beth.

27 June

A morning walk in the rain, up the hill and across into Bagborough Wood. Beneath the trees, rain beating on the leaves, my footfalls on the wet earth made no sound and I twice found myself looking through breaks in the brush at deer, as near as the window here at the turn of the stairs, several seconds passing before they became aware of my presence and leapt away.

I am differently frightened. Frightened of anger, of bitterness. Mustn't run, mustn't hide.

Near the big farm at Schopnoller, I gathered cherries from the low-hanging branches of a handsome tree, and on my return scattered them on my kitchen table. The cherries range in colour from dark red to yellow.

A striped snail has climbed to the top of my front door, relatively safe there from being eaten by birds. Wonder what it finds to eat.

28 June

Not honest words these days.
  Paper pasted over the cracks.

29 June

Cleaned the house. Nobody is coming to stay, I did it for myself. Most of the hoovered-up spiders were already dead. Took down to dust the terracotta jug and was surprised to find it unmarked, expecting to see on its base an imprint from the Watcombe Pottery, Torquay. 'Knowledge is Power' was painted in the 1870s by the designer Dr Christopher Dresser across the lintel of his study door. I like to believe he designed this jug of mine, as Dresser-documented examples of the same type are in the Victoria and Albert Museum.

The sheen on the cherries has dimmed. I'll tip them into my compost bin.

30 June

The old rose-arch which I saved on my first days here is a mass of loose white flowers, its boldest stems climbing into the branches of two adjacent trees, a laburnum no longer in yellow flower and a buddleia yet to bloom.

2 July

I'm troubled by the preciousness of these notes, last month's just now re-read.

Tight. Contrived. Fragility concealed.

And anger. And violence. As if it was somebody else who not long ago threw into the back of his car a bale of dry straw and gallon can of petrol, to burn himself alive.

Mustn't pretend 'he' is not me. Cannot charm my way, Harrovian-style, and refuse to articulate the rank distress still here every day.

It'll change, I will change. Slowly, slowly.

4 July

Rich and his assistant Phil called this afternoon to advise on the next steps to take in caring for this borrowed land of mine. They like what I've been trying to do, and we've decided to mark out on a map the separate sections, make a general plan of what trees to plant where, when to cut back which bits of undergrowth, and how to conserve and enhance nature's way with the place. I feel appreciated, sense their green hands guiding me back from the brink of another bout of despair. Rich says I should keep a written record of all that we do on my land. He sees us season by season work, watch, explore, experiment together, here at Lower Terhill.

I will pay for the work by a system of barter, scaling down my unpaid months of labour for them earlier this spring into fewer hours of their skilled attendance through the autumn.

12 July

Back from a week away on yoga retreat with Beth, I open my front door and enter to the scent of warm wood. On the bedroom landing, as in the rooms themselves, I notice with renewed pleasure the different colours of the boards, unsealed, sanded by hand by Beth to varied textures: schoolroom-style for my study, honey-smooth in my bedroom. She has an eye for the secrets which old materials reveal when worked upon with patience.

Beneath the cane laundry basket from out on the Levels, a butterfly hides, trapped by my closing of all the windows before leaving. It survives. I cup my hands and release it into the garden air, where it flaps its tortoise-shell wings in dizzy flight off over the ridge of the byre.

While we were on holiday the bullocks broke down a section of the iron fence to their field, and rummaged through my woods and garden. Carl, cat-sitting for three days before our return, stretched out on Beth's settee reading a book after supper, heard the sound of munching by the window and turned to look out onto the surreal twilight sight of a dozen all-black cattle feeding on the lawn. Unable single-handed to persuade them back into the field, he telephoned my landlord, who alerted Michael, the Cothelstone cowman. But he too was defeated in the dark, and had to leave the invaders on the loose until morning light.

The damage could have been worse. Sad, though, to lose rows of young lettuces, beetroot and spinach, cultivated by Beth from seed. The trampling of my wilderness also hurt. The empty beehive was knocked over, the occupied hive nudged askew.

I'm not sure why I'm as fond as I am of the podgy box hedge which separates the lawn from the vegetable

316

patch. The bullocks tore gashes in the hedge, and I'm in need of an efficient pair of new shears to cut it back into shape.

Looks as though one only of Beth's four artichoke plants outlived the stampede, nurtured in her greenhouse from seed, planted out a month or so ago on cleared patches of ground, not due to bear fruit until next summer. And the winter greens we were expecting to eat on into February next year are all uprooted.

13 July

Look up from the hammock at the sound of a bird, a single rising note, repeated, a plaintive cry, not loud. The bird is above me, hidden by the leaves of the rescued oak that filter the sun and splash synchronized shades of green. The sound is uncommon and I want to see the bird which thus speaks. I do see it, see the smallish bird's sharp swooping flight, elusive, keeping close to the trees, the sight as special as the sound. A rarity, I feel.

15 July

A bumblebee lies dead this morning on the computer keyboard. Open the window and place the corpse on the brick sill, to be eaten by the wren which bobs about the lane.

I've noticed three types of bumblebee gathering nectar from the purple, trumpet-shaped wild flowers that have recently appeared in my butterfly meadow: the usual kind, with honey-brown fluffy head and smallish black-brown body; a bigger bee, with lion-like ruff and striped tan and tea body; and the largest, a black-headed monster, with creamy-brown ribbon at its waist and thick jack-knife legs. I happen to know the name of the purple flowers favoured by the bees, but do not wish to use it. Not today. Another day, maybe.

16 July

Struggle to write.

Nobody makes me.

Know, at present, no other way of being. Can't stop, don't want to stop.

Remind myself that I actually am a published author, of three novels and several non-fiction books.

17 July

In tears in her kitchen, Beth sobs at the sight of ants shuddering in the throes of death, their bellies swollen with poison. She carries out each ant to the path and, with a stone, administers a 'blow of merciful grace', the *coup de grâce*. She felt, she says, for her ants, nesting in a hole in the quarry-tile floor close to the heat of the Rayburn, where the oil pipe disappears underground. They were doing no harm, she had lived untroubled at their side for a month or more, why now poison them? An injustice, to herself, she feels: the murder of her own feelings.

18 July

There's lots to be done, day-by-day things, resistance to the doing of which merely makes it worse.

19 July

Saturday morning shopping in Bishops Lydeard. Was once so proud of my local shops and claimed that Clive's Bakery and Delicatessen was the best of its kind hereabouts, its homemade meat pies, fruit tarts and chocolate-coated flapjacks recommended by me to everyone. Since expansion of his premises the quality has deteriorated, and I've come to see that Clive cares mostly about money. Not unusual: to work for a living, save for a bigger house, smarter car. His stock may not, in fact, have changed much at all. The significant change is in me, in how I see things. Sweat breaks out on my face as I stand awaiting my turn to be served, not only in Clive's place, also at the butchers.

It's me not them.

They work hard and seriously.

Sweat pours in recall as I write. Can feel drips collect in the crook of my elbows, in the hollow of my collar-bones. Fifteen minutes ago I was cold, five minutes ago hot, and now I'm again cold, vest and shirt damp in the chill air of a rainy night.

Should have driven to Wellington, where nobody knows me.

So easily unbalanced.

The smallest setback threatens disintegration.

It took an hour to write these few words.

22 July

Type as fast as it comes. To get it out, unedited. Want to say that I do recognize the world outside. While living in here I live out there too. Both worlds are, for me, fear-filled. I'm frightened. Very. Today the news of renewed fighting in Monrovia, the capital city of Liberia, where 100,000 refugees are living rough, poorly fed, the supply of water disrupted. A spokesman for the Red Cross said they'd been piping in 1,000,000 gallons a day of fresh water, until last night, when their pump-station was blown up. Dysentery, cholera, death will follow within a few days if reconnection is not made to an uncontaminated supply of drinking water.

On the radio news the screams of mothers bent over the punctured bodies of their children. Report of corpses piled in protest at the defended gates of the American Embassy.

Elsewhere in the Today Programme's bulletin: exploitation of Chinese immigrants in the vegetable fields of East Anglia.

Disparate images spin.

None of this, not the decline of the grocer's shop in Bishops Lydeard, not the calumny of international traffic in cheap labour, not the years and years of the West's unconcern for murderous unrest in Africa, none of this is cause of my flooding despair.

I cling on, afraid of being washed away.

Must ride it out. Quietly. Mustn't dramatize. Yesterday I was able to conceive of holding to stoical acceptance of difficult times.

Stoicism. A good word.

To identify my state with refugees in Liberia is a frantic mistruth.

I am unwell, but I am neither starving nor exploited
nor a victim of war.

23 July

Another birthday is near: the day after tomorrow.

My ex-wife Elizabeth's too, on the same day – Beth, as I used to call her. Then-Beth and now-Beth.

A postcard to send to her lies on the desk in front of me, a coloured photograph of part of the garden at Rodmarton Manor, clipped box hedges lining a path leading to a summerhouse with conical roof of cut Cotswold-stone tiles. On my visit the other day I came across a stack of the tiles behind one of the greenhouses, at close quarters thicker, rougher than I'd imagined in looking up from the ground to the roof of the Manor. Wanted to steal one, bring it home, hang it on a nail on the wall, through the hole already pierced in its curved top-end, for securing to battens on the roof.

Getting tense again. Anxious.

Must stop. Must do something different from writing this stuff to myself.

My mother has kept for several years on her mantel-piece, behind a pottery lion given to her by Elizabeth, the postcard of an adolescent girl wearing a white lace dress with black velvet sash, tied-back blonde hair hanging to her waist, standing in a pale room. A painting by James MacNeill Whistler, reminiscent to me of one of Goya's Spanish princesses, the card unwritten upon. I've no idea what this picture means to Mother.

I should ask.

But I won't.

Where did she get it? From me?

24 July

On his early morning walks researching the movements of deer across the Quantock Hills, and out at
work during the day with SWS, Phil has been gathering
samples of wild grasses, the seeds of which he suggests
we introduce to the butterfly meadow. Next week he'll
call to take detailed note of all that grows in the various sections of my wild garden. He's already thinking
about native shrubs to plant, envisaging this as a model
conservation project, the way of the future. Order, they
reckon, is losing its appeal.

I'm wary of 'shrubs', which I associate with the hybrid
hell of garden centres.

It's ages since I sat on the bench beneath the Monterey
pine: not at all this summer, and seldom last. The wood-
en slats are green with mildew and marked my jeans.
I've scrubbed the bench down now, with the brush which
lives beside the outside tap and a kitchen bucket of warm
water laced with organic cleaner. Maybe I'll begin to use
again this once-favoured place.

The scent of the old red rose by the wall to the lane
is so strong that I feel, eyes closed to draw in breath, its
smell could be solid enough to see.

A pair of rosebuds unfold on my oak table, standing
in a small cocktail glass decorated with pink enamel elephants. The glass belonged to my father. When I was a
child he often used to wear to teach in school a dark-blue
tie embroidered with the rear end of a pink elephant, its
tail hanging free, an emblem of membership of some
club in Cambridge. He liked this tie. My mother loathed
it. The accompanying glass is one of the few things of
my father's in my home. Another: a teak cigarette box

from a houseboat on the lakes of Kashmir, the place of my conception. Neither of my parents smoked, and the packet of cigarettes they used to keep in this box, for dinner guests when my father became a headmaster and they officially entertained, stayed there for months, grew stale. The box, never put by me to use, I keep in the drawer of a cabinet in the end room downstairs, where in the winter I sit beside the wood-burning stove to read. One thing of his, a wide-rimmed blue glass fruit bowl, I do like, use every day. It was given to my father by his father, picked out from his Dad's stock as a travelling salesman in commercial chinaware. My father, the youngest of four sons brought up in the suburbs of Birmingham, was the first in his family to go to university, proud and overawed to have made it to Cambridge.

I, in contrast, presumed my right to be there.

I bought for myself, some years ago, more *Pink Elephants*, a set of eight mail-art folding cards of found images by Gilbert and George, for each of which they composed a different drinking verse. One of them goes:

> Felt a trifle queer last night
> and couldn't eat a thing
> couldn't drink a thing.
> Lay very still for a few minutes.
> Drank a lot and later
> quite made up for it all.
> Cheerio

Beth has made for the set an ingenious frame, of end-cut layered cardboard.

26 July

DISCOVERY FOR SALE: handwritten in capital letters on a sign outside a house on the road across the levels to Glastonbury. PERSEVERANCE WORKS: the address in Shoreditch of the friend of a friend, passed on to me over cream tea this afternoon.

Found a new word I like: haulm – the haulm of a potato is its once-green shoots, which die back into the earth when the tubers are ready to be dug.

27 July

In the long grass close to where I sit in the sun, Bertie leaps to trap between his front paws a butterfly. He sets it free. Catches it again, in his mouth. Spits out the butterfly, its wings too damaged to fly.

28 July

Shaky. The worst for weeks.

30 July

On a dusty pull-in by the road into Taunton a traveller has parked his converted horsebox, an old vehicle with crafted coachwork, the oval relief on the hood of the cab colourfully painted: a bridled head within a frame of horseshoes.

The tailboard has been removed from the back of the van to make space for a narrow veranda, onto which opens a cross-braced door and small window, the bright-print blind, drawn. Riding by on my bicycle I see, in a field nearby, a man in a camouflage jacket walking a dog, the dog alert, the man pale-faced, thin, hair teased into blonde dreadlocks which descend almost to his hips. Pen Elm Hill this road is called, less than half a mile from the paratroopers' defended barracks.

31 July

On the turf path leading into my wild-cherry grove, wet with dew, I pick up by its hind leg the headless body of a rabbit, the flesh of the neck raw, a recent cat-kill. Further along the path is the rabbit's head, chewed to the bone.

1 August

Phil came by this morning to add professional details to the rough map I'd sent him. We spoke of cutting down all the sycamore, laurel and dead elm in the copse beside the lane, half-cleared by me, and transplanting there some of the ash and hazel saplings which multiply in other parts of the wood, in years ahead to be coppiced for the building of bean and sweet-pea trellises. He wants me to think up names by which to call each section of my Terhill territory, as shepherd Janet does of her fields at Aisholt. Phil began to list the wild plants currently growing, with the intention of recording each year new arrivals, some species introduced by us, others already present in the soil, released to flower by selective cutting and clearing of dominant regulars.

I was tense, uncertain, unhappy. The drizzle smudged Phil's map.

I know, of course, the value of formal record-keeping. It's just not the kind of thing I want to do.

I can't, don't have the knowledge. And don't wish to acquire it.

I'm looking for ... I don't know ... something else, something different.

3 August

In the hot sun hundreds of hairy caterpillars have hatched on the leaves of the bank of nettles behind the stables, entwined four or five deep around some of the green stems, a feast for the birds. Butterflies are out now in numbers. Watch three very small small tortoiseshells flit from head to head of the whitey-blue flowers of oregano by Beth's kitchen door. The chequered turquoise and dark brown bands at the base of the young butterflies' wings are not yet as bold in colour as they will be.

4 August

Cat carnage: on the gravel this morning by the garden gate a dead bird, without a head; and at the edge of the lawn the corpses of three shrews.

6 August

Stopped my car fifty yards on down the road from the end of our rutted lane to allow a man and two women on horseback to pass. The man was mounted on a grey stallion, which knocked my wing mirror as it passed. The rider smiled at me: my GP, Dr Merchison, from the surgery in Bishops Lydeard.

Animals at night raid the brick compost bins which Beth and her brother built this spring. Earlier today I followed a trail of celery, tomato skins and potato peel across the lawn to the laurel-shaded path beside the kennels, close to a well-worn badger run.

8 August

The traveller's van has not moved. Maybe he part-time works on the land, baling straw through this week's dry heat, or market-gardening, harvesting the summer greens and other vegetables which explode-grow beneath polythene sheets stretched across field after field by the road.

The four fingers of my right hand can now fully straighten then close, and the vaguest sense of touch may be returning to the tips, the quicks all healed, none picked. Anxiety contained. Don't know how. Don't trust the battening down, the fierce control. My heart beats dangerously fast, is forced by my state-of-mind and by the prescribed mix of drugs to work too hard. Learnt at Wednesday's check-up at the surgery that Dr Ahmed wrote a month ago to my doctor to advise the phasing out of amitriptyline, to prevent damage to the heart. I was never told. I'm worried. Fear the return of sleepless nights. A cardiogram has been arranged for next week.

I want, so much, to free myself from dependence on medication.

In therapy I believe, and in friendship, and in perseverance with the taking of these notes, difficult though they are to write, mind dulled by the struggle to hold my nerve. Five weeks have passed since I last saw Jim, who is off on his summer break. I'm missing him. We start on Tuesday again our work together. He has just passed sixty, could have retired.

Therapy is his life. He's good at it.

9 August

Beth tells me she has removed a dozen or more large yellowish-green caterpillars from the young leaves of her purple-sprouting broccoli, not due to be ready to eat until January. She tossed the caterpillars onto the tangle of bindweed, thistles, ground elder and hemlock beyond the vegetable patch, hoping they might there find alternative food, enough to persuade them to pupate, later to hatch into this year's final brood of butterflies.

Cabbage whites?

There is another breed of caterpillar also on the broccoli, fewer in number, mottled brown, black and lettuce-green, scaled rather than smooth. Don't know what they will transform themselves into. Must find out how long the cycle of change is from egg to caterpillar and on from cocooned pupa into the brief life of the butterfly. Some pupa over-winter, as do some butterflies whose lives, therefore, are not so brief. And particular species of butterfly migrate long distances. Do they lay eggs here, and do these butterflies, when their time comes, fly back to wherever their parents migrated from? I know very little.

10 August

It's a Sunday morning, ten o'clock, the air heavy in the windless heat. This evening it is predicted that the weather will break. Fifteen minutes ago I came up the two steps through the always-open half of the doorway into my study and was halted mid-stride at the sight of dozens and dozens of small white-fronted black-headed birds swooping in to the eaves, where they hovered for several seconds, then flew away in a wide arc, chattering. They kept returning. The occasional bird alighted on the top of one or other of the three partly open windows, tucked in below the roofline. Smallish birds with forked tails and, in flight, sharply tapered wings. I know what they're called: house martins. All the same, I checked in a reference book.

I want them to think next year of building their characteristic nests below the iron gutters of my house. They've gone this evening, are on the point of emigrating to a warmer continent.

I'm afraid this is the wrong thing to be doing.

If only I could write un-self-edited. Each sentence in my head, each phrase, almost every word withers, has to be revived, propped up, frogmarched onto the page.

Need to say to myself: you're OK, you're doing OK, this is OK.

Am I? Is it?

Feels ... Can't say how I feel.

Vulnerable. Fragile. Mistaken.

Many of the crinkled leaves of broccoli have indeed, I saw after breakfast this morning as I wandered in confusion around the garden, been eaten to shreds.

11 August

The soldiers in the barracks at Pen Elm are marine
commandos not paratroopers. Armed guards patrol the
perimeter fence.

14 August

Beth spotted crawling across the byre yard the other day a giant caterpillar, its articulated scales in mottled camouflage-greens, with a pair of cartoon-like eyes – circular, with black half-moon pupils and white corneas – either side of its head, from which projects a tapering trunk, waving around as it concertinas its passage across the warm stones. We looked it up in Michael Chinery's *Pocket Guide to Insects*: clearly the caterpillar of an elephant hawkmoth, a beautiful pink and khaki creature that can, apparently, often be seen resting at dusk on fronds of honeysuckle.

Never seen one myself. Then I've never looked. Did see, though, this afternoon, another of these big caterpillars feeding, as the book predicts, on a stem of rosebay willowherb.

I've begun to read *The Aurelian Legacy*, bought over a year ago, about the early collectors of butterflies. Of Robert 'Porker' Watson (1916-1984) the authors write:

> Watson aimed not for a perfect collection but a collection of perfect specimens. Damaged ones, however rare, he always released. His setting was described as a miracle of perfection, despite his being virtually blind in one eye. Like many leading field lepidopterists of earlier times Watson was a first class shot and fly fisherman. He was also a hospitable and liberal man, holding open days when entomologists could view his collection, and often sending away young visitors with gifts of store boxes or setting boards. Among entomologists, Watson's name will always be associated with the striking red form of the Cinnabar Moth, which he bred over some twenty-five years. The

Watson collection of British butterflies and moths, housed in sixty-five Hill cabinets, was eventually bequeathed to the Natural History Museum, London.

15 August

Duck crowd the shelves and windowsills of Dr Merchison's consulting room in Bishops Lydeard. Plastic duck nest in wicker baskets, ceramic duck swim in glass ponds, painted wooden duck waddle and peck at scattered corn. Half a dozen ugly threesomes hang in arrested flight across his blue walls. My doctor likes to shoot duck, displays cups and medallions won in this and other country pursuits.

He's a lousy doctor, who drinks too much. He has never once spoken to me of my attempt to die, although it was he who before then had subscribed anti-depressants, for the first time in my life. He never asks me how I'm feeling, what I'm thinking. Doesn't look at my wrists.

16 August

Big caterpillar has disappeared. Eaten by a bird – or changing shape.

Checked the nettles by the stables, and not one of the hundreds of those other caterpillars are still there either.

To where do caterpillars slip away to entomb themselves in a cocoon? When? At night? How far do they have to travel?

At kindergarten I think we must have kept silkworms, as I've a memory-feeling of the tension of waiting and watching each day in class for the transformation promised by our teacher that I just didn't believe was possible. No such thing was allowed at home. No pet-anything permitted, other than my mother's spotless cat. Not even a to-be-beautiful butterfly.

17 August

Walk out after breakfast around the newly mown paths, and there's a hint of revival of my old interest in the shaping of this place. Fret at the thought of losing one of the bigger trees in a storm.

It happens, and we adjust.

Too tired tonight to describe what I've seen, will have to make do instead with a list of butterflies newly identified today: gatekeeper, wall, meadow brown.

Twice this afternoon I arose from my desk to let out trapped small tortoiseshells.

19 August

Named, in draft, the sections of the plan of my terri-
tory: Hemlock Dell, The Wilderness, Cherry Grove,
Kass Glade, Shadow Wood, Poplar Alley, Beth's View,
New Zealand, The Orchard, Groom's Garden, Butterfly
Meadow.

Naming ties things down.

20 August

Down for the weekend, Ginny, Alex's Oxford girlfriend, has adjusted my computer, and I can delete virus-suspicious emails now without opening them.

Names! I'm doing it with people too, as if labelling is all that's needed – *this* butterfly is a meadow brown, *that* person is Jim: end of story.

So dismissive. And Ginny is so much more than just a bright Oxford undergraduate – she is gifted with an ease-of-being that makes her a special joy to have to stay, with Alex.

10 September

Today at Kings Cycles in Station Road, Taunton, I consigned my broken old Raleigh in part-exchange for an
almost-new twenty-one speed town bike. Before me in
the queue to be served was a man carrying a box of dis-
assembled child's bicycle parts, which the enthusiastic
owner of the bicycle shop identified as a particular model of the late 1950s, of outstanding quality, spare bits of
which he had for ages been gathering at his home store in
Wellington. It had been the owner's first bike as a child,
then already second-hand, and he wanted it restored for
his young son now to ride. The man at Kings was happy
to take on the task.

21 September

Called with Beth at YSJ Seeds, hoping to ask their advice before choosing more wild meadow plants. There was nobody around, and I explored with Beth this strange place. She found buried beneath the undergrowth the carcasses of several vintage cars, once common family models of the 1960s, and gathered the shining shards of window glass to weave this Christmas with silver thread into stars. In the village of Winsham we climbed the wall of a deserted garden, ate apples from a tree and explored the dusty contents of old working barns.

We can still have pleasant days together, despite Beth's distress and fury with me at other times.

1 October

Today, 1 October, is the day that foxes, Constance Sayer
says, piss on any blackberries that remain on the bushes,
giving them maggots and making them uneatable.

Recall with sudden clarity the disorientation of the
six electric shock 'cures' at Rydon, the blind fear of each
day-a-week ritual, my powerlessness to resist the cycle
of treatment, the memory loss and distress.

2 October

I've brought myself up to date with readings of the two publications received weekly by post, the *Times Literary Supplement* and *New Statesman*, the latter order recently resumed after a break of five years. This return to standard patterns of reading has happened without intent. As if my head has taken to itself to regrow. Earlier in the year I threw away a back-pile of *TLS*, admitting to myself that they could never be read.

I haven't watched television for twenty years and seldom read daily newspapers, never wish to own a mobile phone.

The philosopher Colin McGinn won't watch television either, not because he's virtuous but because it doesn't work for him. He feels emotionally darkened by the box, not enlivened by it. Not relaxed by it, not even stupefied.

Me neither.

9 October

Whilst attacking the burdock I was stung on the inner lip by a nettle. The burdock grows bushy tall on the edge of Shadow Wood, thick as saplings, brought to the ground with a bowsaw, the debris piled in the bottom pit of garden refuse, near the cedar.

Not long ago, within Carl's memory at home in Leeds, the parents of friends made beer from burdock, by boiling its roots.

While taking care not to distribute the burdock burrs about the place, I've failed, nevertheless, to notice how many of the smaller clinging seeds of cleavers stick to my clothes, lodge themselves in my shoes, get entangled in my hair. At my door at the end of the day I brush off as much as I can, and too many seeds blow onto the butterfly meadow, where I'm afraid they may propagate.

Want to describe the beauty of the chest-high walls behind the kennels, freed long enough by now from the throttling presence of common dock and nettles to reveal the richness of life in the damp native mosses, ferns, lichens, creeping blue-buttoned plants and the occasional wild violets which flourish in the crevices. Broken segments of glass bottles and fragments of iron have been placed by Beth to rest on the flat tops of the walls, lined with their original slabs of slate. There is an outside privy at the kennels, and the remains of a kiln.

On waking early this morning and looking out of my bedroom window I saw in the yard flames rise from the massive beams of the old cattle pen leaning against the brick wall. Wearing only my dressing-gown and slippers I stood for twenty minutes directing the hose onto the embers. Twice last night, apparently, without causing me to wake, Beth had risen to put out the remains of her bonfire, so strong that the concrete had exploded and set alight a thick old timber bulkhead. Frank had heard the 2 a.m. commotion and had also got up, walking over to assess the danger.

It seems I do sleep.

14 October

My heart has given up, swelled in size, ceased fully to function. No sooner does my spirit strengthen than my heart is freed to express its distress and register the strain of these many months. Today my legs are no longer the liquid tree trunks of three days ago, have been reduced by medication to spindly muscle-less sticks, and I've this afternoon returned from another stay in Musgrove Hospital.

Will in time be OK, as I've changed GP and am being properly cared for now. In neglecting to give me my specialist's drug instructions, Dr Merchison endangered my life. He should be forced to retire, disqualified if he refuses. The villagers of Bishops Lydeard don't deserve to suffer his incompetence.

15 October

The autumn leaves of the cat-piss tree by the kennels are graphic, the external shape of the leaf repeated in decreasing outlines of yellow then green then purple.

Nearby, the cooking apples on the old tree fall.

The latest bulletin produced by the Somerset butterfly fanatics informs me that the final broods of red admiral and speckled wood feed off apples in October. They and commas also like the late blackberries.

25 October

Remember that, on the morning after the fire, when I opened the front door to the sun I saw Tom seated on the red tiles of the barn floor, surveying his domain. He looked at me, white bib and paws prominent, and with his usual decorum walked over, came in, talking, and followed me up to my study.

I've begun to clear the lane, pruning and shaping the two hazel trees, cutting the holly and hawthorn further back than ever before, revealing not only remnants of a dry-stone wall, in herringbone pattern, but also the curve of the ditch and its hidden banks of fern. Found the work tiring, took frequent stops for breath. Satisfying, though. The same with raking and clearing the butterfly meadow, strimmed three days earlier by Phil.

A bat has been stuck inside my house for three days, flying back and forth from room to room each dusk. By stealth, I persuaded it to escape last night through the double upper doors of the study.

26 October

Saw an unusual butterfly, orange the dominant colour, its flight distinctive. It dashed from the vine which Beth has planted on the sunny gable-end of the byre, to the elder behind the compost and then up into the ash. Didn't see it for long enough to identify.

Micro-cobwebs spread unbroken from the rose in the glass bottle on my kitchen table, to the bronze candlesticks and over to the pierced pottery fruit bowl, given to me years ago in Israel by Vera, made by a friend of her daughter's. I love this bowl.

Will and his wife have been thrown out, forced by bailiffs to abandon their rented home of almost twenty years.

28 October

Do not understand how the force of the unconscious can grow to be so powerful, how it was able, according to Jim, to act as the primary cause in summer last year in sending me to the brink of despair. Mystified as to how I convinced myself that death was a better alternative to life.

Can find no more than a few stray clues as to what has guided me now for three consistent months out of the worst of the darkness.

Want never to go back – must not go anywhere near that dreadful internal place.

Aware that, however different I might wish it to be, there will be times to come of anguish.

And of joy?

Maybe. There may be.

29 October

The two tall ash beyond the byre must be male and female. I don't know which way round. Both are bare of
leaves, while only one of them retains its bunched seed
pods, shoe polish brown in colour. The female?

I have the feeling that things with Beth may have gone
beyond the point of no return. For me, that is. I can't,
don't want to speak for her. The ups and downs have today become too frequent, too violent to continue to be
tolerated. This morning the fury was impossible, and I
fear I may have to call it a day, ask her to leave. While I
know that my behaviour goads her pain, she is *not* crazy,
is herself in control of what she does with her feelings,
however bleak they may be, and I've been reduced to believing there's nothing I can do that she finds acceptable.

Part of me wants to go through the passage door into
her kitchen and simply sit with her, be at Beth's side
through her day of ... whatever it is, as she so often was
for me.

I can't. I too am hurt. My heart is not in it.

Though I know that I am alive in a large part due to
her care.

Things with Beth get worse not better. I pour water
into a bucket with the holes of a sieve.

I write about Beth's distress while unable, at the time and
even now, to describe my own. No mention of standing
on the ridge in the wood, swallowing dozens of aspi-
rin with water from a bottle, the violent slashing of my
wrists with steel carving knife, falling, rolling through
the dead beech leaves and bracken and ferns. Later
waking up alive and staggering back home, soaked
in blood, collapsing on the mat at my own front door,

cradled by Beth.

Or was it a bread knife? Whichever it was, Beth threw it in the bin.

On my way back from posting a letter I wandered down the country alley to the back of Keepers Cottage, and saw Will's wife feeding their horses. Walked over to speak to her, told her how sorry I was to hear that the troubles had come to eviction from the house. Eighteen years they'd lived there, she told me. 'Can't let it get you down, can you?' she said. 'That's life.' They are living in Taunton now, close to the children and grandchildren, and she rather likes it, she says, with a smile. She has dyed red hair and looks younger than her age. I have never known her name.

November: the eleventh month of the year. A visit yesterday with Beth to Castle Drogo, Lutyens' monolith on a promontory overlooking the ravine formed by the River Teign, the Estate's land reaching out in the distance to the beginnings of Dartmoor. The house is built of grey-flecked Devon granite, the stone undressed inside as well as out, relieved only by Lutyens' restrained mouldings and massively beautiful oak doors with long iron hinges. We went for a two-hour walk, down and through one of the oldest unaltered deer parks surviving in Britain, its sixteenth-century walls intact, rich in rare lichens, left to grow undisturbed.

Cothelstone Hill was once an Elizabethan deer park, with a tall surrounding stone wall.

A phone call to Alex this morning provided an unexpected resolution to my dislike of Christmas: I can borrow his flat in central Paris, and pass the five festival days there alone. Need now do nothing false. Not wanting to stay here in Beth's proximity, I won't have to resort instead to inviting myself to stay for Christmas with friends with whom I really do not wish to be.

3 November

Keys, the hanging seeds of the ash are called.

4 November

On Akiko's recommendation I'm reading Raimond Gaita's *The Philosopher's Dog*. Akiko is one of the few people from whom I accept suggestions of concerts to listen to, books to read. The trust between us is unusual, our very meeting unlikely: a reclusive Japanese interpreter and ... me.

I cherish our friendship, embodied today in the pleasure of reading a paragraph by Gaita about bees:

> In our imagination we elaborate on the association of bees with flowers and warm days, and because they die when they sting we readily forgive them the harm they cause us, even though we know they can be deadly when they swarm. Perhaps that is why my father consented to their stings, never wearing protective clothing when he caught a swarming hive in a nearby tree or when he took the racks from the hives. Although he was never bitten as severely as one would have expected, he suffered enough painful bites for his refusal to don protective clothing to excite concerned curiosity. When I asked him why he refused, he said that he did not think of them as enemies against which he needed to protect himself. I did not fully understand his answer. Nor I suspect did he. But it had to do with, and was certainly of a piece with, his tender compassion for them.

Reminded of the bee recommendation from Elizabeth, of a novel by a friend of hers in Notting Hill, Sara George's *The Beekeeper's Pupil*, which I enjoyed reading, the voice convincing, an account of growth in both knowledge of the behaviour of bees and in the courage to love. Elizabeth and I see each other now, when we can.

364

She visited me in mental hospital. Our contact has life again. In December I'll have lunch in The Hague with her mother. I am happy that this is so.

5 November

The summer birds are flown and not all the wintering
ones have yet arrived, the weather still warm. I again
feel drawn to name the birds here. This morning in
the sun on the telegraph wires sat one yellow-fronted
and one white-fronted bird, both with long wagging
tails, preening themselves: a grey and a pied wagtail.
They flew away at the arrival of a hunter-bird, which
then perched on the bevelled top of the post and gazed
around, its breast flecked light brown and white, head
similar, white again on the underside of the wedge-tail,
diving after errant young voles in the grass. Watched
it through field glasses. An immature sparrowhawk, I
discovered from the book.

Don't know what best to do, unable to help Beth, my
presence seems to make her darkness blacker. Do nothing? Not expect to get things right?

I myself need help in this. And will seek it, from my
friends.

6 November

Beth and I took an hour inspecting room by deserted room the abandoned coach house, gathering in bags dozens of rusted nails and keys and things for her to transform into the art she makes. Took a forgotten chair, the adjustable back of which Beth will repair and reupholster, to replace her tomb-like armchair in the sitting room. Weeks ago she mounted in meticulously cane-lined frames the dried-flat bodies of two shrews she had found squashed beneath her carpet, carried into the house by her cats.

7 November

Wordless not long ago to myself, now I'm unable to hear
or be heard by Beth.

The reverse side of the occasional fallen leaf of sycamore is white.

8 November

Acceptance is the key, Beth feels. Mutual acceptance
that there's nothing either of us can do for each other.

Unwilling acceptance.

Hurt acceptance.

Her cares are concentrated on getting through each
day without falling into the void of nothingness or ex-
ploding into self-punishing anger with me. We are each
a threat to the other, she feels.

More, there's always more, much more.

Mutual recognition of a capacity for despair was doubt-
less the original attraction.

9 November

Isabel, I've discovered, is the name of Will's wife.

Picked today in the vegetable patch an all-purple mushroom, bell-shaped with divided gills and striped stem. Never seen such a thing before. Violet webcap (*Cortinarius violaceus*): the book identifies – one of two differently occurring forms, the first found under hard woods, the second under soft, the only all-purple fungi in Europe – 'both are quite rare and though edible, are not recommended'.

Just now a good sound: the kettle purring as I come downstairs on changing after a damp afternoon in the garden, confirmation that I did indeed remember to switch on the water for a pot of tea before putting on dry clothes.

The other day a professionally togged bicyclist drew up beside me on the road and said: 'I'll give you one essential tip about bicycling. You're struggling in too high a gear. The most efficient way is always to change down into as low a gear as you need, never dropping below 20 revs per minute.' Can't manage this myself. Never used the bottom ten of my twenty-one gears.

This evening Beth and I went to a performance by the local Choral Society of Donizetti's *La Bohème* at Queen's College Taunton, where our family friend of childhood was bursar. My mother, sister and I stayed there several times. Much has changed, but his home still stands. On turning away at the garden gate, I remembered once taking constant care to ensure that the runt of his boxer bitch's litter of puppies received its share of milk. My presence felt vital to the puppy's survival. I never discovered what happened after our week's holiday was over.

11 November

Yesterday morning, sleep-deprived, I wrote to myself in detail about how I feel around Beth. And showed it to her.

She wasn't pleased.

I can understand why: this focus on myself, on my own feelings is wrong.

This morning I was able instead to express, in simple words, my thoughts of how she maybe felt and of what it might be possible for us together to do to push through the gloom.

We spoke.

Not right of me to have attempted yesterday to decide for her. For myself, though, there are things I need, for both our sakes, to do.

Delicious rack-of-lamb!

Daring to aim to cook decently!

15 November

Anger. I know what it feels like, spit spraying as I shout:
'Fuck off! Just fuck off, Beth! Leave!'

Which is not exactly what I'm aware of meaning, but
is, at this moment, an accurate expression of how I feel:
that I want her to go away and leave me alone, leave my
sight, leave my hearing, leave my house.

No, not the voice of reason.

19 November

At my desk straight after breakfast, I recall the encouragement with which I responded to Beth when we first sought to be together, and remember my enthusiasm about her setting up home over in the cottages at Cothelstone Manor.

I held the same felt-wishes for myself here in the restored completion of Erkindale. Managed to sustain none of these feelings.

Passed, bicycling in the rain to Taunton, at Nailsborough a dozen bunches of black grapes hanging over a highish garden wall. The leaves of the vine had fallen. I've been this way before maybe a dozen times and have never noticed the grapes, in size eatable but out of arm's reach. In the lane a bird on a branch of the oak dropped black-berried shit onto the front of my shoulder bag, the canvas fishing satchel a version of which I've carried with me everywhere for twenty years. It'll bear forever now the stain.

20 November

Yesterday afternoon, while Beth and I were cutting and clearing trees from beyond her bench, Kerry Salmon arrived across the fields from Cothelstone driving his digger, ready to grub out the iron fence for us, remove rubble from the paddock and level the piled earth.

I helped him.

One of the giant tyres on his JCB was punctured by an iron strut and a mechanic was called out from Wellington. While the repair man worked on into the dark, Kerry talked to me, of being the last son of six children, forced to go with his father when his parents divorced and learning as a boy the mechanics of cars from his Dad, before returning after leaving school at sixteen to live by choice with his mother on the farm.

He admires Beth's deliberately half-finished bench, begun a year ago down by the cleared paddock, made of broken terracotta tiles and shaped like a chesterfield, with out-leaning arms and back. I like it too, very much.

Kerry worked again today. I again helped him.

21 November

Awoke this morning clear about how, if at all, I might be able to make with Beth an arrangement agreeable to both of us.

Before lunch, having neither seen nor heard her, after working all morning with Kerry, I searched her silent house, afraid she might have hurt herself. Her gumboots stood beside the back door, her bed empty. Finally noticed that her car was not there, and remembered her regular Tuesday appointment with a psychiatrist in Taunton.

To my astonishment, when we met in the early afternoon, she too had been thinking along the same lines as I had about what best to do.

A break, not violent.
   There's a chance.
   We'll see, we'll see.
   Beth's mood, of course, can change at whim. Her distress is acute, unaltered.
   Worse than mine, at present. Only someone with their own troubles could have focused so devotedly on mine.
   As if she preferred those long months of my dependence on her, spending all her time caring for me, doing what she could to prevent me trying again to kill myself. Such a waste. A beautiful young woman, she *must* move on.

Sebastian, my neighbour, at dusk walked across our intervening paddock to talk, to inquire what was going on. He is down this weekend from his solicitor's job in Bristol on the hunch that it might be the year's mush-rooming moment, late, almost too late, yet perhaps with that precise mixture of humidity needed to bring out in plenty the finest boletus of the season, the mornings damp, afternoons hot.

Recall that when I discovered this tumbled-down place, I at first planned to make the big stables abutting the paddock into a working studio for artist-friends, to be welcomed to stay rent-free for as long as they needed, with their families, at liberty to follow whatever ideas came their way.

Doesn't sound such a foolish dream.

23 November

Bought from a specialist dealer-friend in Cirencester a small single bookshelf to hold my current reading, which I presently pile at one end of my kitchen table. The hinged shelf is adjustable, similar in style to the 1870s work of Charles Bevan, a documented chair and bedside-cupboard of whose I possess here at Erkindale. The dealer had in stock a rarity: a Pugin garden seat, on which I registered my interest, should the collector by whom it has been reserved fail to settle on time.

24 November

Busy days. Days in which I talk too much, indulging in my re-found ability to speak, to entertain. Myself as much as others.

Worried that the basis is still not there, that I breathe thin air, stand a step away from sinking into soft river mud. The pain hunkers down, out of sight. It hasn't gone away.

There's a long long way to go.

Beth's winter black cabbage survived the bullocks' onslaught and should replenish itself on into the New Year.

I enjoy cutting and cooking it.

Probably shouldn't. It might be better to keep away from her and hers for the present.

25 November

Off in an hour to catch the 10 a.m. train for a three-day visit to London.

Anxious. Not about the trip itself, nor about seeing friends. It's all the old hurts which still kick in, the ritual patterns of defence against ordinary threats of the day-by-day.

I've always been distant and defensive.

Am with Beth.

It's me, mustn't take it out on her.

These are the things that touch me, I don't know how, touch parts of me to which I have no controllable access.

I don't know, I don't know.

Disgust on the train at the sound in the seat behind me of a packet of potato crisps being eaten: the open-mouthed munch and metallic crinkle of the packet. The smell too.

Disproportionate reaction.

Across the aisle, an Iranian and an Irish woman chatted. And I listened, can't think why. Hated what they said. Hated hating it.

Felt better after moving seats.

28 November

While I've been away Beth has repaired the glass panel in my study door which she shattered in fury.

This afternoon the sun shone and, with the forecast of a weekend's heavy rain, I left unfinished the work at my desk to stroll up the hill with a wicker basket and knife to gather the last of the mushrooms. In the warmish wet, with winter rays of sunshine angled low, I came across the extraordinary sight of dozens of tall mushrooms on the slope below a line of ancient beech: a child's picture-book image of the nether world, long-stemmed mushrooms with wide umbrella rims, the older ones six inches in diameter, young cousins poking whiter flesh above the turf. Parasol (*Macrolepiota procera*) they're called. Found some violet-brown blewits too, and one good sample of what I discovered to be the prince (*Agaricus augustus*), also deliciously edible.

On my walk back, the long way round, I heard the barking of the hounds in the distance and was gratified to see a grey-muzzled fox race unmolested from the wood to freedom in the far copse. Passed the iron and timber gate of Hugh's which I've asked permission to re-use down here. Parts of two of the oak bars are missing, and one of the iron brackets; Beth can mitre new pieces of wood onto the bars; and on an identical gate, ruined, lying in the undergrowth, I found a spare bracket which a blacksmith could reuse in our repair.

The junk piled high by Kerry in clearance of my paddock has been removed.

A new struggle: to prevent myself being brought low by the morning news, radio almost as threatening these days as the newspapers I abandoned reading years ago. Jonathan Sacks, the Chief Rabbi, appealed for donations to re-house Romanian families unable to move from their one-roomed ex-Soviet flats, unheated, pouring damp, the single bathroom shared with twenty other tenants. Southern Africa is devastated by AIDS, scything life to the ground.

Book of the month is John Wyndham's *The Midwich Cuckoos*, Penguin's 1957 edition of which stands on my shelves in the bedroom, often observed, a work which I delighted to be terrified by when then reading as a teenager.

Slowly, as an idea for the structure of the day clarifies, I cease to quake.

The season has come round again to gather Christmas greenery for Podshavers. Someone has cut down the yellow-berried holly tree. Beth helped me find, up by Durford Wood and back past Schopnoller Farm, occasional strands of green holly still bearing its red berries. Later we will join the Sunday helpers at Podshavers for a four o'clock roast, after the paying customers have left.

Returning after six it is dark, there's a mist shrinking the lights of Terhill Cottages beyond the bend in our lane, and in the crescent moon the red-woods at the margin of my territory look dramatized, pictorial. We hear in the country distance an Evensong peel of church bells.

1 December

Embarrassed to admit to myself that a pair of items in the radio-news this morning raised horror-rumbles in my stomach: the scenes of jubilation in Wellington, my sister's hometown in New Zealand, at the world premiere there of the last in the filmed trilogy of Tolkien's *The Lord of the Rings*; and David Cornwell talking of despair for world affairs, the subject of his latest novel. My reasons are childish. Frightened not so much by the world outside as by my internal landscape.

This is obvious, what to do about it less so.

A feeling maybe begins to revive from the outset of my time here at Terhill, that this is the place for me, secretive, protected, the place where I'll learn that ... We'll see, we'll see.

Fragments, the stuff of dislocated daytime thought. And of nightmare. A boy digs his talons-of-hands into my neck. There are other characters, recognizable, family members. Neck, nexus, the point of connection.

Every person in every dream of mine is me, a self-representation.

Words are returning, less stifled sentences form.

2 December

The light first thing is beautiful, a slim golden break in the winter sky.

Nobody else can know how it is to feel as I do, how it is for Beth to feel as she does, both of us troubled, neither of us able to turn, in essence, anywhere else for understanding but to our own separated selves. We need help, yes, and find it in various places, in part even from each other, but night and day we must learn first to rely on ourselves.

Same for everyone.

It's lonely. There's such a way to go. I've hardly started.

Blown by the North wind the clouds hurry from my strip of sky. I see things inside to do, a bath to scrub, food to be replenished, clean white linen to replace the old blue sheets on my bed. The day unfolds.

Beth is fixing removable wooden fronts to the brick pair of compost bins which she built a year ago on waste land beyond the old privy. The panels are salvaged from Victorian farm doors which we saved. It will make the compost easier to fill to the heat-primed brim, and inconvenience the food-raids of badgers. There are too few worms yet for the bin properly to function.

3 December

Rain two days ago swept leaves and mud into the centre of the lanes, where it rests, dries, becomes the seed-ground for grass and weeds which will grow green in the spring. I like this, the rural look of these single tracks, on which cars draw in to the occasional gaps to let others pass, the centre in general untrammelled, the seeds freed to germinate.

Notice that the grapes at Nailsborough have gone, eaten maybe by birds, or fallen to the ground to rot.

5 December

I asked Jim how he stayed calm in the face of his patients'
repeated despair, their – my – quest for death. Was he
aware, I asked, that on one particular visit I was in effect
saying goodbye to him.

He knew.

There were several times, apparently, when he feared
he might not see me again. For a full six months I was
very seriously ill, it was touch-and-go, Jim said.

6 December

Being not doing. No nearer achieving this. Always I'm drawn to think of what I might do to change things, believing a response is demanded of me. Beth talks of being locked into a soundproofed room, unheard, unlistened to, forgotten, and it's difficult for me to accept that there's nothing I should do.

Me, me, me!
    I bore myself.

Spend the afternoon by Bridgwater Bay with a group of birdwatchers from the Somerset Wildlife Trust. On my way I drive past Hawkridge Lake, near Aisholt, and witness how very little water is in the reservoir, due to the worst drought Janet has seen since coming to live higher up the valley, thirty-nine years ago. Down on the seashore the day is overcast, the water far distant, not ideal for distinguishing the different flocks of birds feeding at the water's margin, out there on the second longest tidal reach in the world – an hour either side of high tide and a sharp westerly wind are the ideal conditions, when the sea-birds hunker down in easy view from the four protected hides. It takes me time to attune to the pleasures of the place. Heard the calls to-and-fro of curlews, noted a century ago for their poetic Englishness, mournful, phlegmatic, postured. Spirits warm to the sight through my binoculars of the spearhead flight of a flock of small black birds, their undersides flashing white as they wheel in flowing formation across the flat expanses, suddenly together dropping to the ground again to feed. Dunlin they're called, five thousand of them currently out there in the bay, our leader tells us, a nice man, head warden for English Nature, owners of both the site here and the land on Shapwick Levels, half a mile from the home and workshop of George Clement, the furniture maker with whom Beth worked for nine years.

Half a mile out are the remnants of wooden chevrons built by the Saxons to trap fish. A man with a telescope-on-legs informs us that he can identify by the water's edge two godwit and a redshank – both have long beaks, and I realize that I'd be unable to separate these rarer birds from the common curlew, several hundred of which I'm astonished to observe grub in a group on the mud, normally seen by me either alone or in pairs. I overhear another ornithologist speak of the lizard orchids he journeys to see every season in the dune-rough of a links golf course along the coast. The man I warm to the most, and keep closest to as we wander from hide to hide, is a retired farm-worker from nearby, who knows the area intimately and prophesizes the arrival of a peregrine falcon to set the birds wildly wheeling. He's happy, for us all, when the hunter-bird turns up twenty minutes later and we catch sight of the dunlin rise in their thousands, the curlew, cormorant, shelduck, herons and other bigger birds staying put. I imagine a conversation between this clever gentle man and one of his several children, grown town-wise away from home. The son teases the father for his boundless love of nature. 'It's all out there, if you know how to look,' the man defends. 'I'm as rich in life's ways hereabouts as can anywhere be.'

7 December

While bicycling in the early morning frost down through Bishops Lydeard to catch the Sunday post, I passed a tallish youngish man dressed in a close-fitting black coat, his blonde hair short, neat-cut. I saw him stop every twenty yards and turn a full circle before walking on, head down, carrying in his left hand a plastic bag of purchases from the corner shop.

In the sun I started the mower, drawn on impulse to cut the weeds on the walled drive ending at my old open-work oak gates, bought two years ago from George Clement and recently installed by Frank on old timber posts. And, by chance, I then found the ideal resolution to the butterfly meadow's summer encroachment of the cobbled path: to cut with the mower a low green grass verge a foot either side of the path. Feel sure that by next spring this strategy will look exactly right.

The other day I purchased fresh mackerel from the fish shop in Wellington and tonight grilled them for the two of us together to eat. Beth wants us to be able to live here as friends. I do too.

9 December

I've been to London for the day, to have lunch with Alex's father, John Winter, one of my oldest friends. He lives in Tuscany, in the hills above Lucca, and deals internationally in early works of art. Newly placed at one end of the top shelf of his bookcase in Bruton Street is a majolica albarello which I covet, painted on the white body in cobalt blue with the prancing figure of a crazy hare, a pair of cypresses to the right and idealised landscape in the centre. John bought the Florentine renaissance jar, he told me, the week after he finally quit Sotheby's. The hare is him, he said, making a leap for freedom.

After lunch I sat for a while on my own on a bench around the corner in Berkeley Square. Bow-tied black plastic sacks of dead leaves were scattered haphazardly across the grass, looking like dozens of Gavin Turk's painted bronze bin bags. Down in the country, I have missed Gavin's company. And John's.

Pleased, before catching my train home, to see at the Victoria and Albert Museum in South Kensington the exhibition *Gothic Art for England 1400 to 1587*. Henry IV's favourite emblem was the forget-me-not and these modest blue flowers, executed in enamel on gold, decorate the foot of one of the richest pieces in the whole sumptuous show: the Reliquary of the Order of St-Esprit, given in 1412 by Joan of Navarre, second wife of King Henry of England, to a son from her first marriage, John Duke of Brittany, thence, in 1830, to the Musée du Louvre.

11 December

This morning I leave to spend a night and a day with my
mother in Lymington.

12 December

I had assumed these self-writings had finished with yesterday's statement, back at my beginning, with Mother.

Apparently not – it seems I haven't yet said to myself
the things I need to if I'm going to get better. Unless I
manage to do this I'll be ill again, in no time, I bet I will.

The hope: by recording muddled feelings of distress,
to soften my anxiety.

Tend everywhere to see irresolvable disputes: Iraqis
kill other Iraqis at their day-by-day business; British
men and women, while persuaded by TV advertise-
ments to eat more than they need, seek to work off the fat
in pools and Pilates, strain their hearts and die young;
the destitute are turned away from the succour of food
and warmth at St Martins-in-the-Field, in London's
Trafalgar Square, too dirty, drunk, and disorderly to
deserve attention.

Contradiction.

On Radio 4 the one o'clock news announced that
Saddam Hussein had been captured alive. Maybe Iraqi
society will exert its independence and choose freedom
from the confines of all the varied forms of dictatorship.

With difficulty.

There are different kinds of coercion, and Western
money-greed is one of them. Why should the Iraqis
succeed where we, the 'civilized' rest of humanity, daily
fails?

14 December

In an album shown to me by my mother is a black and white snap of my sister, me, and our friend Jonah standing beside his boxer dog, somewhere in the English countryside. I am about nine years old. The photograph is labelled The Quantocks. This is earlier than I remember. And I had not expected my sister to have been with me.

I don't blame my mother, she's done her best.

She – of course – is one of the subjects I'm failing to write to myself about.

15 December

Last night I drove to Stogumber Church to attend a concert given by a friend's flute teacher and family, the Craddocks. All four children are gifted, one a recent scholar at the Royal Academy of Music, another a semi-finalist at last year's Young Musician of the Year Award in Cardiff. The church, built at the highest point of the village, is old, its squat red sandstone tower of square section, like many in this area. It looks still to be the centre of village life, solidly endowed for hundreds of years by farmers of the valley, the altar walls elaborately stencilled in Gothic Revival colours.

The church was full. The children played beautifully: on cello, double bass, viola and violin. Bach, Mozart, Samuel Barber, Gershwin, Robert Schuman and others, in solos and duets, and altogether, with their parents, in a family sextet. Two of the girls are twins. I saw the three girls rush home as I left, lugging their instrument cases, keen to get to a party. The family lives near the church, in a house with a courtyard. They were shouting and giggling.

Like children.

They are children. Clever children.

16 December

Find myself dwelling on another item of news which disturbed me a couple of days ago. It was in an article I read in the *New Statesman*, on the journalist William Shawcross, stalker of the standard political path from exultant socialist to right-wing bigot. This piece fuelled my fears, felt threatening.

Just now been down to the kitchen table to re-read the *NS*.

Dislike the smile in his drawn-portrait, its unappetising air of over-confidence.

Shawcross is an old Etonian, son of the chief British prosecutor at the Nuremberg Trials; he lives with his well-connected second wife in a stately home in East Sussex; his first marriage, straight from Oxford, was to Marina Warner, the novelist. The *New Statesman* piece concerned Shawcross's newly published book of crude simplicity on the Iraq War, and mentioned the fact that he has been commissioned to write an official biography of the Queen Mother.

A relief for Warner to have got rid of him?

To write well, it's what we all want, even as we fail.

17 December

I slept last night solidly for six hours, from fifteen minutes before midnight till a quarter to six in the morning,
longer than at any time during the last couple of years.

18 December

Take a coffee in town this morning.

Read the *TLS*, drink and eat at a café in Taunton, taking a pee and packing up and paying with care to arrive on time at my 11.30 appointment around the corner with Jim, in the terraced house into which he has moved from Kingston.

Ring the bell and enter, letting myself in and up the narrow staircase, noticing that the consulting room door is shut and settling myself, as agreed, to sit and wait in the bare spare bedroom. The session goes on for an extra seven minutes before I hear a female voice preparing to depart, and I then tell Jim I'm in no hurry, aware that he must have had unusual difficulties if it was so hard for the client to leave.

When Jim comes back in with his mug of tea to the consulting room he tells me that, as I'm here, it's OK if we start five minutes early. I totally deny that my regular Thursday appointment with him, for over a year now, has been at 11.45. I am so sure of myself, so convincing in my self-rightness that he momentarily believes he may be wrong and checks his diary.

Sudden realization that it is I who am mistaken. Shocked at the power of the unconscious to blind me to the truth of something I know full well and draw me irresistibly early to Jim. My last appointment of the year.

A minor matter, but important, to me. Which is why I've made such a meal of it on the page.

The other day I noted in my current file of quotes a paragraph by Evelyn Waugh from his novel *The Ordeal of Gilbert Pinfold*, which is a kind-of self-portrait:

397

Another thing which troubled him and which he soon began to attribute to his medicine, was the behaviour of his memory. It began to play him tricks. He did not grow forgetful. He remembered everything in clear detail but he remembered it wrong. He would state a fact, dogmatically, sometimes in print – a date, a name, a quotation – find himself challenged, turn to his books for verification and find most disconcertingly that he was at fault.

Two incidents of this kind slightly alarmed him. With the idea of cheering him up Mrs Pinfold invited a weekend party to Lychpole. On the Sunday afternoon he proposed a visit to a remarkable tomb in a neighbouring church. He had not been there since the war, but he had a clear image of it, which he described to them in technical detail; a recumbent figure of the mid-sixteenth century in gilded bronze; something almost unique in England. They found the place without difficulty; it was unquestionably what they sought; but the figure was of coloured alabaster. They laughed, he laughed, but he was shocked.

This is a retrospective account of impending signs of the author's temporary breakdown. Lychpole is a fictional name for Waugh's house at Combe Florey, a couple of miles from here, and the 'remarkable tomb' is one of two sculptural memorials in Cothelstone Church across the fields from me, the more elaborate of which is in English alabaster – not coloured, though, that's the other one, earlier, in stone, of a crusader and his lady.

19 December

On my windscreen last night at the swimming pool Beth left a note, of urgent warmth, concerned that I should have a decent time over dinner at Podshavers after my regular swim.

I was moved.

On my answerphone this morning a message from Elizabeth, wishing me well for my trip tomorrow to The Hague, to stay for three days with Willem Boymans. I plan to invite her mother out to lunch. And then take the train on to Paris to stay alone in Alex's flat for Christmas.

Original Beth and I were married in The Hague, happily.

20 December

On the train to London I remember that, as I left Jim's on Thursday morning, I noticed my Virginia Woolf post-card to him propped against his phone in the hall. There is little other personal decoration yet in his new house in Taunton.

Emerged moments ago from the Channel Tunnel into the French countryside. It is midday, English time.

Getting myself here: such a journey.

The train is bearing me via Brussels to Den Haag, where I'll take a guest bedroom at Kleycamp, the giant apartment block in which Willem lives, beside the dunes north of Scheveningen. I'll then be travelling on by Thalys Express from Brussels to Paris, following the path taken thirty-three years ago on the opening day of my honeymoon, after our first night in the old-fashioned Wittebrück Hotel.

21 December

There's a twenty-four hour nursing service for residents at Kleycamp.

All over Willem's flat are wooden clothes pegs, clipped to lampshades, to hats, to shelves, everywhere, for he cannot concisely see and needs the pegs to hand in order to hang out to dry around the place the shirts and things he washes in the bath. In the flat and on the balcony are piles of driftwood combed from the beach, and large logs cut for him by the woodmen he used to meet on his bicycle rides. The table at which he and guests eat is a polished piece of equatorial wood, four feet in diameter, in which fissures have cracked open in the heat of his apartment.

Willem's memory judders and stalls.

He rallies, talks with wonder at his good fortune, proud that it used to take him no more than an hour and a half out and back on his bike to swim in the sea, drying himself off in a brisk walk along the edge of the dunes. I have several times bathed with him, sharing our enthusiasm for water. A scene runs through my head: of us walking together across the sand, Willem tall, upright, his thin legs browned by the sun, totally naked.

Willem has prostate cancer and often disappears to piss. He drinks too much cheap wine. Henriette, Elizabeth's mother, says booze has always been his problem, provoking anger and despair. In the summer Willem's penis swelled painfully and the medication he took caused restriction in the blood supply to his legs, for which he is fitted twice a day by the Kleycamp nurses with elasticated calf-bands, soaked in balm.

Lunch yesterday with Henriette, at her flat on the ground floor of a grand town house, sandwiched between the embassies of Austria and Oman, where she has lived for twenty years. I've never before been to this home, filled with objects familiar to me from their earlier family house, one of which – the brass carrying-candlestick with pierced white porcelain windshield – I admired, and she said I could keep, with the voice and gaze of a love still warm for her daughter's once-husband, who walked away ages ago, in 1980. I refused, rejecting emotional re-involvement. Good object, though. Almost the only simple shape in her crowded double room, with its moulded ceilings, adjoined by a conservatory leading to the garden.

Elizabeth's mother's kitchen, bathroom and bedroom, all three firmly old-fashioned, are down a flight of five stone steps. She gives only cold suppers nowadays, so she can host drinks for her guests. 'I always missed the cocktails,' she complains. 'I was always cooking. Jan served the drinks.' Jan-Peter, my father-in-law, died in the autumn of 2000.

My ex-father-in-law.

My only father-in-law.

On a pre-breakfast walk this morning through the woods of the Palace of Clingendael, I passed close by a heron, standing on the lawn by the house. Plumed, vigilant, it didn't bother to shift.

Frida, Willem's friend and helper, dislikes the herons, devoted instead to swifts. Once a swift learns to fly it spends the next four years in flight, never leaving the air, sleeping on the wing, she tells me, until mature enough to nest and raise the first of its many broods of children. Remember, as I walk, Willem responding yesterday with child-like pleasure to my noticing on his veranda at Kleycamp a solid box, a munitions container which he had found abandoned twenty years earlier, a relic of the war in which as a young man he was awarded the Dutch 'VC' for bravery. He is guilty, angry, in a sense regretful at surviving the Second World War, the bravest and best of his generation left dead on the battlefield, he feels. Since reading in Melbourne Library in the early 1950s of the post-war Tokyo Trial and its political aftermath, Willem has devoted his life to persuading the world of the significance of Article Nine of Japan's Showa Constitution of 1947:

> Aspiring sincerely to an international peace based on justice and order, the Japanese people forever renounce war as a sovereign right of the nation and the threat or use of force as a means of setting international disputes.
>
> In order to accomplish the aim of the preceding paragraph, land, sea and air forces, as well as other war potential, will never be maintained. The right of belligerency of the state will not be recognized.

Willem's thick cotton shirts are frayed at the collars and cuffs and stained briar-pipe brown. He declines the waste and industrial impurity of soap to wash his body. He is almost blind and his eyes, staring into swirls of mist, show pain. My understanding of how Willem feels is coloured, I know, by witnessing today his struggle to type at the multi-magnified screen and enlarged keyboard. Short letters of riotous temper, to which nobody ever replies – they couldn't, Willem's words combustible, dangerous to touch. He is able to work for half an hour only before the strain on his eyes becomes insufferable. The same with reading, which he does by scrolling details from a page laid onto a horizontal mirror, heavily lit and enlarged, reflected up onto a vertical screen. His leather bootlaces are overlong, tied in a double loop around his ankles. Onto strands of salvaged sea-rope he has knotted marrow-bones, for decoration.

The scruffy modern square near his condominium Willem has nicknamed Place des Invalides, because of the aged residents who totter on their sticks and zimmers from tea shop to bank to hairdresser to chemist to post office.

A month or so ago I would have been incapable of engaging with any of this.

23 December

Willem appears at my guest-bedroom door, six floors below his, at 5.20 a.m. Unable to sleep, he doesn't want to waste this opportunity of our talking some more, before I leave at seven-thirty to catch my train for Paris. He asks me to get myself out of bed and come upstairs for breakfast, entices me with the promise of pressed fresh oranges. I see his eagerness, his aliveness, and quell my irritation.

Because he cannot properly see, Willem's utilitarian kitchen is filthy, the orange squeezer encrusted with the remains of numberless juicings. He wants to talk, doesn't notice that I do not drink.

Because he's old, unwell, we know that we may never see each other again, and at this last moment I manage to sort out my main disagreement, throughout the years of conversation, with Willem's thesis: his belief that the majority judgement at the Tokyo Tribunal, after which five of Japan's war-leaders were hanged, on Christmas Eve 1948, 'universalizes' Article Nine.

It doesn't, Willem now agrees.

Instead, it contains the more limited yet highly significant implication of international approval of the *concept* of A9, and of acceptance that the effective rule of world law must be imposed by a supra-state military force. The victims require as much justice as the victors, and national leaders must be brought to trial more often than the ordinary soldier.

Willem is right. Entangled in his lifelong thread of animosity and guilt, he's never been able to make his argument clear. Too late. He's dying.

Arrive at Alex's flat in Paris – beneath the eaves, with

incised heliographic borders on the walls, which are lined in packing-case planks, unpretentiously bohemian. I am sent from pillar to post in search of a resolution to the heating/hot water failure, from flat to flat, floor to floor, eventually to the Post Office in Rue Beautrellis to determine the international code for a rescue call to Alex, who is spending Christmas in London. While out I buy, from individual shops in the Marais, fine cheeses, fresh bread, olives, wine, fruit etc. and begin to feel at home. I'm seated now at a table in a nearby restaurant recommended by Alex, warm, content, with a rocket salad in front of me and hare to follow.

Effiloché de lièvre aux champignons des bois, eaten with a side dish of mashed potato.

At the top right hand corner of the mirror in Alex's bedroom is pinned a photograph of Ginny, standing at the centre of the nearby gardens of Place des Vosges, and in the other corner of the mirror a postcard of the church at Cothelstone.

24 December

I'm in the Musée Delacroix, converted from the painter's town house on the south bank of the Seine – in the
back garden is the atelier, which he built to his own design in 1857. The place displays memorabilia: pottery
vases which Delacroix bought as souvenirs in Algeria,
and bequeathed on his death to an artist friend; his
gilt-bronze mounted mahogany painter's table, fitted
beneath its hinged top with lead-lined containers, a
deep drawer below; his sketch of the abbey at Valmont,
owned by a cousin, in the nearby countryside to which
the painter regularly retreated for quiet study of light
and landscape; the leather armaments on which he
modelled the dress given to Saracen horsemen in his
big history paintings. One of my tutors at Cambridge,
Lee Johnson, a Delacroix specialist is credited on the
museum's label with authentication of the unsigned oil
sketch of an Arab fighter's helmet on a pole.

Try to sense some of the man's radicalism as a painter, the attempt overshadowed by my fusty respect for
museum curios.

Pompidou Centre. Watch for an hour the Peter Fischli/
David Weiss film of 1983, *The Right Journey*, a recent
purchase by the French State from the Swiss artists.
Two actors (it seems from the credits – while watching,
I had assumed to be the artists themselves), one wearing
a brown bear costume and the other dressed as a panda,
go on an adventure, into caverns and caves, down rap-
ids, through woods, across the prairie, over an ice flow,
finally to end within sunset view of the Matterhorn,
playing 'found' instruments – blowing thick sticks
which sound like tubas, beating wood-block drums,

the bear swirling his tail like an aboriginal whirligig, demanding of each other to sing deeper and deeper in celebration of survival. Along the way the two had fought in mud, there was an episode with a pig, the bear had rescued the panda from death and, amongst much else, one of them had puked up poisonous mushrooms.

25 December

Paris, on Christmas morning. I've carried with me two small presents wrapped in brown paper, from Beth, and a card, which on opening I see hints at the work-in-progress she's making out of cardboard boxes salvaged from her job at Brendon Books. One of her parcels is a paperback of William Fiennes' *The Snow Geese*, described on the front cover: 'A profoundly moving account of joy, of one man's rediscovery of the world.' I begin reading it this moment.

The road leading from the Eiffel Tower to the Palais de Chaillot, past much-photographed fountains, is named Avenue Hussein-1er-de-Jordanie. It is the most peopled spot I've come across in the whole of Paris, half the crowd of Arab descent. Leading downhill from the front of the Palace, once the home of the city's commissioners and now a year late in transformation into the Cité de L'Architecture et du Patrimoine, I walk along the Avenue du Président-Wilson. The next building along the thoroughfare is the office of the Western European Union, with a new curved glass-hung extension housing the EU-backed Institute for Security Studies. The names and titles amuse and annoy me.

One of Beth's presents was a CD of the songs of Marlene Dietrich, and I pass a public gallery in which a Dietrich exhibition had closed on 15 December, the neo-classical temple shut now for restoration. Opposite is the Musée d'Art Moderne de La Ville de Paris, also closed, because of building subsidence. Beside it, Le Palais de Tokyo, a contemporary art institute open from midday to midnight on every day of the year except today, 25 December. I aim to return.

Where the fruit and vegetable market used to be at Les Halles, I watch for half an hour in a cool grey breeze a game of boules between friends, working men, joined by ageing spectators, who shake hands, mutter greetings in sonorous throaty voices and offer their friends seasonal cigars. A tropical arboretum flourishes in an underground greenhouse near St Eustache, where in the forecourt lie two dozen Christmas trees, at reduced prices. In a side-altar of the church is a painted triptych by the graffiti artist Keith Haring – I hadn't realized he was so young when he died in 1990, aged only thirty-two – not at all interested in his work.

At dinner at Petit Bofinger, one of the few restaurants open on Christmas Night, over a glass of rosé I begin to read in my latest copy of the *TLS* a review of Judith Brown's new biography of Nehru, whose last Harrow School report apparently read: 'A thoroughly good fellow and ought to have a very bright future ahead of him.' King Hussein also went to Harrow and his youngest brother, Prince Hassan bin Talal, was later in the same house there with me. I've several times stayed with Hassan and his wife Sarvath in the Royal Palace in Amman.

The rumour hounds claimed that my expulsion from school was for bribing the young prince to requisition a Royal Jordanian helicopter to fly me to a dance in Norfolk!

Half-a-dozen oysters arrive, delicious with squeezed lemon and French bread. They have beautiful shells, which remind me of grotto-work in Italian villas, seventeenth century, baroque, such a variety of extravagant external shapes, the insides of the shells washed by white clouds against a grey sky.

It's a twenty-minute steady walk uphill from Le Marais to the cemetery of Père Lachaise. Wandering in from the southern entrance, I'm attracted by the occasional polished black granite mausoleum built amongst the old stone edifices along the main boulevard. Turning to the backs of these new tombs I notice that, when alive, many of the recent-dead had bought a 'Concession à Perpetuité' in this prime location. Unlucky others, having neglected to secure a perpetual lease, have been moved to a less salubrious spot, replaced by today's rich. By people like Roger Strauss, in a colossal structure inscribed merely with his name. And by the family Lathvillière, in a plain tomb inaugurated in 1979, later presented with the body of an infant who lived only eight days, together with the family's most recent corpse, Georges Lathvillière, the boy's father, who died last year.

On the sepulchres I note the names of many nine-teenth-century sculptors, familiar to me from my Sotheby's Belgravia days: Jean Dampt, Bartholdi, Jean Carriès, Etex. And Bartholomé, with his cave-like mon-ument to the war dead. My first book, published in 1975, when I was twenty-nine, was about nineteenth-century bronzes, covering the work of many of these artists.

See hundreds of fresh roses at the base of the com-poser Alfred Musset's tomb. And watch a devotee of the philosopher Allan Kardec remove the dead petals from dozens of pot-plants decorating his memorial of 1870, sculpted by the husband and wife team of Hippolyte Riviol and Amèlie Boudet.

Honoré de Balzac's tomb is topped by a portrait bust by David d'Angers and at the base with a bronze book and quill. The writer died in 1850 and his widow, Eve

Comtesse Rzewuski was buried there in 1882.

I don't have a map of the cemetery, and can't find Delacroix's grave.

Père Lachaise opens every day at 8 a.m.

At home I own a d'Angers medallion dated 1831, the posthumous portrait of a Napoleonic general, Jean-Baptiste Kléber. It hangs in my bathroom.

On my route back to town, down Rue du Chemin Vert, I call at a bar for a cup of coffee and pear tart. People drop by to place their bets for the Rapido. The patron, a dishevelled companionable man with thick spectacles, grey suit and overhanging stomach, rushes into the street at sight of a traffic warden: 'He knows my car. He knows my car,' he calls – my schoolboy French tells me – in the direction of his dusty van, parked on a pedestrian crossing. He escapes a ticket and returns, all smiles. The television, mounted high on a wall, plays soundlessly. The mosaic floor is carpeted in cigarette butts, sugar papers and destroyed lottery tickets.

Along the street a fire engine blocks traffic. Young firemen in golden helmets climb an extended ladder and break through the double balcony doors of a third floor flat. They close the lace curtains behind them. Shop assistants stare from the windows below of Mode Young, Import Export Fabricant, Gros et ½ Gros. I wait for ten minutes, hoping that the fireman will reappear, in heroic explanation.

No movement of the curtains.

Move on, delighting in the French reasonableness of the parking reservation marked in yellow: RAISON.

28 December

Home.

First thing this morning I take a worried walk around my territory, and dirty my fingerless woollen mitts in pulling up errant saplings, noticeable now in the frost-contracted wilderness. I'd worn in Paris the black mittens, with my black mackintosh. Animals have everywhere rustled for grubs in the warmer and wetter earth beneath the dead leaves on the paths. Beth's present, of a sculpted-cardboard open bookcase for my CDs, is wonderful, the salvaged boxes folded in curls to add strength, sanded flat, the MDF shelves covered in brown paper to unify the texture, a beautiful touch.

Awaiting here on my desk to be read are notes of the Somerset Butterfly Group's meeting held on 23 November, assessing the season's worth. There were 17 people at the gathering, and it was recorded in the minutes that on 31 July at Hinkley Point, beside the monolithic nuclear power station, its concrete sides painted a fashionable grey-blue, that 659 gatekeepers were seen in the space of eighty minutes.

29 December

On our three-hour walk in the mist across the side of the hill, Beth and I came across an ancient apple tree covered in mistletoe, growing low enough for me to pick the white berries. Janet has told me of placing mistletoe seeds at Aisholt in slits cut in the crooks of branches of apple and ash, binding them there with coverings of earth, and years later responding with delighted surprise at the bursts of Christmas mistletoe in her leafless trees. Maybe I, in time to come, will experience this same pleasure.

30 December

Last night, late, something happened which was as distressing as anything else in recent months. The details do not matter, and I would not help myself by writing about them. Things must change. They will, they will. Somehow.

2 January

Walked up over the top for coffee this morning with Janet at Aisholt and, at the zenith, the sky clear, saw a shaft of sunlight move with the wind across the snow-covered peaks of the Brecon Beacons off out there in Wales. On my return journey I found, close to the ground in Hugh's high untampered pastures, protected by mufflers of grass, enough waxcaps to make myself a fresh sauce tonight. These slimy conical mushrooms have psychedelic colours: crimson, white, yellow, green and buff. The buff specimens are the tastiest, I read, the yellow and green ones inadvisable to eat. What I call 'the waxcap meadow', down here nearer the house, seems to be without mushrooms this year.

3 January

Friends matter. Good that such things do again affect me.

I really *might* be getting better.

Yes, I must be, or the coming trip to see Shenagh in New Zealand would have remained an unachievable dream

Roasted a chicken, in fresh-picked rosemary, garlic, olive oil, lemon and onion, for Beth and I together to share, the only meat she these days eats. We spent from six till eleven together and despite the other evening I feel that we'll both be alright.

4 January

A card today from my dealer-friend in Cirencester, to say that the Minton-made garden seat can be mine, if I still want it.

I do!

I have another, the one possession I've always kept with me, taking it when I left home and later moved into Vera's house in Wapping and, twenty years later, to Janet's cottage over the hill at Aisholt. Bought for twenty-five pounds in 1972, newly married, it cost more than we could then afford, convinced that it would prove to be designed by A.W.N. Pugin, decorator of the Palace of Westminster. Only five other examples have since been seen on the market, and not until the Neo-Gothic exhibition at the Victoria and Albert Museum in 1994 did proof emerge of Pugin's authorship, recorded in a drawing of the 1840s found in the Minton archives. Today I've become owner of a dark-blue ground pottery garden seat or stool, small side table it might today be called, although originally used as a place on which to sit in Victorian hot-houses – it matches mine of turquoise ground, both of them transfer-printed with identical buff, green, rust and white gothic scrolls, top and bottom shaped a bit like an elephant's foot. Will retrieve it on my return to England from New Zealand.

I love it!

5 January

When I gave Jim's bell a warning ring at 9.59 this morning and pushed to enter, I found the door locked, for
the first time ever, on the last of my visits to him before
flying tomorrow to Wellington for the next two months.
He was there. He'd made a mistake and wasn't expecting
me.

His mistake didn't worry me. Maybe I'll be OK?

6 January

I never again want to experience, with anybody, anywhere, anything near what happened yesterday evening
between Beth and me, on my last night in this country
till March.

Must find the strength in the future to steer clear of
such relationships, doomed to repeated damage, of self
and other.

Nobody's fault. We must both let go.

7 January

Somewhere in the sky between Los Angeles and Auckland, on the penultimate leg of my flight from Heathrow, aware, in feeling that, although the nothingness of despair seems to have passed, I still do not understand what happened.

Today's date, 7 January, does not in fact for me exist, as we crossed the dateline before midnight. In The Hague on 7 January, original Beth and I were married.

8 January

I'm above the clouds, in the sun, on a domestic flight from Auckland to Wellington, to my sister Shenagh.

At Auckland Airport I panicked. While waiting at the carousel for my haversack to be delivered, a sniffer dog – a beagle, brown, black and white – located an illegal apple in my canvas shoulder bag. The detectives black-marked my entry visa, leading a customs officer to remove from my pack the climbing boots, accused of retention on the soles of a particle of cow dung. He fined me 200 NZ dollars for falsification of my immigration form. The delay meant that I missed the connecting flight.

I dashed about in a panic. Not as anxiously as I might, not long ago, have done. Bad enough, though.

I'm calmer now, seated on the next plane. I'll be safe.

Like a child, I was suddenly frightened for no real reason.

10 January

Tins of cat food, the fork stuck in, have been left on the kitchen sideboard and my sister sits at the nearby table reading a government paper, while half-listening to a Leonard Cohen tape – a weekend picture of her home in New Zealand. The morning sun rises behind the steep garden, rays glancing through evergreen leaves, branches swinging in the wind.

Why criticize?

I don't.

This is how it is, here. People come and go: friends of Shenagh's and various family members, including an ex-husband, his books, saucepans, work-bench tools and homemade side tables only recently removed from this house on the side of a hill.

I'm surprised, interested.

Need to have near to hold things of my own, to-me-necessities like pencil sharpener and rubber, left behind by mistake in my desk drawer in Somerset. Will buy on Monday replacements.

Loo paper. I need to be sure there are limitless spare rolls of white loo paper in the house.

11 January

Sam, my middle nephew, is at home on holiday from his job in Auckland. I'm happy in his presence, last experienced at Lower Terhill three and a half years ago, when he was close to the height of his distress, fresh from three terrible days falsely confined by his adventure-school employers to a mental hospital in Cumbria. I failed at the time to understand the extent of Sam's vulnerability, and, without adequate support from me, he was unable to survive alone, journeyed home to his family in New Zealand.

I'm out on the slatted deck, which John, the father of Shenagh's four children, dug into the hillside at the back of the house. It's mid-summer, and I'm reading a collection of Katherine Mansfield's short stories, reflections on the early years of her life in Wellington, fourth daughter of a patriarchal father, a prosperous businessman.

12 January

A household different from my own: communal, and designed so to be.

Fran, the youngest child, is fifteen, already independent – although they all remain committed to being available to each other for the rest of their lives. An assumption none of them question.

Intently aware of where we come from, I'm not surprised at Shenagh's pleasure in the loving intimacy she has created: it is what she has always most wanted in parenthood.

Whereas I remain solitary and unchanged, doing many of the same things here that I do at Lower Terhill: clearing overgrown trees from the land; walking into town to visit galleries, churches, Mansfield's birthplace; irregularly cooking and reading.

Into the ravine up above the rear of the property, a neighbour's cesspit leaks and liquid sewage oozes in a muddy runnel across Shenagh's rough grass.

13 January

I see again an image dismissed by me as worthless during the times of trouble.

Postcard Piece, I've named it. My stored cards assembled on the white walls of a gallery, composed to flow out and up into visual forms that tell a sort-of story. See a printed plan numbered according to picture-type, the back descriptions also listed. On one, possibly two walls of the gallery hang three other of my works already made, framed and glazed: the thirteen-by-thirteen *Leavers* panel, of my and Father's mementoes from our time at Harrow School, his as a schoolmaster my own as a boy, the card-mounted leaving portraits of one hundred and sixty-nine eighteen year olds, now business barons, generals, Kings, judges, and forgotten unknowns. And the four photographs of my prep-school teams at Orley Farm, portraits of formal young boys in each of which I'm captain, framed by posed cigarette card shots of bathing belles and film stars of the 1950s. Also, my personal homage to Gilbert and George's mail-art pieces of the 1970s, in which coloured postcard images from the Tate of the artists in victory pose surround cards of Prime Ministers Wilson, Heath and Thorpe at the Cenotaph on Poppy Day, at their centre a cartoonist's view of the iron lady, Margaret Thatcher. Dream of seeing this exhibition happen.

Yesterday at Old St Pauls, the cathedral built of wood by Frank Thatcher in 1864, I noticed on a pillar a brass plaque presented in 1905 by the Wellington Submarine Mining Volunteers, to commemorate the lives of four soldiers, a sapper and three non-commissioned officers, who died at their work in the harbour.

On the ferry from Wellington to Picton, on South Island. The landscape is so quickly primitive, the cliffs and hills stark, uninhabited, less than thirty miles from the country's seat of government – until we pass an established farm, the house protected behind a copse of tall cypress trees, its sheep pastures spreading across two plateaus and up the bush-fired sides of several mountains, steps leading down the cliff to a jetty on the beach.

Birds fly at speed, their wing tips almost touching the water as they outpace the ship, alighting briefly on the waves to catch fish. Smallish blackish birds, which the book identifies as flesh-footed shearwater, down south in summer to lay a single white egg in a burrow dug into soft soil in the cliffs, where it is incubated by both sexes.

It's different once we steam from the straits into Tory Sound, where each bay has been colonised by two or three people, to build sophisticated bachs, their holiday retreats. Tory was the name of one of the sail-ships carrying emigrants from England to virgin land; it arrived at Port Nicholson, as Wellington was then called, on 20 September 1839, with the young artist Charles Heaphy on board, the man who drew and wrote most about this settler land.

14 January

A night at friends of my sister's. In the presence of strangers I sweat and stutter, my sense of safety still fragile.

Find my way after waking, before the others are up, to a deserted beach, the tide out and grainy sand golden, the smooth sea insisting I swim. Strip down and wade in, naked. No towel, no trunks, nobody here, except at the far end some early water-skiers, the water so clean that the rocks are encrusted with oysters and mussels.

Content.

Katherine Mansfield writes about herself, about her most difficult feelings. All the men in her stories, most of them, are if not absent then disappointing – and disappointed: they in themselves and she in them. The edition I'm reading of *The Garden Party & Other Stories* is introduced and annotated by Lorna Sage, who lived for several months each year in part of the converted stables in the ex-convent of San Francesco di Paolo, just outside the city walls of Florence, on the main floor of which John and Chiarella Winter made for a decade their home, where I loved staying. Sage is dead now, awarded posthumous praise and a prize for her mother-bloody autobiography. She describes here a female character in one of the Mansfield stories: 'The girl's namelessness is interesting and suggestive, emphasizing her archetypal quality, and the ready-made role the world has handed her.'

15 January

Near the Rest House in which we're staying for three nights the bay is tidal and, on the long mudflats across which I walk for my early morning swim, birds with black backs and long red beaks feed. They are called, I know, oyster catchers, and are digging for lugs in the sand. Four shy brown birds rise as I arrive, and fly fast and low to the safety of the headland reeds. They may be godwits, which I see from a chart on the wall are a speciality here. Surprised how few butterflies flourish, many fewer in number and variety than at home in Somerset.

17 January

Heard, faintly, a skylark above the marshes at the outset of our three-day walk along the coast of Able Tasman Peninsula.

A Dutch explorer, Able Janszoon Tasman was in 1642 the first European known to have reached New Zealand; he was cooked and eaten by Maoris on this shore when he tried alone to land.

18 January

Slept last night on the beach for the first time in my life, the sole person there, looking out at the moon over the sea and the lights of boats at anchor. From the sleeping bag it was a few paces to the high-tide sea for my morning swim. There are eleven family friends with us on our walk, sixteen of us in total. One of them is a lovely girl of nineteen, a poet and film-maker, wearing a floppy disc converted into a hairslide, thoughtful, an undergraduate at Victoria University in Wellington.

There's a small bird that lives in the bush, brown, unremarkable – until it on occasion opens its tail in a wide fan, two black feathers at the centre the rest white. Fantail (*Rhipidura fuliginosa*) it is called, the female building its elaborate nest in only three days, composed of fine grasses, lichen, moss and small pieces of bark which she binds with cobweb, and invariably leaves with a ragtail wisp hanging below.

19 January

Sam has departed by water-taxi, bus and then aeroplane to his job as a clerk of the High Court in Auckland, the largest city in New Zealand. He is tall and quiet, a cook and movie-goer, twenty-five last September. He finds it difficult not to allocate to himself emotional responsibility for his father's sorrow at separation from the family.

20 January

We are spending a day and a night at a bach in Awaroa, just us and one of the other families on the tramp. I was allotted a single tent in the garden, four others the larger tent, supplied by the household. It was a stormy night of rain, wind and thunder, and the big tent blew down in the early hours of the morning – although I didn't hear a thing, slept through the exodus from tent to the crowded floor of the bach. It's a bright morning now and I'm taking these notes seated on the prow of a metal rowboat. The sun is beginning to heat the washed air – should have brought my hat, and my heart pills.

Yesterday in the late afternoon I walked at low tide across these fifty yards of sand which is now water, and swam off the golden beach, in the ocean beyond the scrubby spit thick with the nests of oyster catchers. This morning an elegantly ageing woman in a scarlet bathing costume, suntanned, waves at me from the deck of her bach. Martins skim low and close, catching sandflies. Move on, and come across the fresh paw marks of possums' recent scuffles in the strip of fresh sand released by the tide. Gather shells on the beach, which I rinse and sort now at an outside table at the Lodge, drinking a cup of flat white and eating fresh croissant with plum jam. Wander back to my temporary home, delighting in my existence, my independence. Pass five active beehives at the edge of a grass-mown airstrip, sheltered by flowering manuka bushes, the bees gathering pollen from its crisp white blossom.

The bay was settled by farmers in the 1870s, this small alluvial plain then virtually untouched, apart from sporadic occupation by Maoris in the summer fishing season. The white men came by boats and for sixty years brought everything they needed by sea: steam engines for the granite quarry, corrugated iron for the roofs of their shacks and canned alternatives to their regular diet of roast boar from the forest and boiled vegetables from the garden. They battled with rampant bindweed.

Darcy Hatfield, the direct descendant from an original settler, won bronze medal for single skulls in the 1921 Olympics at Antwerp, in Belgium. He hand-built his boats from wood that he and his family cut and milled on Awaroa Creek.

Tiredness. Not in bed till after 2 a.m. this morning, de-layed in the storm-force return crossing by ferry from Picton. Shenagh's daughter and I stood out on the open deck, laughing at the salt lash of the spray.

Spent much of today cleaning and hoovering in the house while Shenagh was at work, preparing for her new job in the Civil Service, as Chief Executive of the Ministry of Women's Affairs.

Fran, my niece, tries to maintain order in the duty-shared kitchen. She is organized, and today passed her provisional driving test, available in New Zealand at fif-teen. It's good to spend time with her.

22 January

Too often I hear my mother's voice issue from my own mouth: harsh, unfair, bitter. Yesterday I heard my sister speak with this same voice, repeatedly demanding her daughter do something, a matter of little real concern, in truth immaterial. Like Mother, Shenagh failed to notice that her need was to be obeyed, thus to clear a space in her own head – it had nothing to do with her daughter.

She'd be shocked, and upset, if I told her this.

It may not be true. Maybe it's my over-recognising something that in practice is not a problem for either Fran or her. My problem, must be.

I'm the one who couldn't bear to be alive.

This family gets so much right, lives in such good basic health.

In essence, Shenagh is completely different from our mother.

They keep their front door unlocked, unless away for days, eliminating the need for endless losing and cutting of keys. They have never been burgled.

Shenagh showed to me the letter written by a one-time colleague, a management consultant, sent on instruction to a dozen specified friends after he was found dead at home from a single bullet to his brain, his disintegration from multiple sclerosis no longer tolerable. My sister was an appointed bearer of the coffin at his funeral, each moment of which was pre-ordered by the dead man. The letter is precise, his decision made and executed without telling in advance anybody, not even his wife of forty years, warning notes for whom he left on both front and back doors. His meticulous letter contains a single mistake: 'besting' replaces the intended 'besetting'. He wanted, Shenagh confirms, always to be best – this was indeed his besetting sin.

I'm writing sitting in an organic café where Sam used to work, eating a bacon and avocado salad, drinking pink grapefruit juice and reading a paperback of poetry by Jenny Bornholdt, just bought, in which I thumb to a poem dedicated 'To Elizabeth', set in the house in the South of France where they had supper together: 'The inventive architecture / of mothers and / daughters. Days / are shorter now.' I've never seen the alterations which Elizabeth and her mother made to this studio in Villefranche, which years ago I adored visiting, inherited from a Dutch great-aunt.

Off after lunch to the City Gallery, where the poet's husband, Greg O'Brien, works. His line drawings illustrate her collection, *Summer* the new book's title. Their names and contact details were given me by Elizabeth, in the long phone call she made on the day before I left.

Later I read another poem, very short, only three lines:

French Gardens
Cabbage trees, lemons.
In something I have written,
'rather' is 'father'.

See two of the exhibitions at the City Gallery, the oil paintings, washes and drawings of Stanley Spencer and photographs by Wim Wenders. Spencer's last known words, written not said to the Vicar of Cookham were: 'I am weary, never bored. Why should you think I am? Sadness and sorrow is not me.' Wenders' photos, taken over a period of twenty years, disappoint. His wordy captions too. In attempting to explain, they reduce. Nothing, in my view, to compare with his early films,

438

Alice in the Cities above all; and nothing either to compare with earlier quotes of his I've elsewhere noted:

> I was not so much attracted by distant things as repelled by here. Here there was a vacuum: that peculiar lack of past. You can't convince a child not to look over its shoulder. But that was the feeling I grew up with: it was wrong to look back.

Wenders' London dealer, Haunch of Venison, is credited with several of the latest panoramic C-type prints, in particular those taken on 8 November 2001, of ranks of yellow bulldozers, their giant grabs reaching out to excavate the rubble of the Twin Towers.

For coffee at the gallery's connected café I met Greg, who is hard at work proofreading the catalogue he has written of an exhibition which opens to the public on 22 February. He's a painter and a poet too, who earns his living teaching art history, curating shows and reviewing books on contemporary work. I like him. We'll meet again, in a couple of weeks, for supper with his family at home in Ha Taitai, a suburb of Wellington. He plans to introduce me to artist colleagues.

23 January

From the nature books, gifts to the household which I bought yesterday on my walk into town to swim, I see that the birds I watched at Awaroa are not martins but welcome swallows, permanent residents of the coasts and marshes of New Zealand.

Jenny's verse is personal and direct, the subject of *Summer* the spending of her days in and around Menton, working at the Katherine Mansfield studio on a six month Memorial Fellowship in the summer of 2002, from where she visited Beth – Elizabeth – and her mother Henriette in Villefranche. She writes with deceptive simplicity, the rhythms complex, several poems illusively resonant of the work of favoured earlier poets.

The country's National Museum, Te Papa – Our Home, in Maori – dominates the downtown waterfront. Six storeys high, with balconies and restaurants and souvenir shops, it's awash with children. *The Lord of the Rings*, filmed and premiered in NZ, is everywhere in Wellington, the Museum included. And yet, amongst the theme-park dross I find two interesting exhibitions containing Maori art, one called *Signs and Wonders*, the other *Made in New Zealand*.

Loved the work in corrugated iron by Jeff Thomson, in particular his *HQ Holden Station Wagon* of 1991, out of which he lived for several years. Dorothea Rockburne, born in Canada in 1934, is a name new to me, creator of the *Locus Series* of six large panels of white paper etched and aquatinted in almost indiscernible off-white patterns and folded along pencil lines to take the stylised contours of low hills, precursor to recent work by Roni

Horn which I saw in an exhibition at the Pompidou Centre in December.

Notice that in the late nineteenth century the Maoris appropriated materials brought in by the white invaders, including red sealing wax, which they combined with their native sharks' teeth to striking effect in jewellery. I was attracted also to the small record-sketches by army officers of Maori rebel flags of the 1860s, in red and blue watercolour, the borders cross-hatched in grey ink.

The leak from the neighbour's cesspit lengthens, seeping farther and farther down the sloping lawn towards Shenagh's house.

The family see lots of films, outings which I'm happy to join. The credits of the Lars von Trier film *Dogville* are accompanied by a Bowie song about America, played as the director pumps out onto the screen image after image of street-life degradation, showing the destructive poverty of the Depression and pioneer hardship in the Wild West.

24 January

At my last meeting with my father, in hospital in Southampton a month before his death, I assured him that he need have no worries about the future well-being of his children, that Shenagh and I would never make the misery of our lives he and Mother had of theirs. I was insistent on my ability to avoid his feelings of meaninglessness and despair, promising that, however alone I might feel, I would surround myself with things of interest. I did not tell my father that I never wanted to see a single aspect of him in me.

Such arrogance, and insensitivity. Look at me now, recovering from confinement in mental hospital, my suicidal despair controlled, never defeated.

25 January

Finished reading the middle novel, *Meg*, of Maurice Gee's trilogy, set in Nelson, where he lives and through which we drove on our way to Able Tasman. Noted in my folder of quotes, from the last chapter:

> The sentimentalist in me will not die. Once it had the shape of my whole life, but now it's a dried-up thing, light as a bat, hanging upside down with its feet clawed tight on my ribs.

The notebook of prayers which I made from Jonah's letters to me included a quotation from Saint Augustine's *Confessions*. I learnt it by heart:

> I am working hard in this field, and the field of my labours is my own self. I have become a problem to myself, like land which a farmer works only with difficulty and the cost of much sweat.

26 January

At John Gleisner's property up the Mikimiki Valley I swam in the clear pools of the river running through his land, and watched a harrier hawk slowly circle, like a glider, above the firs in a plantation on the hill opposite. John is building himself a straw bale house, living at present in a caravan, planting trees which were eaten to shreds by cattle when he was away in Iraq, taking his place in the human shield. The valley is fertile, well-farmed by his neighbours. One side of John's beehive, self-made, has collapsed. The bees are furious.

27 January

The copy of George Orwell's *Diaries* which I picked out from the Oban Street shelves must have been left behind by John, a Quaker and a pacifist, genuine in his egalitarianism. This is John's kind of reading, despite the contradictory mixture of ideas.

An old Etonian, Orwell mentions his yearly interest in the result of the Eton and Harrow cricket match at Lords. And then, in this entry, notices the voices overheard in a sanatorium in the Cotswolds early in 1949:

> A sort of over-fedness, a fatuous self-confidence, a sort of bah-bahing of laughter about nothing ... people who, one instinctively feels, without even being able to see them, are the enemies of anything intelligent, or sensitive or beautiful ... No wonder everyone hates us so.

Orwell apparently had a fixation on rats. Observations on rats litter his diaries. Commentators have suggested that the attack by rats on Winston Smith at the Ministry of Love links the radical author of *Nineteen Eighty-Four* directly with the public school educated egg collector and amateur naturalist.

Shenagh's neighbours at the back are old and poor, amongst the few original house-owners of this area, unable to pay for the repair to their worn-out sewage system. They were forced to prevaricate, assured the council contractors that it had been mended.

Janet White asked me, if I happened to travel to the top of North Island, to contact her special Maori friend, who still lived on the coast opposite the uninhabited island which Janet farmed alone in her early twenties. She told me that the woman's son had become well-known in New Zealand for his enterprise, the first to bring summer-time visitors to bachs on his coast. Michael Aiutu is his name. What I did not know, until learning last night from a friend of Shenagh's, is that Aiutu became a Member of Parliament but has recently fallen from grace, accused by enemies in the local community of under-age sex. Janet met Michael as a boisterous boy, already marked, she said, as the most ambitious child in the district.

Janet Frame died this week, my favourite New Zealand author. Fourteen years ago, when I last visited my sister, then living on the Coromandel Peninsular, I read Frame's autobiography *Angel at My Table*. At university in Dunedin, fearing failure in her exams, she simulated the symptoms of schizophrenia and managed to get herself consigned to hospital. Held there for the next eight years, Frame, who was regularly given electric shock treatment, was on the verge of an enforced lobotomy when one of the professors by chance read her single published short story. He came to the immediate rescue, pronounced her sane and helped find her a bach in which to live and write. Deluged – later – with success, she refused to publish a word in the last twenty years of her life, choosing instead to write solely for herself.

At midday this Friday morning the large Catholic Church off Willis Street in downtown Wellington, St Mary of the Angels, was surprisingly busy, the majority of the congregation women of Pacific origin, with a sprinkling of silver-haired old colonials. The columns are stone-built and painted cream, the roof of wood in the gothic manner, the original pews made from forest trees, like those at the nearby Wesleyan Chapel, where the seats are constructed on an egalitarian curve. A travelling man, gaunt and lame, was careful to be the last to take communion and bent to his knees low enough to receive wine from the chalice to the last drop.

The nave of St Mary's is lined in carved figures pastel-painted to depict the twelve Stations of the Cross.

In construction of the motorway the state authorities destroyed not only Katherine Mansfield's teenage home but also mausolea and tombs in part of the Anglican cemetery, stretching across the steep slopes of equatorial forest, a place of covert beauty. Wellington's few Jews are buried there, alongside the Christians. I walked through the cemetery on my way home.

Further along Tinakori Road I passed the Royal Victoria Bridge Club, close to the site of the second Mansfield villa. It is walking distance from my sister's house, like my mother's club is in Lymington, her home-from-home for the seventeen years since Father's retirement. She's a good bridge player, and reasonable golfer too, annoyed at being unable these days to fix same-age partners to accompany her around the full eighteen holes. My mother refused until last year to tell either me or my sister her date of birth, embarrassed at being older than my father. In August she will be eighty-five, I reckon.

31 January

Half-awake in the early mornings I imagine myself
faced with insurmountable problems which, when I
shake myself and think about them calmly, do not in actuality exist. This morning, at 5.30 a.m., I was fearful of
my birthday celebrations next week, at which I was expected to play a flute solo that I did not know, had failed
to prepare. In fact, my birthday is not until July and I've
never played any musical instrument.

At an enjoyable dinner last night with colleagues of
Shenagh's, in a cared-for house overlooking the sea, I
participated with humour and passion. And yet I remain
suspicious of myself, do not feel any closer to understanding what happened to me and have no conscious
knowledge of how to stop despair again taking hold.
Last night's house overlooks Wellington Bay in much
the same way that Elizabeth's and her mother's studio,
tacked onto the cliff below the Corniche Basse and above
the Vieux Port, surveys the harbour at Villefranche and
on beyond to Cap Ferrat. Views can be brash, dominant.
These two allow themselves to be discovered, appear
and reappear at different angles through the trees. On
holiday visits to Villefranche in the 1970s, alone in the
last of the day's sun, I used to dive off the highest point of
the lighthouse wall at the entrance to the harbour, arch-
ing my body out into the blue water beyond the rocks.

The blackbirds eat the strawberries in Shenagh's garden
as soon as they ripen.

Drawn to think back, not long ago, to my six bouts of
electroconvulsive therapy.

Remember that two or three of us were driven, in a

van, around the corner from the mental hospital to the secretive ECT unit. No food or liquid since the night before, to circumvent the threat of choking. Knocked out by an anaesthetist. Complete disorientation on coming round. Hours or minutes later? Didn't know where I was, couldn't recognize fellow patients, was uncertain of my own name. Memory gradually returned. I've never known what they actually did to me while unconscious.

1 February

Kitchen cupboard doors left open, sweaters strewn across the settee.

Strange that visual details matter so little to my sister.
Strange that they mean so much to me.

3 February

Reading a second Mansfield volume of short stories, *Bliss,* dedicated to her London husband John Middleton Murray and published in 1921, four years after her tuberculosis had been diagnosed. She died from the disease in 1923, at the age of thirty-five, on a curative stay with the Russian mystic Gurdjieff in his chateau at Fontainebleu. In the opening piece of this collection Mansfield writes:

> Linda looked up at the fat swelling plant with its cruel leaves and fleshy stem. High above them, as though becalmed in the air, and yet holding so fast to the earth it grew from, it might have had claws instead of roots. The curving leaves seemed to be hiding something; the blind stem cut into the air as if no wind could ever shake it.
>
> 'That is an aloe, Kezia.'
>
> 'Does it ever have flowers?'
>
> 'Yes, Kezia,' and Linda smiled, and half shut her eyes. 'Once every hundred years.'

4 February

The doctor near Shenagh's office, whom I have twice
visited to monitor my heart, turns out to be a daughter of
the Labour Prime Minister of New Zealand in the mid-
1980s. In conversation she judged me, with a smile, to be
a perfectionist, to my own cost!

Read an acerbic entry by one of the richest of the first
pioneers on this coast, Alfred Ludlam, in his essay of
1865 on local horticulture, quoted in a detailed National
Museum catalogue I bought today, *Wellington's Heritage.*
Plants, Gardens and Landscape: 'I have a few words to say
to the destruction of that pest of all pests, sorrel, one
which appears to flourish all the better for the attention
it receives, in digging it up and carefully collecting the
roots.' My butterfly meadow!

5 February

Everybody makes music in my sister's house, children and parents together. Shenagh and John met playing chamber music in Manchester. Both were married then, to others. She is an LRAM, and regularly plays the piano. Sad that John lives alone now in a caravan, approaching seventy, all seven of his children from his two marriages absent, separately involved in their individual worlds. His cello lies in its case on a bunk in the caravan. He still practises.

Seen at a distance from home in Lower Terhill, it feels inexcusable that a man of my advantages, educationally, materially, physically, acted as I did.

Unless suicidal depression is, in a significant part, chemical?

6 February

I swam this morning in the unruffled waters of Lake Taupo, formed by a volcanic eruption as recent as a hundred years after the birth of Christ, the bottom without rocks or weeds, ripple-bands of grey sand beneath my feet. On the esplanade of the town at the end of the lake tourists drive golf balls two and three hundred yards into the water, the deep basin so even and clear that divers have no trouble collecting the balls every Monday afternoon.

A giant mountain, a pure cone of snow and scree, overwhelms the view. Shenagh and I wander through a mature podocarpus forest, with dozens of the most enormous trees I've ever seen, all natives of New Zealand: rimu, matai, miro and a single totara. Some of the side branches of the totara are shaped into deep wedges, growing up and out like the buttresses of Wells Cathedral, or the dewlap of a Hereford bull.

We arrive early evening at a remote farm of several thousand acres, near Piopio in Waitanguru District, up Leitch Road and several miles down a dirt track – in the heart of the King Country, as it is known, land defended in the nineteenth century by a Maori king for the exclusive use of his people. This high hill territory was acquired in 1906 by the present farmer's grandfather, the entire terrain then covered in untamed bush and forest. A photograph taken in the 1920s shows the farmhouse perched on a stripped-bare mound framed by the skeletons of dead trees, today shaded by a luscious bloom of flower and fruit. Over barbecued ribs of home lamb, the sun setting through branches of a eucalyptus tree, we're told of the three and a half thousand breeding ewes currently out there at pasture, together with fifteen hundred pregnant hoggets set to colonise an adjacent farm recently bought, and four hundred beef cows with their calves, not to mention dozens of dutiful rams and bulls. Patricia and Graeme McQuorcodale, who farm their land alone – with the assistance of seasonal part-timers and passing sons – have named each field: Meru's, Folly, Watsons, Mangawhara, Donnelly's, and the rest, several named after the labourers who felled and cleared the trees.

7 February

I need, first thing, to walk out on my own into the hills. To place myself.

Graeme's five working dogs stand in line in their wire cages, ears pricked in silent expectation of being taken off along the miles of tracks seen from the house to thread high outcrops of black limestone rock. They know I'm not their master and don't complain when I leave alone.

Ten minutes on, in a rocky warren on the nearest hill-with-a-view, I disturb two feral tabby cats. Wanting as soon as possible to reach the heights, I ridge-walk up the centre of the McQuorcodales' western territory, beyond the sprayers' airstrip below me on the right, to the edge of a cliff that looks out onto land owned by a Swedish millionaire, heiress to the Alfa-Laval milking fortune. Her manager has built for himself a ranch on the sheltered bluff.

Alfa-Laval, I later read, claimed in 1930 that three of every four of the world's dairy farmers used their revolutionary machines to separate cream from milk. In Ireland, at old Erkindale, my grandmother's farm, they were still milking by hand when it was sold at auction in the late 1980s.

Seated on the top of a limestone pinnacle surveying hundreds of miles of cleared hills, I hear nearby a sharp bark, and turn to stare across the void at a goat on the next pinnacle. She is dark-brown, with slashes of white beside her eyes, and short pointed horns. Summoned by their mother, the mottled lambs jump off with her to join more wild goats in the shade of a distant ledge. Find in the rocky crevice of a gulley three strong shoots of the yellow flowers of ragwort, poisonous to cattle. Uproot

the plant and wonder, when I discover nearby the carcass of a cow, if it was a victim of this hidden growth.
The skeleton is intact, picked by carrion and bleached
white by the sun, the black hide bodyless. I carry with
me the skull, together with five unusual feathers found
at different points on the trail.

Pairs of black and white duck rise from the swamps,
the female croaking as they circle above me, the male
gurgling a supportive response.

With the curve of my steps back down the track above
the farm I think of Janet, at Aisholt, aware of the widow's
plight of walking home to solitude. It's good to be returning to people, to other working lives, to an audience
for my tales of the walk, four hours after I set out. This
truly is sheep station country, still worked by itinerant
gangs of shearers, of which Janet was one of the few
young women shepherds in New Zealand in the 1950s.

I pause in wonder at what is to New Zealanders a
standard sight: the bright red forehead and beak of the
pukeko, with its dark plumage and iridescent blue breast
feathers. And other birds. With their absurd crimson
combs and too-small wings, wild turkeys are as incon-
gruous a country presence as our pheasants, imports
hundreds of years ago from the forests of China. Wood
pigeons here also have an oriental look, twice the size of
those in England, with green and blue chests, and eyes
like jewels, the fire-red pupils ringed as if in precious
gems.

The yellow and black striped caterpillar of the crimson
and charcoal cinnabar moth feed on the leaves of ragwort, and nothing else, I read.

Janet would love it here, appreciative of the McQuorcodale ethos of hill-farming, their pressures and pleasures similar to hers, despite the difference in size of their properties. Maybe she worked the King Country years ago? It's a landscape that Beth too would adore.

Maori souls make return visits to the living in the form of moths and spiders.

The concrete posts of the older sheep fences have been driven in silhouetted lines across the dividing ridges, hung with eight strands of stock-proof wire. These days, hill pastures are fertilized by biplane, and the soils analysed for their metallic content. Science subverts the natural cycle even here, in deep rural New Zealand.

Negation doesn't dissipate: inside, I continue to shriek 'No!'

I often do it: fold down, close up. Doesn't much matter who I'm with. I can manage for a bit, and then run dry of human concern.

Sitting in the back of the car on the long drive back to Wellington: 'BEWARE! Men in Tights' a notice on the highway warns of the approach to a 'Medieval Market' due at the weekend.

Not funny, not to me. Horrifying, in fact.

Alienating.

People care for me, I know they do, and for each other. I wish I could be more loving, could feel positively about harmless attempts at communal fun.

In the front seats of the car my sister and her daughter sing alternate songs to each other, and laugh, for miles.

9 February

It is the week of Shenagh's promotion away from the State Services Commission to head the Ministry of Womens Affairs. Her boss is a Cabinet Minister and a woman; the Cabinet Minister's boss is Prime Minister and a woman; the Prime Minister's co-head of state, the Governor General, is a woman. Shenagh is the only one of this female chain not New Zealand born, eighteen years ago an immigrant.

10 February

Dinner with the poets Jenny and Greg at their house on the southern hills of Wellington. The evening was personal, special and happy, too present in my mind to spoil by writing about.

Can say, though, that the room was full of the art of their friends, and of work by themselves too: a lithographed poem, a boat-like raku bowl, several oils of abstract waves, and coloured words painted on a cube. I picked things up, handled them as I would do in my own home.

Walked back to my sister's along empty roads which curl up and around the cliff-hung houses of Mount Victoria, then down towards the lights of city skyscrapers, of luxury tour liners in dock, the bay beyond. Down there, the main City streets are deserted. Then up another hill towards Shenagh's house, tucked out of the way of the wind – exactly one and a quarter walking-hours door to door from Ha Taitai to Wadestown. It spat warm misty rain for the last couple of miles.

In New Zealand, early February, of course, is summer.

11 February

I went this morning to Shenagh's Maori welcome to the Ministry, a *powhiri ki a*, with traditional songs and ritual, all the whites managing to give speeches in the native language of this land. For a moment I saw Shenagh as a child, a look on her face of worried surprise, her wide forehead scarred where I pushed her down the flight of ten stone steps at the front door of our house overlooking the cricket fields. She was four, and I was six and a half, in my first term at day preparatory school on the other side of the hill.

12 February

Learn that Mother visited the McQuorcodale farm, taken by my sister to stay with her friends for a night and a day.

Reminded of my mother, I recall harvest time at Erkindale when our Grandmother was alive – me aged maybe ten, walking beside the horse-drawn hay cutter and at the corners of the field whacking Rosie with a stick to encourage her to keep pace with Paddy in pulling the machine. Rosie was a long-legged female bay, Paddy a shorter male grey. The next day I stood on the wooden sled behind the primitive bailer which the horses drew, and piled the squared hay into stacks of six before pushing them off the back. I can see the neat rows in which my stacked bales stood on the stubble, the field sloping away from the barns towards the river. In summer Uncle Dave, my mother's youngest brother, kept his cows down there by the water and the shade from the big willows, a rosette-winning herd of black Aberdeen Angus.

I looked like Uncle Dave, I was told, and was pleased to hear. By the time summer holidays ended I spoke with an Irish lilt to my unbroken voice.

Long after Granny's death, three years after leaving my wife and following the closure of my antiques dealing premises, I journeyed to Erkindale, intending to work free on the farm for the summer. The place was dilapidated by then, the roof leaking and garden a jungle, Uncle Dave and his old helper Bill sleeping in rooms on the ground floor, down to which the rain had yet to penetrate.

Understandably, he did not recognize me, smiling with pleasure when I explained myself, but saying, in

464

a musical drawl: 'Ah, sure, kind thought, but this is no place for the likes of you.' There was no choice, no conversation. I got back into my hired car and drove away beneath the overhanging trees of the drive, spent the night at a country inn in Rathdowney, the nearest town.

While working on the bank in Shenagh's Wadestown garden, releasing fruit trees from the press of undergrowth, I watched a large butterfly display its veined coppery wings. The colours looked bright, although it didn't alight. I think the butterfly might be called common copper. They don't exist in England.

13 February

Two of Mother's elder brothers emigrated from Ireland to virgin land in Western Australia, in the vicinity of a then-little-known national landmark, Wave Rock. One of them, the fourth brother, had been a substitute father to her. She must have missed him. Their father, while he was alive, was a hard-driven man, the source, I imagine, of my mother's distressingly harsh demands first on herself, and then on me. It has never been possible to be good enough for Mother.

My grandfather died when my mother was eleven. During his childhood in the Slieve Bloom Mountains he never learnt to read or write, and worked too hard down in the valley to have the time or inclination to learn later.

This morning wrote a postcard to Shenagh: the blue monogram of 'S' from an exhibition of New Zealand print-design at the National Library. I thanked her for being my sister, said a few other emotional things. I have pinned the card image-outwards to the family notice board, and there's no reason for her to see and read my message. I like this, am happy with the thought of Shenagh or one of her children taking down the card months if not years later and receiving my dateless words.

14 February

An invitation has arrived to the Rosalie Gascoigne show which Greg has curated. The card – a strip of randomly printed plywood packing case – was designed by his teenage son; it's terrific, in itself and in reference to the themes of the artist.

The Director of the City Gallery in Wellington is, I notice, a woman.

15 February

Some questions that people ask are already answers, discussion censored in advance. I find this difficult and am crab-like and withdrawn in response. My nights are disturbed by dreams, whilst conflicting images punctuate my days. Do not mention this, and nobody I meet would guess that not long ago I couldn't really speak at all. Not to anybody – except Beth.

Last night I took the family to a David Bowie concert at Westpac, the giant stadium at the foot of Wadestown Hill, scene the weekend before of the rugby seven-a-side finals. Not the balmy summer's night it was meant to be, Wellington instead at its windiest. Bowie was fantastic, an ageless rocker, he and his band performing at full throttle for two hours. The light and video synchronisation surprised me in its complexity, matched by beautiful use of four-camera projections onto a screen immediately above the stage. Bowie was soaked by the rain. 'If you can stick it out, we can,' he promised with a South London slide in his voice to the Kiwi audience of twenty thousand, half of them in the open-air.

We late-called afterwards at a house in Brooklyn, another suburb with a view, to attend a party given by friends from the Golden Bay tramp. Their daughter, Amy, the young artist, had designed an invite dedicated to 'Björk and Barney', the Icelandic pop-pixie and American filmmaker, together parents of a baby. A short Matthew Barney art-movie played in a continuous loop on their television set. At the Pompidou Centre at Christmas I had bought a postcard of Barney dressed as a carpenter for the last-made of his series of five films, *The Cremaster Cycle*. Blood ran from his nose. He is a close friend of several artist-friends of mine in the East

End, with a following here at the far side of the world. Uplifts me, somehow. Even though Barney's posturing and pomposity irritates.

It's raining again this morning.

While my mother was away on a bridge holiday last week one of her elder sisters died, wife of the man who managed the grain mill where we played as children. As Uncle Dave fell down dead checking stock in the fields of Erkindale a decade ago, only two of the ten siblings now remain alive, my mother one of them ...

16 February

In three weeks' time I'll be home again in Somerset. For the last twelve mornings I've done exercises in my room before breakfast, pulling out the tense muscles of spine and thighs. I wonder if I might follow an emergent plan: regularly to spend three months of the year at the McQuorcodale hill station, writing things for myself in the mornings and working for them on the land in the afternoons.

Not practicable, I suspect.

I'd maybe do better returning to London for part of every week, to work again in the art world.

Graeme McQuorcodale's five trained dogs have learnt six different commands, whistled through his teeth, thirty distinct calls to each of which the individual dog separately responds. He has hound-crossed barking dogs as well as his closer-working collies.

17 February

It's hard living with others. Rather than relax and let everyone get on with things, I sit there half-reading, endlessly anxious, disturbed by the absence of control.

Looking forward to beginning again psychotherapy sessions with Jim. I need him. There's no going back: that's Jim's ultimate argument. Find myself reflecting that, over the years, I've sent thousands and thousands of postcards: a way of keeping in touch with people. And yet, and yet ... two years ago I lost contact, for a time with everybody, several times even with Beth. Thus we die. To live, each must reserve a space somewhere inside for the existence of others. Not sure I'm up to this. Room for not many, anyway. For very few. This worries me.

In mid-afternoon the rain stopped and by five the skies were again the clearest of blue. I took an exploratory walk up through the forest above town, eventually locating the Tinakori Ridge Trail leading me across to the other side, from where I followed winding roads past old houses and down precipitous pedestrian steps to the rear end of the Botanical Gardens. I got lost there too, faced with a steep hillside of ancient trees, a ravine at the bottom. With the help of a woman out walking her dog, found my way to the top stop of the cable car and from there down ninety-two steps to the head of Dixon Street. On this last part of the walk I passed through Victoria University, built piecemeal, like a flourishing hospital, and lower down stopped to inspect St John's Presbyterian Church, designed by Thomas Turnbull in 1885, a mass of gothic arches and pinnacles in painted timber.

Time for a quick bite before the first of two Fringe Festival performances of the night at BATS Theatre. I enjoyed again being in the blackened space of an experimental theatre, some of the packed audience seated on the stairs for the company's inaugural piece: 'Sharing an interest in asserting the autonomy of the stage, the group is dedicated to investigating the language of the uniquely theatrical in the text.' Thought of Elizabeth and of the opening years of our marriage, during which she went to drama school in London - when she graduated and left on touring repertory, earning her actor's green card, I joined her from Sotheby's at the weekends. Before I fled our home she had played Viola at Regents Park, a performance I remember for her innocence and energy. Beth − Elizabeth − is a playwright now, with work commissioned by the Riverside Theatre.

On the walk back I stopped at Regan Gentry's *Skip It*, parked on the main road near the entrance to Wellington City Council's offices. I'd met the young sculptor at the party on Friday, and the next morning we had together checked the weekend fate of his ten day installation, a 1980s sitting room assembled inside an orange Dimac skip, at night the lamps lit and the TV flickering. A telephone periodically rings on the table in a corner. As I stood to look, two passers-by peered over the sides into the rain-spattered space. 'Not bad. Prefer it to your pad, as a matter of fact,' one of them said. 'Bigger too!' the other agreed. In London in 1997, Gavin Turk exhibited an extra-large black skip at the Hayward Gallery in the show *Material Culture*. He called his piece *Pimp*, and it was bought for the Saatchi Collection.

Further along my route back to Wadestown, on Lambton Quay, the city's main shopping street, I touched with my hand Jeff Thomson's *Shells*, unsure whether the rippled surface was in the original wrought iron or cast in concrete, daubed by him in multiple shades of pastel paint and rising above the height of my head. A brass plaque records that this municipal commission was funded 'with the aid of EEC Lighting'.

19 February

Motorbikers in the squalls on the mountain road across to John's land near Masterton wear winter gear, black and white skeleton masks protecting their faces, mouths covered, leaning back into the upholstered seats of their Harley Davidsons.

Received today the third of Beth's parcels of mail from Terhill, including current copies of the *New Statesman* and the *TLS*. I'm pleased to register connections retained with the art market back home, marked by invitation cards in the post from artists and galleries. White Cube announces Gavin's new show: 'a single, large-scale installation that explores the notions of perception and suspension, image and reality'. Beth writes of her days thinking and making things at the place which, for this time, is hers alone. Will we find ways of sharing?

At Joshua Compston's second street festival in Shoreditch, his Fête Worse Than Death of 1994, Gavin dressed up in silver drag, and while excreting artificial sausages from his false bum, with a string of real sausages cling-filmed across his stomach, mimed on stage to the David Bowie song *Scary Monsters*.

20 February

On four of the drier recent afternoons I've continued to cut and shape bushes and trees high on the bank at the back of Shenagh's garden. It's an activity I like doing, almost anywhere. A kind-of sculpting. Nobody has been around during the day to see me at work and I can't think who will notice much difference; all the same, I take unusual satisfaction in the labour, sensing achievement.

Above the bed in the room in which I sleep hangs an oil painting that I used to own, a gift to me by the artist, a Tuscan, who lived in a restored farmhouse on a spit of land in the valley below Impruneta, twenty minutes by bus into the hills south of Florence. A large oak tree grew beside the loggia – La Quercia (The Oak) is both the name of the house, and the title of the picture. I spent the whole of one summer there, making my way most days by Vespa down into Florence to study art patronage in the fifteenth century, the main subject of my third year at Cambridge. I had first arrived at La Quercia on an ox cart, hitching from the next-door farmer a lift down the dirt track in the heat. Francesco Clemente the painter was called, owner of several shoe shops in town. Not the Milanese artist of the same name. 'My' Francesco hated the muddle with his famous namesake. He worked in a studio in the converted granary, separate from the house, playing records of classical music all day long and smoking cigarettes, driving off to friends most late afternoons to play tennis. I used to sit quietly in the cool on the settee and watch him add the finishing touches to his painting of the oak, which years ago I ceased to appreciate and let my sister ship together with her other stuff from Manchester to New Zealand.

This afternoon, half-watching the one-day cricket match in Westpac Stadium, South Africa versus New Zealand, I find myself back in the gardens of Palazzo Cappone, on a break for coffee from cataloguing furniture for a Sotheby's sale. John Winter was head of our Florence office then, and he arranged for me to fly out three times a year to take, in Italian, the auctions we held beneath frescoed ceilings in the main rooms of the Palazzo. Auctioneers, if they're good, have complete control!

Francesco used to view the sales and we often had lunch together, although the magic of my contact with him that earlier summer at La Quercia had gone, and after leaving Sotheby's I saw him only once more before he died. The walls of his house were plastered and oiled to the texture and colour of vellum, the floors of old terracotta tiles worn by time, a small pigeon loft at the centre of the square sloping roof. I was happy there. Felt myself to have been lowered softly into the middle of a landscape by Piero della Francesca, the vineyards and olive groves farmed unchangingly for centuries.

At Westpac they dry the grass beneath the rotary blades of a helicopter and the cricketers are athletes, hurling themselves across the turf in a high-scoring game, names and numbers of individual players printed across their backs, black strip for New Zealand, the South Africans wearing green and yellow.

I don't understand the cricket fuss.

21 February

The third of Shenagh's cats, Leah, a street tabby, has been missing for five weeks. I saw her this morning cross Oban Street and pad up the drive of the house next door, where Sam reckons she has moved in to live, in order to be regularly fed.

Christa Wolf, I discover from the *TLS*, has pursued to its conclusion an idea similar to one I failed years ago to follow. In 1960 the communist newspaper *Izvestia* asked its readers to record in detail the events of a single arbitrarily chosen day, 27 September. Intrigued by the concept, Wolf extended the challenge and now publishes the results in *Ein Tag im Jahr 1960-2000*, in which she writes annually of the events and thoughts of this single day for the next forty years. Her youngest daughter's birthday happens to fall on the day after, 28 September, and much of what concerns her regularly involves family matters.

Wolf tells of feeling her life's work to be a long narrative of defeated hopes.

My idea, back in December 1979, was to buy Christmas presents for ten friends, careful in the choice from amongst London's fashionable shops of items to match the taste of each individual, not necessarily expensive but stylish, and to request that the presents be packaged and gift-wrapped and then to put them away untouched in the dark for the next twenty years. To mark the millennium, I planned to mount a gallery show of the gifts, half-opened, every aspect of design of the earlier period exhibited to pristine effect. I intended to write a detailed descriptive catalogue, including analysis of both the stylistic and the personal choices made, in packing material as well as object.

It didn't happen.

I sold to developers my lease on the premises and turned to other things.

We're at a bach on the beach at Castlepoint, by a stream running through the grass down which I walk to swim and see, on my way to the water, a tall bird with a long pure-black bill ending in a shape like a spoon. None of the four other adults, nor any of the five teenagers staying with us at the bach, have seen such a bird in the wild. Nobody knows what it's called. The bird appears to be guarding the place where it lives, the reeds around trampled to the ground and stained with excrement.

It is beautiful here. The 'castle' is a rock at the end of the point, charted and christened by Lieutenant Cook on his original trip of discovery of New Zealand, between October 1769 and March 1770, in His Majesty's bark *Endeavour*.

22 February

Swam into the rising sun, the sea dead calm. Over my head the strange bird flew in unhappy flaps and glides, disturbed at its morning feed on the shore.

Dressed and breakfasted, I took a handful of plums on my walk up the beach beyond the last of the houses, on and on, to the mouth of a river. Exposed in the sandstone near the top of a crumbling cliff I found several large fluorescent Paua shells. They may have been buried there for a million years, since last this land was sea. Layers of rock are turned on an angle and project along a section of the foreshore, a minor version of the extraordinary formation at East Quantoxhead, back home in Somerset, where the stones have been placed by nature as though the ruins of a Roman harbour.

We climbed to the top of the 'castle', facing a drop of a thousand feet to the sea.

Disturbing.

I don't forget.

I won't forget.

On the trunk of a pine in the forest down through which we walked a notice was nailed: 'DANGER. POISON. Pindone carrot bait. Do not touch or remove. Keep all pets away. By order Wellington District Council.' The government is supported by its people in seeking to kill seventy percent of the country's possums, a noisome immigrant from Australia.

Gavin's exhibition *The Golden Thread* was reviewed in last week's *New Statesman*. Across the entire floor of White Cube in Hoxton Square he has built a labyrinth of rectangular glass panels framed in modernist aluminium, described in the review: 'He raises the issue of looking and thinking: he's a good artist not because the objects he makes are aesthetically marvellous, but because of the ideas they provoke. They are about values, society, art, the artist and power – who has it and who doesn't.'

Reminded that at Podshavers, we decided from the start that there would be no advertising, that no interviews would be granted, that nothing would ever be done to court custom. People must come because they want to be there. If they dislike the wildness of the front yard, if they don't appreciate direct no-nonsense food, then Podshavers is not for them.

Gavin works around the idea of artist-as-icon, is himself enchanting and engaged – it is what he charmingly does anyway, whether people like it or not.

Remember, with disbelief, the fact that eight years have passed since I found Joshua Compston three days dead on the plank bed above his picture store in Charlotte Road. Through him and the events he hatched at Factual Nonsense I met Gavin and some of the other artists who are now my friends. Joshua, with his shock of blonde hair and excess haste, was twenty-five when he died, at his own doing, unintendedly, it is my belief.

All this time I may slowly have been mourning his loss, removal of what his livingness represented to me: triumph over the anger and isolation of his teenage years.

Joshua was a hoarder of things – amongst many:

his collection of early cigarette packets; and all his exhibition invitation cards and other printed ephemera. The sculptor Joseph Cornell, in papers stored at the Smithsonian Institute, described his archive of found materials as 'the core of a labyrinth, a clearing house for dreams and visions ... childhood regained.'

In a letter today from Beth at Lower Terhill she tells of returning to the workshop at George Clement's place, to make at his woodworking machines her kitchen top, from dovetailed cedar, the scent accompanying her throughout the day, in the workshop, in her car on the drive back over from the Levels and in the kennels where she assembled and glued the pieces. It will be in position by now in the original half of the cottage, to the right of the window onto the lane, beside her stack of handmade drawers and a cupboard to contain the water-heater, all made of salvaged timber, rich in seasoned grains and marks of previous use. I'm looking forward to seeing the changes she has made, to seeing her too.

Acutely aware with my sister's family these days of separation: my life is elsewhere, is different. At the weekend at Castlepoint I ran alone in the wind along the beach, and twice clambered to the head of a vast sand dune, hurtling down to the shore.

I can run again, won't let myself be caught.

24 February

Am I aiming at idiocy: connection without commitment?

I *do* find it difficult to share. Feelings, to me, are fraught, bordered in black, like invitation cards to a funeral.

Regan Gentry's *Skip It* survives the weather. Eleven days after being installed on the street the television still works and the cell phone still irregularly rings, remaining unanswered – although the wallpaper threatens to peel from the insides of the open skip, the art is otherwise intact, the citizens of Wellington remarkably restrained. I realize that Wellington City Council, the butt of Regan's skip joke, backs onto the post-modern antics of Civic Square, where the City Gallery flourishes behind the deco façade of the old main library.

Rosalie Gascoigne didn't present her first solo exhibition until the age of fifty-seven. 'Distant memory as well as distant landscape – and the objects that figure in both – shape her allusive and elusive art,' Greg O'Brien writes in his catalogue essay *Plain air / Plain song*, in which her piece *Birds* is given prominence, a collage of cut yellow road signs. Gascoigne remarked, shortly before her death:

> I start doing things with materials I like and then suddenly I remember something usually and I move the work along that path. But it has always been something personal to me or remembered.

She made work from the bones and feathers she collected on her walks. And from shells. In her *Turn of the Tide* at the City Gallery, the striped homes of sea-snails (four hundred and eight, I counted them, the vertical lines of the bigger ones on the right in eight rows, and on the left, facing in the opposite direction, nine lines of smaller shells) are glued to wood on a rectangle of beaten galvanized metal, mounted on the unseen panel of a packing case. Light shining through the empty nail holes on the sides of the tin free the piece to float in the air.

Turn of the Tide hangs next to my other favourite sculpture in the show, *Pink Window*, the upper section of a glassless wooden frame turned on its side, nailed to it, as if a curtain blowing in the wind, a twisted panel of rippled iron, painted and rusting. The longer I look at her work the clearer I see the patterned shapes, these found objects not arbitrarily placed but composed by experience into meaning. *Pink Window* was made in 1976 and is still in the possession of the artist's family. The yellow of her road signs is reflective and glows iridescent beneath the gallery's artificial light, like the shells of Paua she gathered from the beach in her New Zealand childhood.

The play of daylight on Gascoigne's work is significant, squares of alternately directed sticks of driftwood seeming to be of two different colours, seen as I step through and around them all to be of the same bruised grey.

Wonderful again to be able to look with sustained concentration at works of art. To question and not to doubt.

25 February

A line in the sand divides delight and despair. Must retain somehow the capacity to ride out the fears, the blasts of pointlessness. It is for me to find meaning in what I do, nobody can give this to me.

Anger.

Twice on this visit my sister has been very angry with me. Angrier than her children had ever previously seen her.

Both Beths have also been provoked by me into wild spasms of angry violence.

Leave it. Let it go. Don't want to push and push to justify myself. Best not define, not explain. These things happened, for reasons I may never understand.

I hate anger.

That's it.

26 February

Pankaj Mishra writes in the *New Statesman*, in his review of Penguin's revised translation of Gustave Flaubert's novel *A Sentimental Education*: 'Frédéric's political voltes-face remind one of the radicals of our own time who turn bewilderingly into courtiers to the rich and powerful.'

The tabby called in briefly to its old home last night, to say hello.

Notice this lunchtime, on my walk into town, the tall metal letters 'KS' and then the words 'Kate Sheppard Apartments' across the top of a building being converted into urban lofts, the balconies of the double-storey flats directly facing parliament on one side and on the other the bay.

KS? Who was she, who is she?

27 February

Its name is the monarch, the big butterfly I occasionally see. This afternoon, near the kindergarten, a mother directed her daughter to watch the creature's bumpy orange flight, calling out its name.

On a long walk through and beyond Otari Native Botanical Garden I pass, off the back route into the City, two New Zealand icons: on one side of the track the green playing fields of Western Suburbs Rugby Union Football Club; and on the other, tucked pell-mell beneath trees and bushes, the hillside gravestones of Kaori Cemetery. There is almost nobody around, the air wonderfully clean, fresh, clear – on the rugby field and in the graveyard.

People are also buried in the wooded grounds of Victoria University, the bodies of teachers and statesman of the 1880s.

On an early plane to Auckland to spend two days with Sam, dropped by car at the airport by Shenagh, the rest of the household asleep in the dark before dawn when we left. Recognize that I don't actually know my sister, not in day-by-day experience. We each hold special knowledge of our childhood, have consistently exchanged in adulthood information about the passage of our lives, but in the fourteen years since my previous visit to her in New Zealand we've spent only three consecutive days together, during her busy stay with me when I still lived in Shoreditch. She was good to be with, and I enjoyed sharing with her my connection to young artists, was happy to communicate pleasure at the increasing public recognition of their work. This, though, was heightened time and, in truth, neither of us had any idea what our normal days are like, had little knowledge of the person the other in reality is.

We know more about each other now.

When my father flew out on his own to see Shenagh, not long after the operation on his first broken hip, the family then lived in the suburbs of Auckland, on one of the streets below the park at Mount Eden. He wet himself on the flight, both there and back, the onset of Parkinson's Disease making it difficult for him to control his bladder.

My sister felt loved by him, felt love for him.

The latter is what matters: how we feel, not what is felt for us.

My parents claim they loved me, but I did not feel it, have never felt love from them.

Nor do I feel it *for* them.

Sadly, I do not love my mother or my father. Even in

memory, in his case.

In the late afternoon I rest and read for an hour. Saw, in a closed-eye moment of day-dream, a wooden tent-peg which I desperately needed to drive into the earth.

Auckland sprawls, lacking the tight shoreline which is an ever-present feature of Wellington.

The friends I was staying with pointed out in the night sky the Southern Cross, a perfectly linear constellation of stars. It puzzled me that I had not noticed this before.

29 February

It's a leap year: today is Sunday the 29th of February. On the lacquered black piano in the room in which I'm staying for these two nights in Auckland stands a photograph holder, empty, the frame painted with grey images of feathers on a mustard ground.

Down on the harbour, in the warehouses of the National Maritime Museum, I very much liked a walking stick made from the spine of a shark, with a pattern of drilled holes in the shaft and carved teak handle.

Maoris lined the insides of their Kahawai fish lures with the fluorescent shell of Paua.

In glass cases there are scale models of the steamboats which used to trade the waters of the South Pacific, and I am taken back to my Sotheby's Belgravia days, to cataloguing such things for auction in the Collectors Sales, a title and category which I invented in the early 1970s. Most of these Kiwi ships were made in Glasgow, their funnels shortening as the mechanics of steam streamlined. Can see, as if yesterday, the collection of tin toys sent for sale by the Maharajah of Hyderabad, in their original cardboard boxes, unopened, made by Bing in Germany immediately before and after the First World War.

A later memory crowds in: of my appearances in every one of the BBC's first twenty-four programmes of the Antiques Roadshow.

I continue to wrestle with whatever it was which impelled me to leave this seeming success, against the wishes of many others – my parents, in particular, who loved the bridge club kudos of having a son on prime-time TV.

In the Museum they exhibit the wooden hull of the eights boat which won for New Zealand a gold medal in the 1972 Munich Olympics, and a fibreglass model of Auckland's Black Magic, the only sailing boat built outside the United States that has – to date – successfully defended the Americas Cup.

A day late, I realize that the Southern Cross cannot of course be seen in the skies of the northern hemisphere.

1 March

I was shown, in the weekend national paper, large colour photographs both of my sister in her new job and, in the arts section, of Greg, talking of his time as a surfer poet in the hippy heyday of the 1970s.

Both of them look good.

I never guessed, until seeing some here in the National Museum, that the weavings and ornamental dress of Polynesians could be of such beauty – their painstaking use of shells and teeth in complex patterns is wonderful. Maori artefacts, from New Zealand itself, are more primal, more powerful, in ways.

Find myself drawn to sit on the benches and rest, from where I continue to watch and to think.

Maybe I haven't slept well on the folding couch. Maybe the constant presence of people has exhausted me. My heart, I trust, is not again protesting.

I am looking forward to arriving home on Sunday at Lower Terhill.

I stare for a long time at the traditionally carved whale-bone handle of Te Kooti's battleaxe, which he presented in the late 1870s to a British General. Te Kooti, the most notorious leader of the Maori rebellion, saved himself and his fighters by taking sanctuary in the forests of The King Country, before eventually being pardoned by the occupying forces. With the blade of this axe he had slaughtered many Pakeha, as Maoris called the stubborn white tribe which had invaded their lands.

In the park at the centre of which the museum stands, overlooking the waters, two teams of twelve-year-old boys play a cricket match. At Orley Farm, in my last prep-school term, I scored the most runs the school had ever witnessed, took the most wickets and caught the most catches. I deserved, I felt, to be awarded all three of the season's cricket cups but was permitted to win only one, for batting. From then, thread by thread my competitive nerve snapped. By now, long solitary swims in the sea is the exercise I like best. And working in my wood, at home

2 March

I've received, wrapped in a silk bow, a joined pair of oyster shells and a poem, from a close woman friend of Shenagh's. For me alone. I like them both: the shells and the poem.

I love dates like today's, numerically neat, balanced.

I'm back with my sister in Wellington. A hoe lies on the bank, hidden by flowering bushes, dropped there by Shenagh while I was away in Auckland. Does it matter? My mother would think and say so, in a temper.

It's late; the cats have not been fed; they cry in the dark at the glass garden door.

3 March

Seated on a tall round stool at the bar of a café tucked behind the City Gallery, I look up from my glass of wine and see that the sky is blue after another rainy day, the wettest summer Wellington has known. There is no natural object within my sight. All is man-made: the green marble point of a stone pyramid; a concrete and glass segment of the concert hall; the corroded copper of a metal Palm tree. I like what I see, its geometry, the arm of a yellow crane in the distance, set against the clouds now bowling by.

As the sun's rays lower they skim the curved line of a chrome roof.

4 March

On the bank below the nearest house to Shenagh's there is a damaged native beech, a large old tree its branches bare of leaves on the weather side. It will recover. In the meantime birds flock to it, and I spotted this afternoon two, perhaps three kingfishers alight to eat cicadas noisy in the sun; these long-beaked creatures are whiter than in England, and smaller, have different habits. Scruffy turquoise-tinged tui, the largest of New Zealand's honey-eaters, fail in their attempt to chase away the young kingfishers.

I see from the book that it was a spoonbill that we saw at Castlepoint, a bird which has demonstrated impressive powers of recovery since being declared in 1975 an endangered species, both in North and South Island.

Leah, the tabby cat, has just been here again, on a fleeting visit.

5 March

My last full day in New Zealand. The morning sun catches the tops of trees and patterns the ferns I have uncovered at the brow of the bank. Last weekend, while weeding in the garden, Shenagh noticed my work, told me that she lacks the vision to see how such changes as these need to be made, my many marks on the land barely noticeable and yet, in visual effect, transforming.

Like this praise – although I already take private pleasure in what I've done, have often sat in one of the canvas chairs on the deck and gazed around, spotting slight improvements to be made and clambering up the bank with the bowsaw to execute them.

Shenagh and I had supper in town, brother and sister alone together for a couple of hours on my final night. We both cried at the table.

6 March

I'm in town for a farewell swim before the thirty-seven hour journey home to Lower Terhill. My regular swimming haunt in Wellington, a twenty-minute walk from the house, has been this 1930s open-air pool, with clapboard changing cabins, swan-neck shower stalls and a pebble-dash flight of concrete steps on which to sit in the sun and watch others. Front crawl for twenty-five minutes, a session of stretching exercises, shower and off soon to the airport.

I have gained in strength here, am impatient for the future.

We'll see, we'll see!

On the plane. Resolutions. I will send postcards to whomever I like whenever I want. I will invite to stay whomever I wish whenever I choose.

7 March

Almost back, today's date lived through twice.

Swirl of half-remembered things.

Versions of events, each view personal. The details matter such a lot to the individual and so little in general. It's important that we try to hold to permission for difference and not seek to impose on each other our personal stories.

Shenagh is seldom alone, I almost always am.

Two people can disagree, see shared things conflictingly and yet can both be unmistaken.

Staying with Shenagh has been good for me. My sister is a blessing.

I am frightened that I may be sad, lonely, disconnected from the lives around me at Lower Terhill.

If so, so be it, I wish not to despair.

It is not the place itself which hurts, this I now know, learnt by spending these two months in New Zealand. There is no escape.

8 March

First sound heard from outside on waking in my own bedroom, curtainless, is the cooing of a pair of wood pigeons – the second, from the third from top branch of the Scots pine, the croak of a raven.

I cannot manage to operate the bicycle pump on these new-style valves on my bicycle. The front tyre of my car is flat and I severely cut my hand trying to undo the nuts. A moment of panic. Calm down. Must calm myself.

I have done.

The clothes pegs, pink, white and green, I used laboriously to insist on placing in pairs to match the colour of my laundry. Today I find it possible to take from the bag each peg as it comes in hanging my washing out on the line.

Proud of myself.

9 March

Looked from my study window in the early morning to see Hugh and Michael seeking to shift a flock of forty sheep from the old orchard and along the lane to new pastures. The two men flapped plastic sacks to direct the sheep and called to them, hoping they'd think they were about to be fed. The animals wandered through the gate in dribs and drabs, some feasting first on the verges, others running back into the field and refusing to follow instructions. Michael, who prefers his cows, cursed the stubborn flock of sheep. Eventually they trotted off down the lane behind his pick-up truck.

Found in the wire tray on my desk the last of the cards I had bought of Matthew Barney, dressed as *The Entered Apprentice* for his Cremaster 3 film, made in 2002. He is wearing a leather apron, with pouches for tools, standing against an Art-Deco lift door. Send it to Amy, the young artist in Wellington who gave the Björk and Barney party and loves his work.

10 March

This early morning's dream, taken note of in pencil before falling again to sleep, contained no women, I notice. We are all male, boys and men. In the dream I make a passionate speech and return back up Harrow Hill to my cave. I am close to tears. Happy. I don't know what the darkness contains, the mouth of the cave overgrown with ferns. I am not afraid of entering.

Through bare branches I noticed in the middle of Taunton a walled garden and sat on a bench there on the mound of a Norman keep, to eat for lunch fresh sandwiches and a piece of cake bought at the Women's Institute Market around the corner in Bath Place. A notice dated the keep to 1160. On the sheltered moss grew dozens of the most delicate blue spring flowers I have ever seen, a form of wild crocus, I presume.

Continued on my bike to Musgrove Hospital to be fitted with a heart monitor.

11 March

Beth struggles.

12 March

It's snowing.

13 March

I struggle.

14 March

Tired.

In the evenings I nod off to sleep at my desk.

I'm drawn to the books I attempt to read, but my mind cuts off.

15 March

High in the grey sky above fields past which I cycle to Taunton to see Jim, I hear skylarks sing cascades of notes. It is spring, warm, I am out on the bike without a coat.

Alex telephoned from Paris. He's been puzzling about the parking places I noted with the mark RAISON, and rang to say he reckons they must be street-damaged versions of LIVRAISON. In translation: 'unloading'. More prosaic than 'reason' as I'd willed it be, drivers justified in parking if they articulated a convincing French argument!

16 March

In too many places postcards are changing size. At the National Portrait Gallery's exhibition of the artist Tom Phillips' collection of WWI postcards, their reproduction cards have moved to a larger format than the original, after a century of satisfaction with the standard size. Bet Phillips is furious! How could the NPG make their copies larger than his standard originals?

17 March

On exhibition at the refurbished Camden Arts Centre, in the main space, is a chandelier and computer work by Cerith Wyn Evans, titled *Rabbit's Moon*, similar to the piece I saw at White Cube last November, to accompany which Michael Clarke had created a dance that I watched he and his company perform. At Camden, on the single computer screen, is a quote from *Keywords* by Raymond Williams:

> The earliest meaning of image in English was, from the thirteenth century, a figure or likeness ... There is probably a root relation to the development of intimate, but as in many words describing these processes (c.f. vision and idea) there is a deep tension between ideas of copying and ideas of imagination and the imaginary.

Cerith Wyn Evans was a supportive friend to Joshua. At Cambridge I attended, for a year, Raymond Williams' legendary lectures on the English novel. I love lateral links.

The buses in London have been transformed, charges reduced to a standard one pound for every journey and congestion more-or-less removed through Ken Livingstone's code-zoning system. Such a pleasure now travelling on the top deck of a red bus, in spring sunshine, watching from above places familiar to me day-by-day for thirty years. Much has changed. Much too has stayed the same. In my eyes.

18 March

What is it that makes special, makes especially beautiful, to Beth and to me, the patchwork of salvaged wood she has built to fill the vacant wall of the shed backing onto my to-be-orchard?

Two concentrated days of work, this wall with chicken-wired windows and steps up to an iron-hinged half-door, rusted chains and nails in the places they've been for a hundred years on certain bits of the ... collage, yes ... It is art, a work of art. I'm very pleased with Beth's creation.

She lives to make things, does it all the time. Not to sell. Beth is bad at selling.

Another thought: about a different aspect of this art thing: about Carl Freedman's gallery on the ground floor of my old Charlotte Road home, which I visited yesterday when I was in London. A friend criticised Carl for failing to make it possible for passers-by to gaze in from the outside and decide whether or not they wished to look at each exhibition. What matters is that people already *know* that they wish to enter. The black steel door is plastered with graffiti and Carl has raised a blank white wall flush with the inside of the plate glass window. The building is confusingly divided into two entrances, and the numbers of the street travel down one side to the junction with Great Eastern Street and then up the other to face Rufus Street. There is no facade sign. Nothing is clear. Available to the determined, the only kind of person Carl needs to meet, he protests.

He's right. You've got to want to. That's what art is.

19 March

I can do distance; not too good at close.

20 March

Wind and rain beat against the prow of my study jutting into the lane, so hard that water seeps beneath the closed window. I stand to look out down the curved line of the lane and am content to see the blackthorn beginning to push into white flower, in many more places than past years, a response to my careful clearings.

Bumped into old Constance, yesterday. Ollie's ghost doesn't visit her at night any longer. This winter, though, birds still from time to time tapped with their beaks at his bedroom window, expecting to be fed.

21 March

The other day Jim gave me a Xeroxed copy of Freud's essay *Mourning and Melancholia*, the final draft completed on 4 May 1915. I read it last night, and for a second time again today, taking note of several quotes, including:

> In mourning it is the world which has become poor and empty; in melancholia it is the ego itself ... This picture of a delusion of inferiority is completed by sleeplessness and refusal to take nourishment, and – what is psychologically very remarkable – by an overcoming of the instinct which compels every living thing to cling to life.

Walked over the hill this afternoon to Aisholt for tea with Janet. Helped on the farm, where she works through the nights on her fifty-seventh season of lambing. In the brightness of a spring afternoon she put on rubber gloves to pull, by its projecting feet, a lamb from its mother's womb. Over our mugs of tea by the Aga she told me of the time she spent down on the coast at the edge of The King Country, in the 1950s, the only non-Kiwi in her shepherds' squad. On the deserted island which she then went to farm, up in the Bay of Islands, Janet kept three working dogs, one of which was a hunter-barker, like Graeme MacQuorcodale's. She has always loved her dogs. Dart, the elder of her two current Collies, coughs blood, has not long left to be alive.

If this distress continues to recur one of us must go.

Maybe it should be me. Maybe London is the place I need to be, leaving Beth to her life here in Somerset.

Art is for doing not merely for thinking about, philosophising around. The ivory tower is a myth.

I remember Angela Carter argued in her collection of essays *Nothing Sacred* that you can't call yourself a writer unless you somehow publish your words, as the point of all art is the wish to communicate, that it should be called something other than art if you write only for yourself to read. If you do not at least aim to publish you are not a writer, Carter said.

I agree with her.

Which means, I suppose, that these pages are 'something else'.

What?

But I *am* a writer, of nine published books.

Sent a note to my dealer-friend in Cirencester, asking him when it would be convenient to him for me to collect my Pugin garden seat. I've decided also to buy one of his bookcases for the study – I'm not sure which, certainly an architect-designed creation, something to match the bold oak bookcase on the other side of the door, made by Gillows for the Palace of Westminster, also the work of A.W.N. Pugin. Maybe I'll wait to make the drive until after I collect on Thursday my new car, a VW Golf Estate, 1.8 cc, S registration – the only problem: I swore never to own a red motorcar.

Beth hurts, is in pain. How long can she sustain the strain?

I found it possible today *not* to rush to defend myself against an attack which I know to be unfair, unmeant for me. This helped us both, as I refused to be drawn into the chaos of Beth's damaged feelings, despite her tears and my compassion.

From a dusty crevice in the trunk of one of the redwoods I watched an overwintered ladybird crawl into the spring light. How has it managed to survive?

24 March

Forgot to say: yesterday afternoon I planted six white rambling roses.

25 March

The roses are of three varieties, the first growing by the porch, two of another type and three of a third. They look content enough with their new surroundings.

I have dug up from the wilderness another undamaged glass bottle, again with relief-cast lettering, this time for Yorkshire Relish, made by Goodall Backhouse & Co. The glass is a watery green colour, the top imperfectly formed. In it I've placed a single white tulip, self-generated in another part of the garden. Yorkshire Relish and Horse Embrocation are of the same design, with different lettering. Found intact a third small Eiffel Tower Lemonade bottle, made by Foster Clark Ltd of Maidstone.

I have heard from Holland that Willem Boymans is ill, confined to bed with pain in his back. He very seldom allows hurt to defeat him. This must be serious. Years ago he raised his bed to waist height, to allow himself easily to get in and out. Able to look from this bed straight onto the sky, he has surrounded himself with chosen objects, in particular the radio, on which he listens to the World Service night after sleepless night. I want to see him once more before he dies, but don't expect to be in Holland again until June. Trust he lasts. Find myself thinking of his meetings in Tokyo in the 1960s with Kenzo Takayanagi, a defence lawyer at the Tokyo Trial twenty years earlier, by then Chancellor of one of the largest Japanese universities. I placed both of them as themselves in the early part of my novel *The Folded Lie*.

Takayanagi was a fine man.

So is Willem.

In the email note that I sent to him ten minutes ago, I

at first wrote fiend instead of friend. He *is* difficult!

26 March

Prince Hassan of Jordan was interviewed on the radio this morning. He is an articulate defender of the need for incessant dialogue in his Middle East, the only way, he believes, of bringing bloodshed to an end. His mood is apocalyptic. If things continue on their present course he fears the terrorist bombing of nuclear material in Iran, Syria, India maybe, or Pakistan, and descent into the Third World War.

I am thinking of Joshua. He was so incredibly alive. Maybe too much?

> Come and wave to your friends as
> the real becomes imagined!
> Come and be on TV!
> FN: No FuN without U and fun can
> seriously make you FN!

Factual Nonsense: he chose a great name for his art gallery. Artists loved the FN bravado. In spring 1996 Gary Hume and Gavin Turk painted his coffin, carried by them and other artists from Charlotte Road to Christchurch Spitalfields for the burial service, accompanied by a jazz band and thousands of mourners, attended by Gilbert and George. I preferred to stay alone at home, two floors above his vacant premises.

27 March

The monarch (*Danaus plexippus*), I read, is a rare migrant visitor to the southernmost shores of Cornwall: 'Such is the excitement that single sightings can be reported several times.'

Saw the other day a black leather golf-bag and its trolley standing unattended on the grass of a picture-pristine village green, outside a cottage covered in early wisteria, with plastic-framed double-glazed windows. There was no person in sight.

Drove quickly by.

I hate golf. As a teenager, knowing no better then, I was very good at it, with a handicap of seven. By my early twenties I refused to play the game, with my parents or anybody else.

Worked it out: to stay steady I need to feel safe and, at the same moment, free.

Not easy.

Only possible, if at all, by living alone, and celibate.

For me, that is. Know nothing for anybody else.

28 March

The mown grass verges to my path beside the butterfly meadow look as particular as I hoped they might.

Two years it would take, I was told, for the nerves to regrow from the spinal column back down through the shoulder to my damaged right hand. There is feeling still only in half of my third and the whole of my little finger. The others, and my thumb, suffer burns and cuts without registering pain. And the muscles of my thumb have perished. There are no signs of sensitivity to touch in these fingers and I struggle to pick up dropped pencils, frequently mishit the typewriter keys. Twenty-one months since that self-destructive day. The feeling has gone forever, I fear.

I'll manage, I'll find a way. It could have been irrevocably worse.

Hill-walk again to visit Janet, to have lunch with her and the mutual friend who originally introduced us two.

On that day the friend had first driven me over to this side of the Quantocks, stopping at her favourite spot, where she was appalled to see that the statue on top of a sandstone grotto had fallen to the ground.

This favourite place of hers I later recognized as the head of the park here at Cothelstone, where the statue has been restored by Hugh, my landlord. Nearby, when I passed this morning, I saw my first butterfly of the English season. Not sure what it was, as I was not close enough, its hesitant flight through the rays of the sun an uplifting sight.

A memory: of spending the millennium night in Janet's cottage at Aisholt with Alex, who was staying with me in escape from London. We cooked a meal, talked and read, drank a glass of wine together somewhere around midnight.

When Janet visits me now, she often brings the field mushrooms she gathers while feeding her sheep; I took to her today a gift from the garden of a brown paper bag full of Beth's purple sprouting broccoli. In November Janet is returning to New Zealand to stay for three weeks alone on her island, still deserted, now a national nature reserve.

30 March

Due in Cirencester at midday to collect my Pugin pottery garden seat.

Back home now at my desk, looking up every other moment to enjoy a favourite pair of pine hall chairs, a place for which I couldn't find until today buying in Cirencester an open bookcase. Its columnar supports to the shelves are painted in red and gold with stylised flower-heads and now stands to the right of the studio door, either side of which the chairs perfectly fit.

The royal-blue-ground of the pottery seat looks terrific, in the room downstairs.

On wandering through my friend's stock at Cirencester, I put into my 'to-buy' pile an oval cardboard box decorated in sky-blue and gold, the top printed:

LINCRUSTA-WALTON TABLE MATS, A Dainty Novelty ... a set of these mats is a valuable, though inexpensive present, and will give great satisfaction alike to the recipient and donor, for they will WEAR WELL! WASH WELL!! AND LAST FOR YEARS!!! Solid in Colour! Solid in Relief!! Solid in Value!!!

He gave the box to me!

I've left high bids at the Christie's South Kensington auction today on several pieces in a consignment of two hundred and ninety-one lots from the disbanded Poole Pottery Museum and Archive, begun in 1873 as a tile factory on the coast near Bournemouth. I hope so much that I buy two particular lots, the first a blue plaque, its white tube-line letters stating 'Camden London Borough Council. In a house on this site lived MARY WOLLSTONECRAFT, author of *A Vindication of the Rights of Woman*. 1759-1797.' I want the next lot too, comprising three plaques, one of them on an unusual rust-coloured ground, again with white lettering: 'The House of the Royal Society for the Encouragement of Arts, Manufactures and Commerce, foundation laid 28 March 1772, completed 24 April 1774. Robert & James Adam architects.'

2 April

This morning Rich and Phil planted for me a native
hedge and, elsewhere, my three new trees: a medlar, a
mulberry and an Indian bean tree. I transplanted ash
and cherry saplings in a potential wedge-shape leading
towards the hedge that now flanks the back lane to my
landlord's coach house. Work is due shortly to begin on
conversion into Hugh's family home of these beautiful
buildings and their cobbled courtyard; the Jacobean
manor across the fields will be redecorated and let. Last
week Beth and I constructed posts on which to hang an
Edwardian iron garden gate to the mown path passing
through a gap in the planted hedge, the thick old posts
flanked on one side by an evergreen prunus and on the
other by holly.

Thomas, Beth's cat, died two nights ago, and is buried
in the kennel run, beneath a big Quantock stone. I liked
him, and am glad he seemed to like his life here.
    Beth is going to be fine. I mustn't dramatize.

Yesterday and today a spate of internal placings, through the rediscovery in stored cardboard boxes of things I like and had forgotten I still owned. On the rosewood hanging cabinet, also bought the other day in Cirencester, I've positioned a selection of the oddities kept from art events with which I was involved on the streets of Shoreditch, erratic flights of imagination by youthful British artists before the world had heard of them: the Tracey Emin badge CLARITY = HARMONY; Gavin Turk's original one-Bull and ten-Sheep notes; a pair of Beck's beer bottles dot-painted by Damien Hirst; Contemporary Art in a Can, the Heinz-type small food tin with the image of a Gary Hume picture; Sarah Staton's papier-mâché Camel cigarette packet; Abigail Lane's the Complete Arthole's bottled Eye-for-an-Eye; a silver-foil envelope of Survival Seeds; and several more artists' play-things.

Names.

Everything I own is named.

Unpack from tissue paper Joshua Compston's blown hen's egg, painted by his schoolmate Zebedee Helm, designer of the Factual Nonsense logo. Place it too on the small rosewood cabinet, now hanging in my sitting room.

The cabinet itself doesn't have the name of designer or maker. Definitely 'by' someone. By someone good. The square turquoise tiles on the doors were designed and made by William de Morgan, in his iznik style of the early 1870s. This at least I know.

At the back of a deep shelf in the storage cupboard I find some earlier artwork too: Peter Blake's drawing of the Great Theatre Company's production of *Frankenstein*;

and Gilbert and George's litre of Chinese wine, person-ally-labelled with images of the pair. I select places of display for all of these. Also for the kelim saddle bag from the Sinai desert, with a cowry shell border, given to me twenty-five years ago on my first stay in Jerusalem, in the house close to the Damascus Gate.

Changes have been made in every room during these two last days. My house is alive again, is mine. I have arrived back home. It will now be possible, if I wish, to leave.

We'll see, we'll see.

4 April

Not finished. Far from done with life.

I think, though, I'll stop right here this writing to myself.

On a good, numerically balanced date.

5 April

Caught!
An addiction?
Not sure I really want to stop.

In town by bike this morning I bought from Kings Cycles a black rubber patch and tube of vulcanized glue to repair a cut in the side of my gumboots. They are my oldest boots, the pair I like best, French-made, dark green in colour, slim at the calf. I'm pleased to have saved them from the dustbin.

6 April

Heard from my sister that the sewage leak across her upper lawn has been fixed. This weekend one of her sons dug a T-shaped ditch to follow the natural lay of the land, placed pierced drainpipes at the base and filled in the trench with pebbles, topped by turf. Problem solved.

7 April

There's always more to say.

8 April

The Wollstonecraft plaque was bought at three times my bid, a dealer-friend told me, by Yuri Geller, the bender of spoons. The Royal Society roundel I have installed on an outside wall of my house, below the window to the stairs, to the right of my front porch.

Yesterday, in London, for lunch at the Museum of Garden History I sat beneath the branches of a medlar tree, *Mespius Germanica* the notice said, its presence in England first recorded in the year 995.

Planted mine in West Somerset in 2004.

Need a quince too. Must also be an ancient tree, I reckon, both names with the ring of age.

Acknowledgements

The author is grateful to Helen Knight, Frances Richardson and Corinne Schneider for use of photographs taken at Lower Terhill.

Fitzcarraldo Editions
8-12 Creekside
London, SE8 3DX
Great Britain

ISBN 978-1910695-89-0

Design by Ray O'Meara
Typeset in Fitzcarraldo
Printed and bound by TJ Books

fitzcarraldoeditions.com

Fitzcarraldo Editions